THE FOX COURTS TROUBLE

THE FOX COURTS TROUBLE

Philip Walker

The Book Guild Ltd
Sussex, England

The Book Guild Ltd
25 High Street,
Lewes, Sussex

First published 1994
© Philip Walker 1994
Set in Baskerville
Typesetting by Southern Reproductions (Sussex)
Crowborough, Sussex
Printed in Great Britain by
Antony Rowe Ltd
Chippenham, Wiltshire.

A catalogue record for this book is
available from the British Library

ISBN 0 86332 950 0

AUTHOR'S NOTE

All legal cases described in this book are fictional and bear no intentional resemblance to actual case histories.

1

It really was not Jeremy Carrington-Fox's day. It began badly when his car refused to start and things only got worse. The car episode was doubly frustrating as it had only returned from the garage three days before with a horrendous bill Sellotaped to its dashboard. He had been warned that Porsches were expensive to repair but he had not realised just how much it would cost him. The car had appeared to be such a bargain when he first saw it – low mileage, really smart and only four years old. He had overstretched himself to buy it and could well do without the repair bills. Vanity had won a Pyrrhic victory on that used-car forecourt, for which he was now to pay in more ways than one.

When he arrived at twenty past nine at the office, he assumed that Mr Fifoot's summons was to do with his lateness but he was wrong. In truth, he was facing redundancy. The old fellow was charm itself. Dreadfully sorry and all that but it was only natural that Charles wanted to join the family business as soon as his last term at law school was over. Times were tight enough and the practice hardly warranted employing a junior as it was . . . . Jeremy would, of course, be receiving a month's pay and, as he was due for a fortnight's leave, he could finish at the end of the week.

Jeremy went back to his pokey office and looked at the

conveyancing papers on the desk with the delight of a hyena finding a carcass cleared by the vultures. Who really cared about Mrs Thistlewaite's house in Oxfordshire anyway? She might have done but Jeremy certainly did not. In fact, he resented doing any conveyancing work at all. He seemed to get only the most boring jobs. Here he was, with an upper second in law and an incisive brain eager to grapple with the complexities of the criminal mind, relegated to Mrs Thistlewaite's semi. Even when he got to court, he usually ended up defending some idiot on a speeding charge and it usually cost them far more in legal fees than his advocacy saved them.

He absent-mindedly sharpened his pencil over the desk and blew the shavings clear of the documents. Ten past ten. Almost another seven hours of this before he could escape to his flat. Then what? The prospect of cooking a meal, doing his washing, watching the television and going to bed – alone. Oh, hell! It really was not his day.

The telephone was a grateful relief.

'Mr Carrington-Fox, I have a young lady down here.' The voice dropped and sounded muffled. 'Least, I think she's a lady.'

'What does she want, Miss Finch?'

'She says she's supposed to be in court this morning but she decided at the last minute that she wanted to see a solicitor first.'

'Does Mr Chessington know she is here?'

There was a pause followed by some semi-audible arguing. It was not Miss Finch who spoke next but a distinctive, brazen voice saying, 'Sure he does but I don't think he liked the looks of me so he says you're to see me. ''Ere, listen. I need a solicitor bad and I ain't going to take no for an answer.'

There was a slight pause.

'I'm sorry about that, Mr Carrington-Fox. She grabbed the phone off me.'

Jeremy Carrington-Fox closed his eyes and drew a deep breath. 'Send her up, please, Miss Finch.'

He braced himself. A wispish thought played briefly on his mind. Mrs Thistlewaite's semi would have to wait. Today was not all bad. The thought evaporated into the air at the sight of the apparition in the doorway. The young woman – at least, he, like Miss Finch, assumed it was a woman – was grinning slightly at him, holding the doorknob with one hand and supporting the architraves with the other. Yes, she had to be a woman. The wide hips and thickened rear quarters confirmed that but there the femininity ended. Her face was devoid of all make-up, while her hair was close-cropped and tousled; her hands were large and grimed. He ran his eyes down the denim jacket, the loose-fitting jeans and finished at the large tennis shoes, once white but now almost beyond recognition, caked as they were in muck and oil.

'Well, now you've had an eyeful, do I get to come in?'

'I suppose so, if you think I can be trusted enough to deal with your case.'

Normally, he would have got up and shaken hands in a manner that Uriah Heep would have envied. As it was, he remained seated. He had never treated a client like this before. On the other hand, he had never had a client like this before. What was more, she had eyed him up as much as he had done to her, hence his slightly off-beat comment.

She grinned deeply, showing a hint of her white teeth. 'You're all right, you'll do me. My name's Paddy, by the way.'

She strolled in and sat down.

9

'Nice to meet you, Paddy. Now, how can I help?'

The remnants of the grin melted away. 'I was supposed to go to court this morning. I got there and, well, like, decided not to go in.' The East End accent was pronounced.

'Why ever not?'

'I chickened out, I suppose.'

The admission caused visible pain. Pride had been at stake.

'So you decided you needed to see a solicitor?'

'Yeh.'

'You've left it a bit late, haven't you?'

'Guess so but I'm here now. You will help me, won't you?'

The voice was not so brazen. He did not answer her directly but, instead, went on, 'Why did you have to be in court?'

'They wanted me for GBH.'

He mentally took a step backwards. 'And were you on bail to appear today?'

She pulled out from her jeans a screwed-up piece of paper and tossed it across the desk. He straightened it out. It was a summons.

'You know what it means if you don't turn up?'

'Yer, of course I do. They come and get me.'

He felt a sudden compassion for the girl. For all the brave front, she was scared. He reached for the telephone and lifted the receiver.

'Tea?'

'Got any coffee?'

'Miss Finch, could you bring up a couple of cups of coffee, please?'

He turned back to his client. 'Now, tell me what happened.'

'You mean how I got done?'

10

'Yes. How you got done.'

'Well, I had this car to pick up – you see, I work for my old man – he's got this garage up in Lewisham. Some guy in Hillingdon Avenue was offering this Cav for sale through the trade so Pa got me to fetch it. I caught the train and got instructions how to get to the place from some guy selling flowers outside the station. He reckoned it wasn't far so I started walking. I was about a hundred yards from the garage when these two fellahs come up to me. They made some rude comments and I told them to . . . to . . . ah, go away, only I put it a bit stronger than that. Then one of them says how I should wash my mouth out and how they'd teach me some manners, like. The one with the beard poked his finger right under my nose so I took a swing at him. That's all there was to it.'

'That hardly seems to justify a charge of GBH. Sounds more like self-defence to me.'

'Yer. That's what I called it.'

'How badly were they hurt?'

'One had a bust head and the other got a broken leg, two broken ribs and I doubt if he could use his balls for a couple of weeks.'

He took a second mental step backwards.

She clearly felt the need to justify herself. 'I did call an ambulance when I got to the garage and I didn't do a bunk. I could have, y'know.'

Another tack was called for.

'How did you cause that sort of injury to two men? I mean, you couldn't have meant to do them any real harm?'

He was rapidly trying to work out how one young woman could be attacked by two yobos and come out unscathed, while putting the pair of them in hospital.

'Not to the first one, anyway. I pulled him over me

11

shoulder and he just landed head first.'

'What about the second one?'

'I just kneed 'im in the balls. When he doubled up, I swung my shoulder-bag into his ribs – I had my tools in it so it really winded him. He just groaned and sank to the ground. It was bloody funny, actually. There he was, lying on his back, kicking his legs in the air and making one hell of a racket, the big baby. I know I shouldn't have but I just couldn't resist it. I gave him a McBear roll.'

'What, when it's at home, is a McBear roll?'

There was a ring of pride in the voice. 'It's my speciality – you dive forward, taking your opponent's foot in your hand with you, and do a shoulder-roll over. I heard his leg crack at the joint as I went.'

Jeremy took another dozen mental paces away from her. No wonder Chessington would have nothing to do with her. She was a raving psychopath and, what was worse, he was alone in the room with her. He grabbed the pencil and started scribbling madly.

'I must get all this down. I shall need to get all the details right if I am to have any hope of representing you.'

She seemed to understand this. At any rate, she was more than cooperative in helping him get each point in order. Meanwhile, dear Miss Finch excelled herself – she managed to produce the coffee in record time. He had hardly got two-thirds of the way through when she arrived, putting down the tray and retreating with both decorum and commendable speed. By the time the note-taking had come to an end, Jeremy had regained his composure – not that she had ever noticed he had lost it – and was ready to face the ultimate question.

'What do we do now?'

'Go down to the court and see if we can keep you from being locked up.'

She suddenly looked terrified again. 'I couldn't stand that. You won't let that happen, will you?'

'I'll try not to. Frankly, you are lucky not to have been kept in jail at the beginning, given the charges.'

'The cops that came with the ambulance said it depended whether these fellahs pressed charges or something. They took a statement then said I could go but I would be hearing from them. Then I got this copper round from the local nick and he had me go down there and answer some more dumb questions, then they said something about police bail – I think that's what they said. Then this letter came through the post.'

She indicated the summons.

'Here, do I really have to go inside the court? I mean, couldn't you get it put off for a bit?'

'I'll be quite honest with you; I'd like nothing better than not having to stand up in court with you in the dock. Looking like you do, I give little for my chances of keeping you out on bail but, short of illness, we have no choice.'

She was looking pitifully at him. It threw him how this young woman could cheerfully talk one minute about breaking somebody's leg as though it was a common occurrence and then be near to tears the next. She was like some trapped animal. Yes, that was it, a trapped animal. On the street, she obviously could look after herself, though God knows how she managed it. That was her territory but courts were something alien to her: she was out of her depth just at the thought of one.

'What if I couldn't walk?'

The cockiness had returned.

'Then I might be able to ask for an adjournment on the grounds of your incapacitation. However, there seemed little wrong with you when you came up those stairs.'

She got up and took two paces towards the door.

Suddenly, she pulled up, gave a sharp cry of pain and would have fallen if she had not caught hold of the filing cabinet.

'It's my ankle. It keeps doing this to me. Can you get me into the chair?'

He rushed round the desk, initially most concerned for her well-being, and supported her by wrapping one hand about her waist. With infinite care, he helped her turn around and eased her back into her seat.

She looked up impishly. 'Is that enough for one of those adjournment things? Do I have to go now?'

The brazen hussy! He suddenly wanted to laugh, decided against it and tried to look serious. It was impossible. She was gently grinning and talking wildly to him with her eyes. The suppressed giggle came with a spurt of froth between his teeth. He wiped his face quickly, embarrassed and red at his lack of control. The wretch laughed fully and openly at him. He had no choice: he joined her. Why, he did not know, but he actually liked her even if she had scared the pants off him when they first met.

'You'll have me out of a job behaving like this.'

Damn it, he was out of a job anyway in a fortnight.

'OK, OK, I'll phone the court and tell them that you are unable to walk.'

He suddenly thought about his fee.

'No, that will not do. I'd better go down there and straighten it out in person.'

That way, he could apply for legal aid. He doubted that she had any significant money: this was clearly Green Form time. The state could pay this bill.

'Come on, you'd better come as well. You can stay in the car while I go inside.'

He stopped, almost in mid-sentence.

'Oh, damn. I've just remembered. My car wouldn't

14

start this morning. I had to leave it at home.'

'That's OK. Mine's down below.'

'Then let's go.'

'Hey! Aren't you going to help me down the stairs?'

'Why should I?'

'My ankle. I can't walk on it properly.'

'There's nothing wrong with your ankle.'

'Miss Finch don't know that. We ought to give her a good performance.'

He sighed. 'Give me your arm.'

Immediately, she wrapped her left arm completely round his chest and leant hard against him. He had no choice but to support her under her right arm. He found his hand resting on her breast. He was not sure whether to feel embarrassed or to enjoy the experience. The truth was, he was awkward with women as a rule. He might lie in bed at night with salacious thoughts running through his head but, in the real world, nobody paid much attention to this six-foot-two-inch gangling creature who had little except his brains to recommend him. He decided he would take the whole affair as the most natural thing in the world. As it happened, Paddy appeared to have the same attitude. Thus it was that Miss Finch looked up to see the pair apparently coming down the stairs in each other's arms.

'It's all right, Miss Finch. Paddy has a damaged ankle and can't walk properly. I'm simply helping her to her car.'

Oh, God! he thought. I called her Paddy. I don't even know her surname. That is hardly professional. Her name had to be on the summons. Why the hell didn't I read it properly? He racked his brains. The name McBear came to mind.

They got through the door and he closed it behind them, taking in a deep breath as he did so.

'Where's your car?'

'There!'

She pointed across the road to where a red 325 BMW was neatly parked on double yellow lines. From where he was, Jeremy could see the plastic sheet hanging under the windscreen wipers. She had been booked. He unhooked himself and walked across the road, fervently hoping that he was not recognised. Paddy had no inhibitions. She strode purposefully forward, wrenched the ticket away, screwed it into a ball and tossed it neatly into the gutter.

She caught his look. 'Don't worry. We never bother about traffic offences in our family.'

'They'll trace you from the number-plates.'

'I doubt it. This set belongs to an Astra from the scrapheap.'

He winced. She felt the need to elucidate.

'I somehow collected nine penalty points on my licence for speeding and Pops said he wasn't having me losing it so he switched the plates. It means I don't have to bother where I park either. Great, isn't it?'

Jeremy managed to contain his answer – a feat of amazing restraint.

She stopped suddenly at the driver's door and tossed him the keys.

'You'd better drive,' she said. 'It wouldn't do for me to be seen at the wheel with a damaged ankle.'

He hesitated. A vision flashed before his eyes of explaining to the officer how he came to be driving a car with forged plates, no doubt lacking a MOT certificate and, for all he knew, probably stolen. As it happened, it was legally obtained, it did have a certificate – her father had done it personally – and it was in fine mechanical order, as were all the McBear cars.

'You can drive, can't you?'

This was clearly not a time for a faint heart. Actually, he found the car most pleasant. It certainly moved away smartly. Not sure of the wisdom of conversation, he held his peace at first but found the desire to chat became overwhelming.

'Goes well, doesn't it?'

'OK, I suppose. Straight-line acceleration is reasonable but it handles like a pig in the wet. I only use it when there's nothing better in the garage.'

'What do you normally drive?'

'A Sierra Cosworth. It's Pops's, really, but he lets me use it when he don't want it. What have you got?'

'Mine's a Porsche. Unfortunately, it's proving a bit unreliable at the moment.'

'I'll have a look at it for you, if you like.'

'You!'

'Yeah, why not? I told you – I work in a garage.'

'Yes but you don't repair them, surely?'

'What do you think I do all day, ponce about looking beautiful?'

No, he did not think that. Before he had to answer, they reached the corner of the road leading to the court. He escaped by changing the subject.

'We're nearly there. Now listen. You stay in the car and don't speak to anyone and certainly don't hit anyone! With luck, I'll be out in about fifteen minutes.'

He was in the driving seat in more ways than one. This was his territory. He left her still looking apprehensive but consoling herself with heavy metal coming from the stereo at around the hundred-decibel mark. He loped casually in through the glass swing doors and made himself known to the usher. That done, he sat quietly in the corner and viewed the assortment of villains lined up for the day.

Inside the court, the clerk took the note from the

17

usher. He read it with little apparent interest then turned to address the bench.

'I am sorry, sir, but it appears that there is a problem with number eighteen on the list. The defendent is, apparently, not well.'

He said it in a voice that implied he had heard it all before and did not believe a word of it.

'Counsel asks if he may be allowed to address the bench.' He shrugged his shoulders. 'It's up to you, of course. It might be that he will suggest a suitable alternative date. It could be helpful.'

The voice strongly suggested that it would not.

The chairman had a few hurried words with each of his fellow magistrates then addressed the open court.

'We will listen to counsel for Ms McBear.'

Jeremy was eloquent. He won sympathy for the accident. His client had, he explained, fallen awkwardly while in his office and had badly sprained her ankle. Indeed, he was not sure if it was broken – only an X-ray would decide the matter (he was careful never actually to say she was in hospital or that the ankle was to be X-rayed; he just left the impression). The young lady had been most upset at having to miss her appearance. Would the court please accept her apology?

He waited for the perfunctory nod from the chairman of the bench then smoothly went on. Naturally, she would be pleading not guilty to the charge. Given the circumstances, perhaps the court would be so good as to give a formal adjournment for two days when pleas could be taken. He intended to apply for an oral committal. There was no need for the affair to be dragged out. If the prosecutor could supply advanced disclosure quickly, he would be able to proceed almost immediately. His client was most anxious to have her good name cleared as soon as possible.

He emerged ten minutes later, more than pleased with himself. He had even got his legal aid application in hand. He broke the news to Paddy.

'We have two days' grace then you will have to plead. That will only take a couple of minutes. Bail shouldn't be a problem. They didn't raise any objection during this morning's hearing – they just continued your unconditional bail – so the prosecutor is not likely to press it next time. For my money, we've had a lucky break, so don't say too much!'

'You'll be there on Thursday, won't you?'

'Of course.'

'Shall we go and look at your car now?'

'Really, it doesn't matter. I can take it back to the garage that did it last time.'

She snorted. 'Cocked it up, most likely, and they'll want to charge you again for putting right their mess. Hey, you don't trust me, do you?'

'Of course I do. It's just that I don't like putting you to any trouble.'

There the resistance ended. Without knowing quite how he had let himself in for it, he found himself driving the woman the twelve miles to his flat in Orpington, where she surveyed the red 944 parked in the driveway with a critical eye.

'Did you bang it or was that done before you got it?'

'It's never been in any accident. I was guaranteed that when I bought it.'

She grunted disparagingly. 'Then you were conned. It's had a paint job done on the off-side wing and the front bumper isn't original equipment. See how much brighter it is than the rear one?'

As she pointed out the evidence, he found his anger at being taken in by the salesman tempered by a grudging

19

admiration for her quick eye.

She had the bonnet up and surveyed the interior.

'Turn it over. Let's hear what's happening.'

He did. She quickly held up a hand for him to stop. For the next quarter of an hour, he watched fascinated as she deftly went to work. She carried out a series of tests, none of which seemed to please her, but, at the end of the time, the engine fired on the second turn of the key. Despite the rough note, it did not stall when he took his foot off the throttle and she seemed content.

'It's only a temporary job,' she announced. 'The electronics had gone. I've bypassed them with a get-you-home kit. You'll not get any performance from it but you'll be able to follow me OK.'

'Follow you?'

'Sure. This is going to take a couple of hours with proper equipment. Just follow me back to our garage and I'll do it there for you.'

A thought suddenly struck her.

'Here, I'll tell you what. You get me off and I'll get this car right for you for nothing.'

The words were still going through his head as he turned up Lewisham High Street. He had to be a maniac. What was he to tell Fifoot? That he had played hooky for the afternoon to go off with a female client who offered to fix his car? He could just see that one being swallowed. He looked at the car clock. Astonishingly, it was only twenty past twelve. Perhaps he could get back at a semi-reasonable time and claim he was hanging around the court for most of the day.

The realisation of the time brought on sudden stomach pains. Despite his rather thin build, he had been born with an appetite that was close to being insatiable. Lunch was certainly a clear priority. They turned down a back street and moved away from the shops. The route wound through a series of narrow roads festooned with parked cars in varying states of decay. The area looked far from salubrious.

Just as he was wondering how much further they had to go, the BMW took a sharp turn up a narrow alley and came out in the backyard of a garage. They wriggled past two lorry cabs in various degrees of dissection and parked in the middle of an area that had once been poorly covered in concrete. Around them were a dozen or so cars but his attention was caught by two in particular. Adjacent to his Porsche was a trailer carrying what had once been a yellow American car that sported a rainbow bodywork and had its radiator clearly visible where the back seat ought to have been. Lurid, red flames were painted on the front wings, the glass had been removed from the windows and a yellow nine figured prominently on the door. In front of that was a two-year-old Cosworth Sierra that was jacked up with the front wheels missing but, otherwise, appeared in excellent condition.

Paddy slid back the rear door to the garage and called out, 'Hi, Pops! I'm home!'

Pulling her head back from the doorway, she addressed Jeremy.

'Best if you wait in the office. You'll only get that suit dirty if you hang around here.'

'Actually, I was thinking of getting some lunch. Is there anywhere reasonable to eat around here?'

'Yer, but I'd better come with you if you don't know your way around.'

Before more could be said, a deep, booming voice called from just inside the door, 'Paddy. Did it go OK?'

A great bear of a man emerged, rubbing grease from his enormous hands with a rag the size of a lady's

21

handkerchief. He must have been all of six-foot-four and around seventeen stone. That would have been enough to intimidate most people without the knotted shoulder-length hair and six-inch ginger beard. He was dressed in a boiler suit over a T-shirt that sported a 'world peace' slogan. With this fellow around, anyone would think twice before declaring war.

'Hi, Pops! Meet my lawyer. This great guy is going to get me off. He's already got an adjournment and I didn't even have to go into court.'

Jeremy hardly liked to explain that they were far from getting her off and there had been nothing clever in getting an adjournment. Better to leave alone for the moment.

'That's great, Pad.'

He turned his attention to Jeremy.

'I'm right pleased to meet you.'

He wiped his hands down the boiler suit and extended five black tentacles towards his visitor.

'What's your name, son?'

'Carrington-Fox – Jeremy Carrington-Fox, actually. I'm pleased to meet you, too, sir.'

The last word was strangled under the finger-crunching grip.

'Well, Jerry, you're most welcome here. I really love this girl and anyone who can make her happy is a friend of mine.'

The other massive arm wrapped round Paddy's shoulder and squeezed her tightly. She seemed to enjoy it. Jeremy checked his fingers, found to his surprise that none were broken and decided the safest way to keep them like that was not to inform the Bear that he had got his name wrong.

'What brings you here?'

Paddy explained. 'Some bugger has mucked his

Porsche up. Idiots didn't know what they were doing so we've brought it up here to get it right. We've made a deal –'

Have we? thought Jeremy.

'– he'll get me off and I fix the car.'

The next four sentences were technical garbage to Jeremy. However, Pete clearly understood the lot and nodded his head sagely.

'That's gonna take some time, lass.'

'Jerry wants some lunch. I said I'd take him to Luigi's, if that's OK with you, Pops?'

'Tell y'what, lass. I'll fix the car while you take him to Luigi's and then you kids go to the cinema or something. I've nothing much on this afternoon and I ain't hungry. When you get back, we'll all go off for the evening. What do you say?'

His beard parted to show a row of gleaming teeth. Any Tyrannosaurus Rex would have been proud of them. Jeremy hardly liked to say no. His return to the office today was now, beyond doubt, out of the question. What the hell – he had been given the push already so why should he feel beholden to Fifoot, Chessington and Mainwaring? He decided that it was his middle-class standards that gave him a sense of guilt at skipping work.

'That sounds great, Pops. What do you say, Jerry?'

'Luigi's sounds good but I'm not sure about the cinema. Anyway, before that, we need to talk about your clothes.'

Whoops! The thunder-clouds had gathered.

'What's wrong with Pad's clothes?'

'Nothing if she wants to work in a garage but she won't cut a very good figure in court looking like this. How can I persuade the magistrates that she is an innocent girl who was set upon by two muggers if she looks like some

23

spanner-wielding Amazon warrior?'

He addressed himself to the smouldering volcano beside him.

'If you want to walk out a free woman then you'll turn up in a smart dress and put some make-up on your face.'

'Like hell I will. I don't wear dresses.'

'She will. Pad, you do as Jerry here says. If it takes a dress and lipstick to get you off then you do it. He's the expert.'

He pulled a wallet from his pocket and proceeded to peel off a dozen or so notes. They appeared to be mostly fifties with an assorted mixture of tens and twenties in the middle. Whatever, it was more money than Jeremy was used to seeing except in a bank. He thrust them towards the lawyer.

'Here, son. Take this lot, pay for the meal and then see she buys whatever you think she needs.'

Paddy opened her mouth to protest, caught her father's eye and shut up. Whatever she did, she knew better than to argue with her honourable progenitor.

*

Jeremy Carrington-Fox stopped the Porsche with an uncharacteristic flourish at around a quarter past three. He was not in the habit of revving exuberantly at that time of night but he had not enjoyed himself so much for a long time and he could not resist a final burst.

The past twelve or so hours had been very different but great fun. He had had excellent food and fascinating company, starting with Luigi's. He had found the place quaint – that is, once he had grown accustomed to the rest of the clients – and the meal had lasted for the best part of two hours. During this time, he moved from the initial reaction of near petrification at the assortment of fellow diners to a relaxed appreciation of back-street banter. There were enough potential clients in the Italian restaurant to keep him in business for a couple of years but, once they knew he was Paddy's lawyer and under her protection, he was taken into the family in a way that is only found in such close-knit communities where most outsiders are considered aliens and the few who are accepted are sworn friends.

The afternoon had been fun, too, in its own way. The only slight blot was having to contain his laughter for fear of not being well enough to defend his client. Her reaction to the dress section of the departmental store was one of total disgust, accentuated by the production of a series of articles that he insisted she bought. He more or less escaped unscathed from this store but the mention of a wig was painful.

'Wig!!!'

He received the blast at a range of two feet and at over a hundred and twenty decibels. He reeled back from the onslaught, caught his breath and managed to play his trump card seconds before his annihilation.

'Father's orders. Do what's necessary.'

There was a pause as she considered the situation.

'I'll not wear a wig and that's flat.'

'I'll settle for you buying one and fight you over what we do with it later.'

'I'll not do it and that's an end to the matter.'

They returned to the garage shortly after five with three carrier bags in the boot.

'Did you have a successful trip, kids?'

'Wonderful time, thanks, Mr McBear . . .'

'It's Pete, Jerry old son, it's Pete. Nobody's called me mister for years. Don't feel right.'

'Sorry – Pete – no problems. You sure have a pretty daughter when she's dressed up.' He stepped smartly aside and continued, 'She makes a great blonde – no one

25

who knows her would recognise her.' He winked without her seeing.

'Go and get togged up, lass. I want to see what you look like.'

'To hell I will!'

Pete eyed the transformation at the top of the stairs approvingly.

'Son, you've managed something I've failed to do since her ma died, God rest her soul, and you've only known her for a few hours.'

'I look a right wally.'

'No you don't, lass. You look really good. I reckon you could pass for one of those female Russian shot-putters. What do you think, Jerry?'

Jeremy had no opinion. He was busy salvaging the wig from around his face.

'Get changed then, love, and we'll be off. I ain't taking you out in that gear.'

The Bear turned to his guest.

'If you go in the fridge you'll find three cans of beer. Break 'em out, son, will you? You might like to go down to the workshop then and try the motor. It never ran so well, I'll warrant.'

'Even when it was new?'

Jerry laughed but Pete was serious.

'Maybe. Depends how well those Jerries knew their craft. It certainly goes OK now, anyway.'

Jerry decided the beer needed pouring. He nonchalantly took his can, drew a few sips and sauntered down to the workshop. Sure enough, there was the Porsche with the bonnet still up. The whole engine looked very clean; someone had done a neat job. There were a few bits he did not recognise but that was not surprising: his mechanical knowledge was immorally low. He felt a mild tinge of excitement. He was still admiring it when his host strolled down.

'Like it, son?'

'Yes – thanks. What can I say?'

He knew what he wanted to say but somehow it hardly seemed right. He was not expected to go overboard in thanks. A schoolboy urge was building inside him: he could not wait to give it a whirl.

'That's OK, son. If you are our family lawyer then we've got to look after you.'

He stopped as if an afterthought had struck him.

'I've fitted an anti-theft device as well. Little invention of mine – it stops the sort of bums who like to joy-ride in someone else's motor. I'd better show you how it works.'

While he was doing so, Paddy arrived, dressed in black shiny trousers and a black leather jacket. In a funny way, she looked all right. At least, she no longer passed for a second row forward, more a female bouncer.

The Bear drove with remarkable restrain. Nevertheless, it was clear he could drive and knew where he was going. The car slid artistically from lane to lane as they cut their way into the heart of the city. Jeremy knew roughly where he was until they had crossed Oxford Street, then he was lost. The car was cutting up side streets and down back alleys to emerge in some main boulevard for long enough to find the next short cut. At last, they pulled up in front of a narrow doorway sporting a neon sign that had seen better days but was still able to advertise 'The Magic Lantern Club'.

They went down a flight of stairs to find a man who, but for the colour of his skin, could well have been the Bear's twin brother. Immaculately dressed in evening jacket and bow tie, he stood amiably enough in front of the door but his true purpose in life was in no doubt. He recognised two of the trio immediately and grinned

27

broadly.

'Hey, man! How are you doing? Haven't seen you for ages.'

'Is our table ready, Samson?'

'As ordered, man. You enjoy yourselves.'

He opened the door to an evening of food, drink and bawdy entertainment that only ended around two. Pete reckoned that was late enough for any daughter of his.

2

Paddy was at least on time. 'Be at the office on the dot of nine,' he had said, and there she was. What Miss Finch was thinking Jeremy would never know but, as always, she was the soul of tact and diplomacy.

'Mr Carrington-Fox, I have Miss McBear in reception. She says she has an appointment with you for nine o'clock but I don't have anything in the diary.'

'That's my fault, Miss Finch. I forgot to put it in yesterday. Please ask her to come up.'

The young woman entered without knocking and greeted him like a long-lost friend.

'Hi, there, Jerry. See, I've made it and I've even parked legally.'

The summer dress flowed gaily while maintaining sufficient dignity to satisfy Jeremy. She had the wig on properly and a touch of lipstick but, otherwise, no make-up. He had not left this to chance but saw to it that Pete knew exactly how she was to dress. She also wore the chic shoulder-bag. He had given a lot of careful consideration to it and wanted to make sure that it looked substantial enough to have inadvertently caused injury while being unquestionably a lady's bag.

'Shut the door and come and sit down. We have a few things to go over.'

'Like what?'

'Like what you are going to say and not say later on this morning. Mostly, it's about what you are not going to say.'

'I thought you said it would be very quick today?'

'It ought to be. Now just listen. When we get called, we will walk in together but I shall have to go into one of the front benches and you will be shown into the dock. First thing, remain standing until you are invited to sit down. The clerk will ask you your name and address – you give that and nothing more. He'll probably tell you to sit down then. Don't say anything, just do it. Let me do all the talking. At some stage, you will be asked to plead. You stand up for that. Whatever he says, ignore it until he asks you whether you are guilty or not guilty – he'll give you a load about the section they are prosecuting you under first – then you just say "not guilty", nothing else. Have you got that?'

'Cinch. Can't go wrong!'

Oh God! thought Jeremy, that's a kiss of death if ever I heard one.

However, he constrained himself to a stern look and then briskly looked at his watch.

'Right! We'll be off straight away. That will give me plenty of time to talk to the clerk of the court and see if we can get in early.'

Luck was with them: they were the second case to be called. There was no trouble getting through the door and the obvious apprehensive look she gave as he left her before she was ushered into the dock lost her no marks. She remembered to remain standing. Jeremy was relieved. Perhaps his pre-court preparation had been worthwhile.

'Cynthia Anne McBear. Is that right?'

'Yes.'

'Is that Miss or Mrs?'

'Miss, of course, stupid. I'm only nineteen, y'know. Do I look daft enough to have got myself married?'

He should have had a couple of paracetamols before he had come in.

'Just answer the question, Miss McBear.' The chairman of the bench gave her a hard stare as he spoke.

'I'm sorry. It was just such a dumb question.'

Perhaps he should have taken four paracetamols. Fortunately, the clerk appeared eager to progress. He looked in the direction of the prosecutor.

'Mode of trial?'

The prosecutor rose ponderously, searched needlessly amongst a pile of papers, then addressed the court.

'Your worships, you may feel your powers are not sufficient to deal with this case . . .'

Jeremy was on his feet. The prosecutor paused and, as Jeremy started to speak, sat down again.

'If it pleases the court, I feel I might be of assistance here. It is my understanding that my client wishes to plead not guilty and feels that it is right for her to ask for Crown Court trial. However, the defence will contend that there is no case to answer. Therefore, I would ask for an oral committal in this case and I should like to ask for a formal adjournment for two weeks to allow time for study of advanced disclosures. Then, if I may be allowed to suggest it, we should be in a position to set a date for the hearing.'

The prosecutor nodded in agreement, only half rising to indicate support for the idea.

The clerk looked up.

'Would you stand, please, Miss McBear.'

He waited for her to rise before continuing.

'Cynthia Anne McBear, it is alleged that, on the twenty-eighth of April 1990, you hit Arthur James

Pallister causing him actual bodily harm. This is contrary to section forty-seven of the Offences Against the Person Act, 1861. Also, you assaulted Terry Michael Pallister causing him grievous bodily harm. This is contrary to section twenty of the Offences Against the Person Act, 1861. Do you understand these charges?'

Paddy looked across at Jeremy, who nodded.

'Yes.'

'Do you plead guilty or not guilty?'

'Not guilty. It was self-defence. They attacked –'

'Yes, thank you, Miss McBear. There is no need to say anything more at this stage.'

The clerk consulted the desk diary.

'May I suggest the sixteenth for resumption? Ah, would that be long enough, Mr Carrington-Fox?'

Jeremy was on his feet.

'Perfectly acceptable, thank you.'

It was the prosecutor's turn to rise.

'May I suggest that the defendant is not required to attend on that occasion?'

'May I thank my learned friend for that helpful suggestion.'

Jeremy sat straight down once more. It was going well again. Perhaps the paracetamols were not needed after all. He must remember to buy the prosecutor a drink for keeping Paddy out of court for the next session. Then again, perhaps he was trying to avoid the hassle for himself.

'The case is adjourned until the sixteenth of June. Is the defendant on unconditional bail?'

'Yes, sir. Er, there is no objection to that continuing, I understand.'

The prosecutor half stood again and muttered, 'No objection.'

'Your unconditional bail is continued, Miss McBear.

You are not required to attend court on the sixteenth but you will be notified of the date of the next hearing after that and you must attend then. Do you understand?'

She nodded.

'May Miss McBear leave court?'

The clerk looked up for the perfunctory nod and proceeded immediately.

'Call Brewster and Gill.'

''Ere, can I go now?'

'Yes, you may leave court.'

Jeremy was signalling urgently. Anything to get her outside before she upset anyone. As it turned out, there was less need to worry than he thought. She could not get out of the place quickly enough.

'Oh, thank God that's over! Now I can get out of this stupid dress and get back to work.'

*

In a way, it was quite funny. He actually felt deflated when she drove off. Life was different with her around. It might be unpredictable, even hairy, but it was not boring. He had had a great day out with her and her father which had been totally unorthodox by his standards yet he would not have missed it for the world. Now he was facing the depression of redundancy. It was an insult to his person. He was eager to work but he had none and no prospect of any. He had also been unethical – he had had the legal aid made out to him and not the practice for the continuation. In truth, he did not doubt for a moment that Paddy would have anyone else now or that Chessington would want the case but it was still unethical. He did not care; it was a form of petty revenge for being given the boot.

He went back into the office and set to work clearing out the files and putting in order the work the partners in the practice would have to complete. He did it honestly

33

enough but without any great conviction. Just before five, Fifoot came in.

'Ah, Jeremy, how's it going?'

'Everything is in order, Mr Fifoot, except the Thistlewaite, Brown and Calderdale files.'

'Excellent. Look, I have felt quite badly about having to ask you to leave. You've done some good work since you have been with us and we will all miss you. Clear those up tonight and take tomorrow off. That's the least we can do and, remember, if I can be of help in recommending you to another practice, you have only to ask.'

He beamed as though he had just given him a golden handshake.

'That's most kind of you. I'm going to miss you all, too, sir. I'll have these done in an hour and will put them on your desk before I leave.'

'You won't forget to leave your keys, will you, Jeremy?'

'I won't.'

'Well, I'll say goodbye in that case.' He held out his hand.

'Goodbye, Mr Fifoot, and thank you.'

The last comment had been intended as heavy sarcasm but Fifoot took it at face value, smiled and left the room. Jeremy decided it was probably for the best: there was no sense in upsetting anyone on his last day. He would leave the keys, shut the door and shake the dust of the place off his feet. Secretly, Jeremy vowed he would work for himself from now on, however hard it was.

As it was, it took nearly two hours to clear the office. Partly, it was due to the interruptions: there were the formal and uncomfortable goodbyes with Chessington and Mainwaring, neither of whom really wanted him to go and made it as clear as they could without direct disloyalty. Whatever they say, thought Jeremy, they were party to the agreement to replace me. He would not bear a grudge; it would help nothing. Miss Finch was a different matter. She was genuinely fond of her young boss and needed his large handkerchief before she eventually left.

Suddenly, the office was quiet. He finished the last of the files, collected the three together, put them on Fifoot's desk, took a final look at his own room, then descended the stairs to the deserted reception area. He would miss it, he knew he would. It was two years since he had joined the firm as a very raw recruit from law school and, in that time, he had come to feel part of the place. He shrugged, threw the keys on the desk and let himself out. Tomorrow was a new day.

In point of fact, tomorrow took a long time to come. He tossed most of the night and found it hard to sleep. When he did, he dreamt he had Paddy in bed with him. He tried to fondle her and she whipped his arm up his back and wrenched it. He woke in a cold sweat and with pins and needles in his arm where he had been lying awkwardly. It took a hot drink and a shot of brandy before he settled in bed once more.

He eventually awoke feeling far from rested and out of sorts with the world in general. He went through the ritual of dressing, washing and having breakfast. No need to rush, he could read the paper at leisure. He had nowhere to go; that is, unless he went down and signed on the dole. That thought was too depressing. He suddenly decided on lunch at Luigi's, preferably with company.

Thus it was that a red Porshe, after four wrong turns, pulled up outside the rather dilapidated forecourt of the McBear garage. From inside, the hiss of a welding torch could be heard over the sound of metal on metal. He

35

cautiously walked in and surveyed the scene for those delicious moments before he was noticed. The big American car was on the ramp, having what looked remarkably like half a bedstead welded onto its underside. From the pit, Paddy's head just showed as she hammered at a rusty exhaust, piece by piece removing the useless system.

The Bear turned the torch off and moved from under the car.

'Hey, Pad! We've a visitor. Great to see you again, Jerry. What brings you up here?'

Pete grinned broadly.

To Jeremy, there was something rather wonderful about this place. It was all so naive and homely in a rough and ready way but it had character.

'To tell the truth, I was bored out of my mind and I got to thinking about Luigi's. Reckon I owe you so I want to take you two out on me.'

'What time is it, son?'

'Just gone eleven.'

'Right you are. Go in there and make yourself useful by putting the kettle on. It's about time we had a brew-up. How's the exhaust coming, Pad?'

'It's a right bugger. It's rusted onto the retaining bracket but I think we're winning.'

She hit the bracket with another resounding blow and the clip came away. She climbed out with the agility of a mountain goat and grinned at him.

'Did you say something about Luigi's? Does that mean I don't have to fix the sandwiches?'

Pete snorted. 'Do you ever?'

'Ah, come on, Pops. I do it sometimes.'

They all laughed easily.

Over the next hour, Jeremy brewed the tea, washed up the dirty mugs and sorted out the office. Even he could not make it last that long so he spent the rest of the time until lunch idly watching the pair work.

'I'm racing this beauty over at the Wimbledon circuit on Sunday. If you've nothing else to do, why don't you come over and watch? Better wear some old clothes, though.'

'I'd love to.' He paused. 'Are you really racing that? I don't mean to be rude but it looks fit for the scrapheap.'

'That's where it came from, Jerry old son. I'm driving in a Demolition Derby.'

'What's that?'

Paddy shouted from the pit, 'Come along and find out!'

He resolved to do so.

It was around a quarter to one when they eventually arrived at Luigi's. Jeremy did not know it but that meal was to result in big changes in his life. He sat down to lunch as an unemployed solicitor, feeling slightly sorry for himself, and left with the prospects of his own practice, an office and an over-optimistic view of the future.

The conversation had somehow turned to his predicament. It was Luigi who actually started it; he had come over during the meal and sat with them, business being slack and, anyway, he fancied a chat.

'You should have an office around here. There are enough criminals to keep you overworked all the year.'

'Easy said, Luigi, but you have to be known.'

'That's not a problem for Luigi. He will spread the word, he tell all his friends that a new lawyer is good and looking for work. If you can get Paddy off then they all come to you.'

'And where do I find an office?'

'That's easy, son. If you really want to set yourself up round here then you can start in the garage. There's a spare room at the side. Just needs cleaning out a bit.'

He wound his spaghetti round his fork and tried unsuccessfully to stop the strands falling away as he brought the food up to his mouth. Thank God it did not seem to matter here if your manners were not perfect.

'You're joking, aren't you?'

He was already getting used to being wound up by the inhabitants of this part of the world.

'Straight up. Would Luigi kid you on something serious like this?'

'You clean out the room, son, and it's yours.'

'Wait a minute! I'm skint, remember. I've no money coming in. How can I pay you?'

'You clean the room out and you can use it for fifty pounds a week or ten per cent on what you take, whatever is the least. How's that for a business deal? If you don't get any clients, you pay nothing. The worst I get out of it is a clean room. I only use it for storage at the moment.'

They returned to the garage. Jeremy saw the room, promptly went out and bought a T-shirt and cheap trousers and spent the next two hours sorting it out. Once he had disposed of the old bicycle and an assortment of car parts and thrown out the old furniture, it was ready for a good clean. By three o'clock, he was in the car, driving back into the town. Less than two hours later, he was back in the garage, having seen the bank manager for a loan, ordered two hundred business cards, bought a desk, two chairs and a filing cabinet for delivery early next week (all on extended credit) and loaded up with decorating materials. When Paddy came through the door with a mug of tea, she found him up to his eyes in paint. As she put it down on the floor, there was a knock on the open door.

'I'm looking for the new solicitor. Luigi says he works here.'

He put down the paintbrush. 'Fox – Jeremy Fox. How can I help you, Mr Uh . . . ?'

He had already decided to drop the Carrington bit and it would not be long before Jeremy had given way to the diminutive as well.

'Freddy Field. I got this.'

He held out the summons. Jeremy glanced rapidly down it. A drinking and driving case. No problem. He would get a £850 fine and a two-year disqualification. Routine.

'I know you can't stop a disqualification but I need to put it off for a couple of months. Can you work it?'

'Why?'

'The wife's pregnant and I want the car for when she starts.'

Not so routine. The summons was for next week.

'There's no trouble paying, like.'

He had read Jeremy's face and drawn the wrong conclusion.

'It isn't the money. I don't think I can keep you on the road for that long.'

Jeremy carefully avoided adding that nor did he wish him the opportunity of driving if he drank like the summons suggested.

'You will try, though, won't you? I don't care what it costs.'

'I'll try, Mr Field.'

Here was his second client.

*

In the following week, Jeremy Carrington-Fox underwent a transmutation, not least in name. The only thing in this area that was double-barrelled was liable to be sawn off and used by his prospective customers – to all callers he was simply Jerry Fox. He had had visits from six clients, accepted five of them, and had been called out at three in the morning to go to Lewisham police station, where a would-be client refused to say anything until his lawyer was present. This was Fletcher, known to all as Froggy for no reason that anyone could remember. He had been caught behind the counter in a local jeweller's, the tools of his trade in his bag, but wanted to plead loss of memory and claimed he had no idea how he got there. He thought he must have walked in his sleep. It was all the same to Jeremy; the fee would be good – this one was destined for the Crown Court.

He had turned down but one client, a certain Samuel Wallace. Wallace was an enormous fat slob of about thirty-three with perpetual tears in his eyes. It was not clear how he had found Jeremy – certainly, Luigi had not recommended him. His case was simple: malicious damage to his neighbour's car.

'I won't have to go to prison, will I?' he bleated.

'I doubt it very much, Mr Wallace. Even if you are guilty, you are only likely to get a small fine and be ordered to pay compensation. I can't say until I have a few details of the case. Let me get some facts down on paper first. What is it you were supposed to have done?'

'I reversed my car into the next door's Mini and crunched it up a bit.'

'And did you?'

'Oh yes, but it wasn't my fault.'

'Ah, an accident?'

'No, you see she is a witch and she put a spell on me.'

Jeremy stopped writing.

'Am I to understand you intend to ask a court to

believe that you were bewitched?'

'Yes, that's right.'

The pen was returned to his coat pocket.

'Then, Mr Wallace, I shall give you some free advice. Go to court and plead guilty. Don't mention the spell; magistrates don't usually know much about such things. Simply apologise, grovel, say you were drunk . . . .'

'I never drink, Mr Fox. Alcohol is the work of the devil.'

'Say your wife had just left you . . . .'

'I ain't married, Mr Fox.'

'Then say you were under drugs – I know, don't say it, you never take anything more than an aspirin. Say any damned thing you like only don't mention the spell. If you grovel enough, even burst into tears . . .'

'That will be easy enough, Mr Fox.'

'. . . you might get away lightly. You can expect an order to pay the compensation and a hundred pounds' fine – anything less and you can come and pay me the balance for my advice – otherwise, there is no charge.'

Was it a wise move, turning down a hundred-pound fee? he thought. Sure it was, the woman might have put a curse on him for defending the twerp. That was one case he was best leaving to others. Thinking about it, Chessington might have been interested.

He spent one morning at the court, successfully putting off Field's disqualification. He had him plead not guilty and demanded trial by jury with an oral committal. This pushed his luck enough with the bench but he riled the prosecutor by wanting all the witnesses present. That caused the prosecution to ask for a week's adjournment – turned into two by the clerk – in order to find out when the witnesses could attend court. He came out triumphant.

'This is going to cost you,' he said. 'Once you change

41

the plea to guilty, the bench will hammer you with costs. Mind you, if I play it right, we ought to get a month's delay before we can get a date for the hearing and then, if you need it, you can always let it go to the Crown Court.'

'You're a good 'un, Mr Fox. I won't forget what you are doing for me.'

Just tell your friends, he thought, but contented himself with, 'It was nothing, Mr Field. All part of the job.'

Life in the little office was not all milk and honey: he was made to earn his keep in other ways. For most of the day, he had no one in the office so he had to occupy himself. The shelves were fitted by Tuesday afternoon and the telephone was on order. He had time on his hands; time that Paddy ensured was not wasted. Thus he got used to buying a cut loaf and a variety of sandwich fillings every morning, either on his way in or during the first hour. By the Friday, his tea was a connoisseur's delight and his tuna, lettuce, tomato and cucumber sandwiches were a speciality. He had even managed to sort out some order to the garage books. As far as he could see, only about a tenth of the business was shown; the rest depended on a cash-in-pocket or barter basis, with the latter figuring highly.

What appeared to be developing into a slightly eccentric but passable life was to twist in a way neither he nor the Bears could have foreseen. It was two-thirty the following Monday night, or, to be more precise, early that Tuesday morning. He was awakened by the continual depression of his doorbell. More asleep than awake, he staggered to the hall, fumbled for the light switch and slid back the door as far as the security chain would allow.

'We need you, Jerry old son. We've got trouble.'

He pushed the door closed, removed the chain and let Pete in.

'What's happened?'

'It's Sandra. She's rung to say she's got trouble with the boy-friend. I guess, from what she said, that it's bad trouble – enough to make it good sense to take you over. Paddy's gone on while I came for you.'

'Slow it, Pete. Who the hell is Sandra?'

'Didn't I tell you? She's my other daughter.'

One was bad enough. He would have declined the GBH case if he had known he would be involved with two McBear women. Indeed he would. What he did not know was that the second had trouble that made Paddy's pale into insignificance. Nor did he know just what trouble he would get himself into by insisting on taking his small, black, zip-up court case.

3

Keith Parsons sat nonchalantly behind the wheel of his Granada listening to the dulcet tones of Elaine Paige emanating from the tape player. Calmness was the hallmark of the man. That, mainly, was the reason why he had this job. It needed discretion, professional coolness and, not least, a degree of courage. He also possessed other more important qualities, though these are not usually so valued by the law-abiding public. His real virtue, in his employer's eyes, was his ability to maintain a perfectly respectable position whatever he was doing, the implication being that it was not always totally legal.

The bow doors of the ferry opened steadily, allowing the late evening light to percolate in. The front vehicles slowly pulled up the ramp onto the dock. Today, he was lucky. Fate had put him very near to the front of the queue. He started the engine and dutifully followed the caterpillar leading into the customs hall. The majority of the cars were filled with tourists returning from holiday and, mostly, these turned for the green sign, leaving him first in the line for the red counter.

The officer was very polite. He was expecting a traveller returning with excess alcohol in the boot, a couple of hundred extra cigarettes or a few expensive gifts and lacking the nerve to risk the green counter - a common occurrence Gordon Mitchell had handled countless times a day.

'Good evening. Two things to declare, officer. I've brought back some perfume for my girl-friend and also the item on this sheet.'

He handed the typed piece of paper through the window and waited. He expected the pause. It happened every time and this was his nineteenth run at the game.

'I see, sir, and do you have the necessary documentation?'

'Of course. Do you wish me to come into the interview room?'

He knew the form as well as anybody.

'Er, yes, sir, if you don't mind.'

Parsons coolly opened the door, walked round to the boot and withdrew the black attaché case. Without a word, he followed Mitchell through a sturdy door labelled 'private' and closed it behind him. They crossed to the door immediately opposite and entered an inner room with no windows. The neon strip threw a stark light over the metal filing cabinets and the lone table in the middle of the floor. Behind it was a substantial wooden chair and in front of it were scattered three rickety chairs. Without waiting for any instructions, he placed the case on the desk and unlocked it. The lid sprang open and revealed a small pouch and a couple of bottles of rather expensive perfume. Ignoring the latter, he untied the cord at the neck of the pouch and carefully poured the contents onto the worktop.

'Beautiful, aren't they, sir?'

Even customs officers did not see one and a half million pounds' worth of diamonds every day and this officer certainly found them intriguing.

'There's a certain fascination with them, isn't there,

officer? They seem to possess a life of their own. Things of great beauty, indeed.'

He pulled out a loose-leaf file from the bottom of the case and extracted a sheaf of paper.

'You should find everything in order, I trust.'

Mitchell took a small chemical balance from inside the cupboard, levelled it carefully on the desk top and spent the next twenty minutes carefully weighing each stone in turn, checking it off against the sheets in front of him, occasionally fixing an oval stamp to the forms, and simultaneously filling in a sheaf of his own forms. Finally, he seemed satisfied.

'All in order, sir. If you will sign here – and here – and here.'

He put the papers into a drawer, returned the copies to Parsons and watched as he scooped up the stones.

'Doesn't it worry you, sir, carrying that lot?'

Parsons smiled condescendingly. 'Not at all. You get quite used to it, actually. There's little risk. After all, nobody outside the two firms knows what I am doing.'

He laughed half-heartedly.

'Oh, and you fellows, of course, but you're not going to broadcast it, are you?'

He packed the case, locked it and took out his wallet.

'What do I owe on the perfume?'

A calculator appeared from Mitchell's pocket.

'Er, yes. I'm happy to call that two pounds fifty, thank you, sir.'

Parsons held out the five-pound note.

'Give me a moment, sir, and I'll get your change.'

Mitchell left the room without fuss, crossed to the exit and emerged into the open once again. He signalled to a senior officer nonchalantly chatting in the corner of the customs hall, who walked across.

'You wanted a word if any diamonds were brought in. I have a man in the interview room.'

'Thanks, Gordon. Just let him go normally.'

The dark-haired young officer slid back into the interview room, where Parsons was pacing idly up and down as he waited for his change. He accepted it, along with the receipt. No more passed between them as he walked coolly back to the car. Without hurrying, he replaced the case containing the gems in the boot, got back into the car, did up his safety strap with studied care, started the engine and sedately drove out of the port. He took a left turn at the roundabout and smoothly accelerated as he climbed the Jubilee Way out of Dover. He allowed himself a brief smile then settled back on the leisurely drive towards London. Whatever happened, he would obey the speed limit to the letter and do nothing to attract any attention. Anonimity was the name of the game.

At first, he paid no attention to the red Sierra a hundred yards behind him. Indeed, he was not immediately aware of its presence, even though he was on the alert for such events. It was, however, a particularly clear evening and, despite it being well after nine, neither he nor the Sierra had initially switched on full-beam headlights. There was nothing especially unusual about another car also exactly obeying a speed limit. He carried out his usual practice of slowly reducing speed by a few miles an hour. This should have caused the Sierra to close on him but it did not. It was still a good hundred yards back. There was a second test. He checked his mirror carefully then increased speed over the next two miles to more than eighty. The red Sierra was maintaining its distance.

He dropped back to seventy and thought. The drill was

to pull into the first service station to make the swap. There was always the chance that the Sierra was innocent, the driver subconsciously keeping with him. In which case, there was no reason to alter the plans. If it was not, then there was no saying they knew what happened once he had crossed the Channel. The switch was still possible and he could drive on without fear. One thing for sure, if they did know his instructions and he broke them now, then they would also know he had spotted them.

He dipped under the bridge and climbed the hill towards the service access road. He put the trafficator on early.

Give the guy plenty of warning as though I don't know he's there, he thought.

As he filtered left, he noticed the Sierra slowing to follow him. He parked and went round to the boot without looking up. He knew he was being watched now but he trusted they did not know that he was aware of the fact. He might, he told himself, still have the edge on them. Be natural, that was still the name of the game. He took out the black case and carefully locked the boot. His pace towards the door of the restaurant section was even and unhurried. Inside, he walked up to the drinks section, took a pot of coffee and a bun, paid for it and sat down as close to a corner as he could get. As he entered, he had just caught the reflection of the two men from the Sierra in the glass door. It was enough. They had been behind him at the counter and it was now the most natural thing in the world to look up from the coffee in their direction. There was no way they could know they had been spotted.

In point of fact, Parsons was more interested in searching out his contact than worrying about the pair following him. He had no cause to worry. Roger Pratt was sitting at the far end of the smoking area, blowing fine circles into the air and reading a paper propped in front of the now empty plate. He was convinced the pair from the Sierra were police; there was nothing to fear once the switch had been achieved. They could happily stop him for questioning: he would be, in all things, exactly what he claimed to be.

The mime was perfect. Despite the lateness of the hour, there were still a dozen or so other travellers in the room but nobody else in that restaurant had any idea that the four men were in any way linked. Each pursued his own activity in total oblivion of the others. Ten minutes passed. Pratt stubbed out the cigarette, folded the paper and quietly got up. He put his attaché case on the table, opened it and put the paper inside, checked the lock and walked normally out towards the toilets. Parsons swallowed the last of his coffee and prepared to follow suit.

Instinct stopped him. Wait a few moments. The two in black leathers and carrying crash helmets – they had finished their meal very abruptly and left a lot on their plates. It could be innocent but he was becoming just a little paranoid. This was not like his usual self but, perhaps, this was not such a routine trip after all. From where he was, he could see the exit clearly. Anyone leaving had to pass his line of sight. Three minutes passed. Then four and then five. The adrenalin was pumping in his veins. Roger knew well enough to wait for him but the two in the leathers should have gone ages ago. They also must have gone into the toilets but they should have come out by now. He would give it another couple of minutes.

Something had gone wrong. No one had emerged from the entrance and the men had not come back to the restaurant. He got up calmly, picked up the attaché case and walked steadily to the door. He reckoned on having about fifteen seconds' start before the two following him would leave. That was all he wanted. He stopped at the entrance to the toilets and looked behind him. They were just getting ready to leave. He reached in his pocket for his ignition keys then walked very briskly to the car park. He hurried towards the Granada, pressing the infra-red door-lock button as he went. He pulled the door open, threw the case on the passenger seat and scrambled in. For all his haste, there was nothing to alert the casual observer that anything was wrong – he just appeared to be in a hurry. The car started just as the two men came running towards him. He was away.

He accelerated the car hard towards the join of the slip road and the dual carriageway. Luck was with him and he slid out easily. He put his foot down, watching as the needle rose to nearly ninety. He looked in the mirror. It seemed clear. He was down the hill and climbing towards the motorway roundabout. Which way? He looked again in the mirror and saw a set of lights coming from under the cover of the bridge and closing. Whatever was under the bonnet of that Sierra, it was having no difficulty in staying with him, even narrowing the gap gradually. The engine had to be powerful to come from behind like that.

He swung the wheel left and the tyres protested under the heavy cornering. Down the slip road and onto the motorway he went. The Sierra was closing; he could not outrun it. All right. Keep calm. Slow down and play for time while you think. He dropped to seventy and watched his mirror as the Sierra closed upon his tail and stayed there.

They're in no hurry, he thought. They know I can't outrun them so they're biding their time.

He passed a lone patrol car sitting on the hard

shoulder. Unfortunately, he could hardly stop and ask for help. Not with the case still on board and he was not prepared to jettison it yet. Indeed, he was now fairly certain that the two behind him were from Special Branch.

He reached for the car phone and started dialling. The voice at the other end simply said, 'Yes.'

'Trouble at the switch point. We had unexpected company and I've a couple of unwanted companions on my tail right now.'

'Can you lose them?'

'No, I've tried that and failed. Whatever they're in is souped up and can out-perform me.'

'What about Pratt?'

'I left him. He doesn't know where I am.'

There was a brief pause.

'OK, where are you now?'

'I'm about three miles past the Ashford exit on the M2.'

'Come off at the next exit and take the Maidstone road. When you approach the first roundabout after you have crossed the M20, switch your lights on and off several times. I've a friend in the area who owns a garage. I'll see to it that a blocking vehicle gets behind you. Take your time and stop worrying. If they haven't tried to intercept you so far then they will probably not try until you stop. My guess is that the cops have picked you up and want to see where you lead them. We'll worry how they got on to you later. Meanwhile, we need to lose them.'

Keith relaxed a little. His partner in the little venture, Jameson, was taking his line of reasoning: it reassured him. If it was the police then he was in no real danger and the block was being put in hand. He checked the mirror. They were still there, right enough, but they were quite content to play a waiting game.

The road flattened out at the top of a long, steady climb and swung round lazily towards a downhill stretch of deceptive bends which he knew well. It was worth one last try to slip them. Whatever else, it was good psychology. They would hardly expect a blocking vehicle immediately after he had tried to lose them. If he were unsuccessful, they would relax marginally in their over-confidence at staying with him.

He dropped the car down a gear, flicking the brake with the left foot. In the same instant, he floored the right on the throttle. It gave him another fifty yards before they realised what he was up to. He came out of the bends with his tail sliding wildly, counter-steered and continued accelerating. The ruse had worked. He had a lead of a good two hundred yards, with the traffic lights over the M20 access in front. He was prepared to shoot them on the red if necessary but it was not. He still held thirty yards on the closing Sierra as he reached the roundabout. If nothing else, he had made it easy for his helper to protect him.

Lights on, lights off, lights on, lights off. Just for a second, the nightmare of no one being there swept over him. He rolled the car fiercely round the curve of the road and noted with uncontainable joy that a black transit van had moved out behind him; the driver had timed his arrival at the junction with perfection.

For the first time, Keith realised that he was sweating. No need to worry now, pal. Just take it steady and watch the block car take him out. In his mirror, he could see the Sierra try to swing past and then cut sharply back the other way. Already there was a hundred yards' gap behind him. The Sierra moved out again.

The two shots dispelled all confidence. In an instant, he knew that his tail was not police. Five seconds later, he knew he had lost his protection. The van swayed violently to the side and careered off the road, going through a garden fence and ending in the middle of the front lawn.

There was no point in trying to slip his pursuit now. There was one chance and one chance only. He had to go to earth quickly. There was Sandra. If he were lucky, he might just make it to her flat. She lived about half a mile away across the town. As he was thinking all this, he carved his way through the mini roundabout, ignoring the hoots of other cars, and accelerated hard down a side-road to the right. If there was one thing to his advantage, it was the town. It nullified much of the following car's superior performance and, while he knew where he was heading, they did not. There was no way they could cut him off.

A fast left followed by a hard right brought him out in front of a block of high-rise flats. He turned down the side, threw the wheel sharply to the left and dipped down to enter the underground car park. As he turned, he pulled the handbrake up hard and braced himself for the inevitable slide. The car slid all right, turning as it went. There was no room for the car to pass the wall broadside. The front and rear bumpers came in contact with the walls and partially straightened the car. He ground to a halt, leaving a small gap either side between the dented bodywork and the concrete sides of the entrance. He had slipped his safety strap before he came to a stop and grabbed the case. Opening the door, he ran across to the lift and stairs. Behind him, he heard the sound of the impact as the Sierra failed to stop in time. They would be shaken; that had to be worth time. He looked at the open lift, jumped inside, pressed the button for the sixth floor and leapt out before the doors closed on him. Now he took the stairs as fast as he could.

He reached the third floor out of breath but without

any dropping of speed. God help us, you had better be in, Sandra my love. He leant on the doorbell and was still pushing it as she opened the door.

'Keith, what are you doing here at this time of night . . . ?'

She got no further. He pushed her in, shut the door quickly and slid the chain. In the next instant, his hand was at her mouth.

'Shut it,' he hissed.

The hand came away. There was something in his eyes that told her he was in trouble. She did not question, she did not even speak, but looked up wide-eyed at him, waiting for some explanation. He took her arm and indicated towards the lounge, turning off the hall light as he went. Once in the lounge, he also turned off the light and, in a hoarse whisper, told her to sit down.

'Not a sound, love. I've some people after me who are not at all bothered what they do. I don't think they saw me come up here but we mustn't take chances.'

She gripped his arm tightly. They had been going out together for eighteen months and never, in that time, had she ever known him lose his cool for a moment. She could feel the fear in his voice and it was transmitted to her. If he was frightened then there was good cause for her to worry as well. They sat like that for several minutes, ears strained for anyone in the corridor outside. Tension mounted higher as they heard soft footsteps but they passed without stopping and the pair relaxed slightly.

At last, Keith spoke quietly but no longer in a whisper.

'Sorry about this, love. Trouble at work!'

He got up and stretched.

'I sure could do with a cuppa. Let's put the kettle on.'

He continued. 'I've been over to Amsterdam again, picking up diamonds from van Hoffner's. I left around

54

ten this morning and had no trouble until I left Dover, then this car gets on my tail. I tried to shake it off without success but I managed to get just enough time to block off the entrance to the car park and get inside the building before they could see where I was going.'

He omitted the incidents at the service station, the block car and the shooting. He was not going to tell her half of what he was involved in if he could help it.

'What are we to do? Do you think we should phone the police?'

'It's not quite that simple, love. You see, the diamonds in the bag are worth more than the declared value at customs. All the diamond merchants do it – there's no way some run-of-the-mill customs officer can value diamonds – you say you have about two-thirds of the value of what you are really carrying. Trouble is, if we call the police, they might start digging a bit deeper.

'No, we'll wait a bit and then I'll see if the coast is clear. If it is then I'll come back and borrow your car – that'll be OK, won't it, love? – then I can finish the job.'

She looked far from happy. They had the light on now and the kettle was beginning to bubble. She shrugged, resigned to his plan without agreeing to it.

'I'll make the tea.'

Half an hour later, Parsons slipped quietly out of the door and she barred it behind him. She had her instructions: wait two hours. If he was not back by then, she was to dial a certain number and ask for Mr Wagstaff. He would tell her what to do. She was not happy and, now that he was gone, she was more scared than ever. She boiled the kettle again, made some more tea and left it to go cold. She put the television on but found her mind continually wandering. She had no idea what programme she had been watching. She knew it was a film but, beyond that, she had little recollection of the plot.

What was more, the clock had slowed to a crawl.

The direct fear she felt as he left subsided fairly quickly and was replaced by a gnawing apprehension that plagued her mind with every passing second. She was worried sick – almost literally – as the minutes turned to first one hour and then two hours without Keith returning. She gave it a full quarter of an hour over the time he had said then dialled the number.

She waited an interminable time before a sleepy voice simply said, 'Hello. Who is it?'

'I was told to ask for a Mr Wagstaff.'

'I'm Wagstaff. What do you want at this hour? Who are you?'

'I'm not to say.'

'Where are you calling from?'

'I wasn't to tell you that either.'

There was a pause.

'Who told you to call me?'

She hesitated.

'Was it Parsons?'

'Yes.'

'OK, what's happened?'

'He left a case here with me two hours ago and I haven't seen him since. Some men had been chasing him. He told me to call you if he didn't come back and he hasn't. He said you would know what to do.'

'You still have the case?'

'Yes.'

'Then hang on to it. Call me again at ten o'clock exactly tomorrow morning and I will tell you what to do with it. If Parsons returns meanwhile, tell him to wait and make the same call.'

The line went dead without another word.

4

Jeremy was none too pleased at having his sleep disturbed, nor was the prospect of another female McBear in trouble one he relished, but his immediate fears centred on the road in front of him. Convinced as he was that the Bear was practising for his next stock-car race, Jeremy tried shutting his eyes. However, the sound of the protesting tyres and the sickening G-forces every other minute caused him to abandon his action. He glanced at the speedometer and then wished he had not. They were in the high eighties and still not clear of the forty limit. St Mary's Cray came and went as a blur of street lights and then they were rolling hard through the roundabout and onto the dual carriageway. Now the Sierra really opened up and Pete was not even considering dipping his lights as they caught and passed other vehicles at alarming speeds. Fortunately, there was little around at that time of night, which was as well.

There is one thing in favour of such reckless flight: it does not last long. Leastways, the car was actually slowing for the slip road for the Maidstone exit before too long. However, this only exchanged one form of torture for another as the motor tore into the town. The Bear was, however, down to something resembling a sane speed on the access to the underground car park, which was as well considering it was blocked. Cursing, he managed to stop the vehicle literally inches from the white Granada. The rear passenger door had been dented and fragments of glass remained on the ground. The impact had pushed the rear of the car tightly up against the right-hand wall, leaving it at an angle of about sixty degrees to the left-hand wall but with a gap just big enough to allow a child to squeeze through.

Pete slammed the car into reverse, backed out of the drive and parked on the double yellow lines at the front of the block. It was only as their Sierra exited from the parking bay that Jeremy noticed the red BMW outside the main entrance. Paddy, at least, had arrived safely.

They entered the block via the main door and took the lift to the third floor. All was in silence and the only light came from the low glow of the night-lights in the lift and corridors. They switched the main light on for themselves and walked quietly along the faded carpet to the same door that Parsons had arrived at several hours before. They rang the bell and waited patiently while the chain was slid back and the door opened.

'Oh, Dad, I'm so glad you've come!'

Pete let his elder daughter throw herself into his arms and he hugged her long and hard.

'Come on, kitten, what's happened?'

He was looking over her towards Paddy, who was viewing the scene with a face full of long-suffering forbearance.

'Don't worry, Pops. That's just it, nothing seems to have happened. Lover-boy was here earlier with some cock-and-bull story about being chased. He left his case and told sis to phone some guy in London if he wasn't back in a couple of hours. Guess what? He wasn't, so she's panicked and got us out of bed.'

'Hush there, Pad. Stop being so bitchy. Sandra never cries wolf. You know that.'

'She has this time.'

'I'll be the judge of that. Come on, kitten. Let's go inside properly and tell your old dad all about it.'

He was talking as though she were still a very young girl. Jeremy noticed with interest how Pete treated his two daughters so differently. This one obviously needed protection.

'I don't suppose there's any chance of a coffee, is there, Pad? My stomach doesn't take kindly to romping around in the middle of the night, especially at the speed it has been travelling.'

'Kettle's in there. Make it yourself!'

'That will do, Pad. I don't reckon it'll hurt you to rustle up a few cups of coffee while kitten tells us what's happening.'

'Please, Cindy. You don't mind, do you?'

'Cindy?' Jeremy laughed gently. 'I thought you told me you'd kill anyone who called you that?'

'You call me that and I will!'

'How come she can get away with it and I can't?'

'She's my big sister, isn't she?'

Big sister? Jeremy could not see it. This female Goliath was at least four inches taller and more than five stone heavier than her sister. He intimated as much.

Paddy flounced into the kitchen, calling back over her shoulder as she went. 'Well, she's my *older* sister, anyway. She was calling me Cindy before they got round to giving me a nickname.'

Over the sound of the running tap, she went on, 'I got this T-shirt with a Paddington Bear on it when I was about three and Pops, here, started calling me Paddy and it stuck. I can't stand Cynthia for a name. Only Ma could think up something as dumb as that.'

'Don't you go insulting your mother none, d'you hear me?'

59

Pete unwound his arms from Sandra and gently led her towards the settee.

'Right, kitten, let's have it from the top.'

'Well, it was about half past ten. Keith turned up all worried and, I think, frightened, only he doesn't admit to such things and is usually dead cool. He said he had been chased by some men in a Sierra and he had blocked them off in the car park then run up here.'

'We didn't see any Sierra when we came in but there's a white Granada skewed across the entrance and something has hit it. I suppose that's Keith's motor.'

'I expect so. Anyway, he waited for a little bit and we had some tea and a chat and then he said he had to go. He left his case here and told me to ring this number' – she passed over the pad with the telephone number on it – 'if he wasn't back in two hours. That was three hours ago and I'm scared something has happened to him.'

'Why did he leave his case?'

For the first time, Sandra took notice of Jeremy.

'Who's this, Dad?'

'This,' said Pete with just a touch of pride in his voice, 'is Jerry Fox, our family lawyer.'

Somehow, Jeremy found the description slightly ostentatious.

'I'm defending Paddy in her own case, that's all.'

'That's not all. He's got her bail and reckons he'll get her off with no sweat.'

Oh, God! thought Jeremy. I'm a dead man if she gets anything more than a conditional discharge.

He smiled blandly and held out his hand. She shook it very seriously.

'I'm pleased to meet you. The case? He had diamonds in it and I think he was afraid these men were after them.'

'And have you tried phoning?'

'Yes. I got this man Wagstaff he told me about and he said I was to call again tomorrow if Keith hasn't shown up by then. Oh, something's happened to him, I know it.'

She began to cry again. For his part, Jeremy was trying to come to terms with a case of diamonds.

'Do you happen to know how much they're worth?'

She nodded. Between stifled sobs, the words emerged in a series of gushes.

'About a couple of million, he said.'

Pete was trying to pacify her again. His large arm was wrapped protectively over her shoulder and his hand was patting her arm absent-mindedly. Jeremy was trying to look as though he normally dealt with clients who carried the odd couple of million around in their briefcases. He was not succeeding.

'Don't worry, kitten. He'll be OK.'

'He won't, he won't, I know he won't.' She was sobbing heavily now.

'Yes he will, kitten. We'll have our coffee then me and Jerry here will go and look for him.'

She brightened a little. 'You will?'

'Sure we will.'

'But definitely not before coffee.' Jeremy decided to be positive. His interjection was bred of need. He still had not come to terms with this couple of million idly lying around in the flat. What was more, his beauty sleep had been grossly abused and he was feeling it.

'Actually, I think we ought to report this to the police . . . .'

He stopped. Pete was aghast. Paddy, who was just entering the room carrying the coffee, stopped stock-still and looked daggers at him. For her part, Sandra appeared pertrified at the suggestion and started to wail again.

'No police, old son. Not popular in this family.'

No, I bet, thought Jeremy.

'You can't call the police on this, Jerry. Keith told me that the diamonds were more valuable than he declared at customs. It wouldn't do for him if anyone started to examine that case too closely.'

Jackpot, old girl, though she was innocent of any first-hand knowledge of what it really held. So far, she had not even had her perfume out of it and that was legitimate. As far as Jeremy was concerned, the whole matter was getting out of hand. No, that was hardly fair. It had got out of hand some time ago. Nevertheless, he was sticking to his guns.

'You brought me along for my advice and you've got it. If you don't want to take it, on your heads be it.'

'Look, lad, I know you mean well but that isn't the McBear way. We'll have our coffee, go down and park Keith's car properly and then scout round and see if we can find him. I assume you've got his home address, kitten?'

She nodded. 'He's got a flat in Chelsea. I'll get the address book.'

'Why don't we phone him to see if he's got home? If he found his car was stuck, he might have had difficulty getting back.'

To Jeremy, this was the obvious course of action and it struck him as odd that no one had thought of doing it before.

'Give me the number, kitten, and we'll see if he's back. Like as not, the thoughtless bastard's gone to bed without thinking about you worrying your head off for him.'

Pete took the address book and dialled the code. The phone rang all right but no one answered. He let it ring for several minutes before he reluctantly replaced the receiver.

'Looks like either he's a heavy sleeper or else he hasn't made it back. Have you done with that coffee, old son?'

Jeremy took a long swig and put the mug on the casual table in front of him.

'Right, then. You girls stay here, now, while Jerry and me go and have a scout round.'

The two men left the flat and started walking together down the corridor towards the lift and stairs. Once Jeremy was sure that the door had closed behind him and they were clear of the flat, he broached the subject that had been running through his mind for some time.

'Pete, you'll probably not thank me for this but I don't see much point in looking for this fellow around here. For my money, he was on the fiddle and someone got onto him and he's done a runner.'

'Could be, old son, but he ain't home and he ain't come back for his diamonds so where is he? His car isn't damaged enough to stop it being driven so why didn't he scarper in comfort? Put this one down to intuition, Jerry, lad, but I don't reckon he went anywhere. Only thing is, he can't have told anyone where the loot is, otherwise we wouldn't have been the first to get to Sandra.'

He paused.

'We'd better search the building. He certainly wasn't in the entrance or on this corridor so I suggest one of us goes up and the other down. Check the corridors, any cupboards and hiding-places.'

Jeremy felt a nasty itch start in the small of his back and spread up his spine. He wanted to scratch it but it hardly seemed good manners. Pete clearly expected to find lover-boy but not in good shape. It was slowly dawning on him that this sort of company might be unconventional and fun in its own way but it was also highly unpredictable and certainly not safe.

'If it's all the same to you, I'll take up.'

'Suits me, son. I'll go down and take the car park as well.'

He pulled a foot-long spanner from the deep pockets of his boiler suit.

'Take this just in case, lad. You never know.'

There was a sudden seriousness about the voice.

'What about you?'

'Don't worry, Jerry old son. They come in pairs.'

Jeremy looked at the spanner and at the giant frame standing next to him. He was not easy. He was thinking that he had left him with the roughest patch to search and it made Jeremy feel slightly ashamed.

'Do you think it might be better if we stayed together?'

'Are you scared, son?'

'A bit, but that wasn't why I suggested it though.'

'No, we'll stick to the plan but yell like hell if you find anything.'

With that, the two parted. Immediately, Jeremy felt even less secure. He was alone with only the low-level security light to see by and all he could hear was the soft pad of Pete's feet on the stairs. He turned the corner and now he could hear nothing. He braced himself. Not likely to find anything going up. Pete felt that as well. That was why he had taken the lower floors. He gripped the spanner tighter and turned his attention to the fourth floor.

The stairs opened onto a corridor to all intents and purposes identical to the one he had left. It was also very empty. He paced the length and returned to the stairs without finding anything. The only cupboard on the corridor was locked. He made for the fifth floor with some slight gain of confidence though neither the

64

solitude nor the silence was designed to raise spirits. Again, the corridor was deserted and the solitary broom cupboard locked.

The sixth floor was also the top floor. It, too, was deserted, only this time the cupboard was not locked. It was with some trepidation that he opened the door, spanner at the ready. At first, he could see nothing inside. Certainly, nothing moved but he needed to check. He moved away, switched on the main lighting and returned to probe the depths of the cleaner's domain. There was an adequate supply of buckets and cleaning materials and a large commercial vacuum cleaner but sight of Parsons there was none. Relieved, he closed the door, switched off the main light and was about to descend the stairs the way he had come when the fire escape caught his notice. Since he was here, perhaps he should just check it.

The door appeared firmly shut. The darkness beyond obscured anything that might have been out there. He tried to squint over the edge of the glass, shielding the reflection from the inside light with his hand. All seemed quiet. He rattled the bar. It was not properly fastened and it yielded under a gentle push. He felt the cool air swim around his face as he ventured gingerly out onto the platform. There seemed little point in exploring further yet, if he was checking, he might as well check each platform. He came back inside, fastened the door securely and walked down to the next floor. Again, he checked the platform, going outside as before. By the time he reached the fourth-floor door, the check had become routine. Indeed, he hardly noticed that this door, too, was not properly fastened. He went onto the empty platform and briefly glanced around. He gripped the safety rail and peered over into the darkness. Nothing. He went back inside and pulled the door towards him. The handle seemed sticky. As he removed his hand, he noticed the red smear. Somehow, he must have cut himself. He cursed silently, moved under the light and examined his hand but he failed to find any cut. Puzzled, he stood still and considered the situation.

The itch in his back had returned. He did not seem to be bleeding. He opened the door again and felt the safety bar on the platform. It was tacky. He pulled his hand away, took out his handkerchief and wiped the metal rail, returning once more to the light to examine the evidence. Certainly, the white linen was streaked with dark red. It had to be blood and it did not seem to be his.

Jeremy made sure that the door could not slam on him then very cautiously started down the outside staircase. He almost stumbled over the prostrate figure hunched into the shelter of the fire-escape door on the third floor, so camouflaged was the black suit in the pre-dawn air. He remained frozen by the sight, within touching distance yet unwilling so much as to move his hand out in its direction. He knew he was dead; at least, he had no doubts – he did not have to examine the body. He continued to stare for some time, not knowing what to do next. At last, he bent down and lightly touched the man's jacket. It was leather. He pulled the body over and jumped back in alarm as the corpse rolled towards him, stopping on its back. He looked down at the face. It was staring up at him, open-eyed, blood congealed down the cheek where it had run from the partially open mouth.

The shock of the discovery numbed him. It was the first time he had seen a body this close. He resisted the urge to vomit, closed his eyes and took in several deep gulps of air. He could feel the pumping of his heart and the sweat on his brow. Slowly, the fluctuations eased. He was getting a grip on himself; his brain was functioning properly again. Time to open his eyes and face reality. This time, he would be in control.

Leaving the body where it was, he ran up the stairs, through the fire exit, closed the door behind him and ran back to the third-floor corridor. He reached it just as Pete was about to knock on the door to Sandra's flat. Jeremy called to him in a hoarse whisper but it carried. The Bear turned round and came back towards him.

'I think I've found Keith. It's going to upset Sandra.'

'Is he alive? No, he can't be – not by the colour of your cheeks.'

'Too true. He's dead all right. Come and look at this.'

Jeremy moved straight along the corridor to the fire exit. He pushed the door half open and had a slight struggle to push the body completely away from it with his foot. He pulled back to let the Bear see.

The big fellow grunted, dropped on one knee and pulled the man through the gap so he could get a better look at him. In the light, the full extent of the injuries showed. Both his hands were covered in blood and so was a large region around his midriff.

'Somebody's stuck a knife through his stomach. Very messy. He bled to death, by the look of it. You're right, old son, Sandra ain't gonna like this one bit.'

Satisfied, he pushed the body back onto the platform and pulled the door to, enough to hide its secret. That done, he signalled back towards the flat.

'Poor sod. I wouldn't mind a few minutes alone with the bastard that did this. Best if we don't tell the girls too much about it, though. I guess the only sane thing we can do now is to get them back to Lewisham.'

'For crying out loud, Pete. We can't just leave a body

lying around. Whether you like it or not, we must call the police.'

'You can call them, old son, but not until we are well under way. You can use the car phone in the BMW if you like. You drive that one on your own and I'll take the girls.'

They were at the flat door. As Pete rang the bell, Jeremy shrugged and said, 'Have it your own way. I can't get out of here quick enough.'

Sandra opened the door for them. She did not ask anything: she just looked at their faces then burst into tears. The Bear moved quickly inside and wrapped his paws round his little cub. Behind the touching little scene, Paddy was questioning Jeremy with her eyes. He nodded shortly and shut the door behind him.

'I found him on the fire escape. He's been knifed. God! Is there any brandy in the place? I could use one.'

'Not now, old son. We still have things to do, including driving home. Time enough for that when we get back to Lewisham.'

The Bear was right. Jeremy pulled himself up hard. Had to keep a stiff upper lip, especially as this lot had not had the benefit of a public-school education. It was for situations like this that he was supposed to be equipped.

Sandra suddenly stopped crying and detached herself from her father's embrace. Her face was ashen but her voice steady.

'Oh, Daddy, what are we going to do?'

'Get you away from here as soon as possible, kitten. Do you feel up to packing a few things?'

She nodded.

'Come on, sis, I'll help you.'

The two girls went into the bedroom and closed the

door. Jeremy threw himself into the nearest chair, dangled his legs as far out as he could get them and let his arms droop over the side. Pete stood looking around the room.

'I can't see that case,' he said.

'Ask Sandra.'

He grunted.

'It can wait. You OK, Jerry, old son?'

'If you want the truth, I feel absolutely knackered.'

'Yer, know what you mean. I'll feel happier myself once we're home.'

He, too, slumped onto the settee and closed his eyes, though he clearly was not going to sleep.

'You won't be mentioning Sandra when you phone the police, will you?'

'No way. A solicitor's first job is to protect his client. She wasn't involved so there is no need. The police will eventually get round to questioning her, I suppose, but she doesn't have to say anything. We could say she spent the night with you and if Keith did call then he must have found her out. She can hardly admit to having seen him without letting out about the diamonds, though, who knows, she might take a different view of things in the morning. I ought to tell the police that he was carrying diamonds when I ring them.'

It was not long before the bedroom door opened and the two girls emerged. Paddy was carrying a large brown suitcase and a small metal-rimmed one in grey. Sandra followed with a small black attaché case. There was no need to ask what it contained: both men knew, or thought they did.

'Right, girls, let's have those cases and we'll get off.'

He ushered his daughters through the front door, waited for Jeremy to extinguish all the lights and to pass through it, followed him out and slammed it before following the small party to the lift. They reached the front entrance without incident and walked through to the road. Here, the McBears bundled into the Sierra while Jeremy took the wheel of the BMW. They had agreed their plan on the way down: drive quietly to the edge of the motorway and stop while Jeremy made his call to the police. He had also been warned to make it short; Pete was worried that the call might be traced.

Dawn was filtering across the sky as the cars sedately wound their way through the deserted streets of the town. They crossed the Medway bridge and climbed up the short hill to filter off along the A20. Hardly exceeding the speed limit, the pair proceeded down the main road and turned off at the entrance to a garden centre. Jeremy switched off and reached for the car phone. He depressed the nine three times and waited.

'Which service, please?'

'Police.'

'Can I have your number please, caller?'

'Sorry, no. Put me through to the police straight away or I hang up.'

'I can't do that, sir. I need your number.'

'Listen, sweetheart' – he liked that bit – 'I've no intention of giving you long enough to trace this call, so do it or I ring off.'

There was a brief pause.

'Police. How can I help you?''

'There is a man on the fire-escape outside the flats of Osbourne House in Maidstone. He's been knifed. If I need to speak to you again I shall use the code-name "the Fox".'

He switched off immediately. It had given him a thrill and he knew it should not have done. He was a solicitor, he must remember. An officer of the court. He should not behave like this. However, officer or no, he was not inclined to be more involved than he was at present. He could just stay out of it without withholding evidence. He thought about the black attaché case. Well, without withholding much and nothing that should inhibit the police inquiry. He would phone back from a call box in the morning and tell them about the diamonds.

He did not like it. It was going against his training and yet his instincts were warning him not to get drawn into this one. Get drawn in? Damn it, he was already. He looked up at the Sierra, gave a thumbs-up sign and started the engine.

5

It could hardly be said that Jeremy had a restful night – or what was left of it, as it was well after four when he curled up on the McBears' settee. He did not have enough room to stretch his legs out straight and the solitary cushion that passed for a pillow had insufficient padding to stop the wooden arm pressing on his neck. Although his mind was in a turmoil, the double brandy at least induced a measure of sleep. The term could only be used in the loosest sense, as he had a particularly nasty dream in which he spent most of the time avoiding a series of vicious attacks from knives with a will of their own that chased him virtually continuously around endless flights of stairs. When he did eventually escape from the sadistic blades, he ran into the road, only to be attacked from all sides by stock-cars intent on doing him no good.

The nightmare was broken shortly after eight. He awoke with sweat on his brow and needed a few moments to reorientate himself. Deciding that consciousness was preferable to more of the traumas of sleep, he washed and put the kettle on. It was just boiling when the Bear appeared, full of the joys of life and apparently unruffled by the preceding night's activity.

'That's the stuff, son. Nothing like a good brew-up to start the day. I'll rustle up some bacon and eggs. Fancy some?'

Words were hardly needed: the facial expression was enough.

'Dried toast and tea will do fine, thanks.'

'Rubbish! Get a decent breakfast inside you and you're set up for the day. Still, please yourself.'

The pan was sizzling with half a dozen rashers of bacon and four eggs when Paddy appeared. She failed to share Jeremy's inhibitions about fat that day (given his normal attitude to food, the poor quality of the night's sleep was only too clear to anyone who knew him intimately – little else could have destroyed his appetite) and tucked in with relish. However, he was not alone with the toast: this seemed adequate for Sandra, who failed to manage even the one piece she took. Her eyes were red and everything about her manner suggested she had had even less sleep than Jeremy.

With the meal finished, Pete and Paddy went off to the workshop as though nothing had happened, leaving Sandra with Jeremy in the upstairs flat. Between them, they cleared up the dishes and straightened the untidy mess left from the night before.

At exactly ten, with Jeremy as close to the receiver as he could legitimately get, Sandra rang Wagstaff. The phone seemed to ring for an interminable age before a voice with more than a hint of an East End accent answered.

'I want to speak to Mr Wagstaff, please.'

There was a slight hesitation.

'He's busy at the moment, can you call back later?'

'He specifically told me to ring at exactly ten,' she replied. 'It is rather urgent.'

'Give me a minute. Who shall I say is calling?'

'Sandra. I am the woman who called him last night.'

There was a pause.

'And what is it about?'

'The case. Just tell him the woman with the case is on the line.'

She waited patiently.

'This is Wagstaff. Do you still have the case?'

'Yes, of course. I thought you were going to tell me what I should do with it.'

'You actually have it with you in the flat?'

'Yes. I said I have.'

'Tell me where you are and I will get somebody down to pick it up.'

'Are you sure?'

'Of course.' The voice sounded slightly impatient. 'Now, give me your address.'

Jeremy held up his hand in front of her face and waved it from side to side rapidly. She looked at him and he shook his head vigorously, signalling to her to put the receiver down.

'Just a minute,' she said. 'There's somebody at the door.'

She put the phone down, questioning him with her eyes. He beckoned her away from the table.

'Tell him to find another way. Whatever you do, don't give him your address or telephone number.'

She picked up the receiver again. 'Sorry about that. It was the milkman.'

It sounded a lame excuse but appeared to be accepted.

'Keith told me not to let anyone know where I was.'

'Don't be stupid! That was only an initial precaution. Now we've made contact, that no longer applies.'

'I – I don't think he would like it if I did.'

There was another pause then the voice came again, smoother, reassuring this time.

'He may be right. Listen carefully. Take the case and

74

leave it in the left-luggage office at Charing Cross station. Can you manage that this afternoon?'

'Yes, I think so.'

'Good, then ring me on this number at exactly five o'clock this evening.'

He gave the number slowly and let her read it back.

'Now don't worry. It will all be fine. Just do as I say and there shouldn't be any problem.'

She read the piece of paper Jeremy pushed in front of her with some astonishment. He nodded and urged her to ask the question.

'Have you got any word from Keith?'

'Be patient, my dear. I expect to hear from him soon. I believe I know where he is.'

He rang off.

Sandra looked at Jeremy with a mixture of puzzlement and alarm. He, in turn, looked grim.

'Can you be sure that the fellow on the phone this time was the same one you spoke to last night?'

She hesitated.

'It sounded like him but I couldn't be sure. No, now you mention it, he did sound a bit different.'

'I've got this funny feeling. There's something not right about this whole affair. If he is who he says he is then he can't have a clue where Keith is. Here, give me that phone.'

He reached across and redialled the number. Again, it was some time before it was answered and it was the same accent as before.

'Good morning. Can I speak to Mr Wagstaff, please?'

'If you will just hold the line, sir.'

They have had practice, thought Jeremy. Much more polished this time.

75

'Wagstaff here.'

'Hello, old chap. Fraser speaking. Look, I've been tied up a bit this morning. I'm going to have trouble making our three o'clock meeting. Could we put it back until tomorrow, do you think? Frightfully sorry about all this.'

'Certainly, my dear fellow. Name a time.'

'Say nine-thirty?'

'That will be fine. I'll see you then.'

Jeremy looked thoughtfully at the telephone for long after the other party had rung off and, for her part, Sandra refrained from interrupting his cogitations. He absent-mindedly let the receiver slide onto its holder. Whoever they were, they were certainly cool. Obviously, they needed to be in the place for some time and were happy to answer the phone if that was necessary. Something big was going on.

'Sandra, go and get Paddy and Pete up here, will you? Tell them to shut the garage for a bit – we need a family conference.'

She had barely left the room when he was on the phone.

'Lewisham police station. How can I help you?'

'Listen very carefully. I am not repeating this and you will need to make notes. I made a 999 call last night from the Maidstone area so I don't know which station would have taken it. I used the code name "the Fox". I have more information. I have reason to believe a crime has been committed at a house in the Petts Wood area. I only have the telephone number.'

– he gave it –

'I suspect there is a man there impersonating a Mr Wagstaff. If the true Mr Wagstaff is not there, there will be a good attempt at deception by men who are likely to be armed.'

He rang off sharply, realising that he had no justification, other than a hunch, for saying the men might be armed.

It was curious: the position was undoubtedly serious but he was getting a kick from all this cloak-and-dagger stuff. It also worried him: he was playing at Jekyll and Hyde. Here he was, an honest, law-abiding, middle-class solicitor caught up in the centre of a murder case, a diamond fraud and God knows what. He considered. He had hardly acted improperly; idiosyncratically, yes, but not improperly. At least, he hoped not. What about removing Sandra from the scene of the crime and not disclosing her part? He shrugged. He would let it play itself out a bit before he did anything else.

The four sat around drinking coffee in sombre mood as Jeremy explained what had happened. Sandra only grasped the full significance as it was retold but Paddy and Pete both cottoned on at once. Wagstaff was hardly the chap he claimed to be if he agreed to change an appointment that never existed.

'What made you try that trick, old son? I mean, how did you get on to him?'

'I don't know, really. I just got that feeling. After all, if you had been waiting for a call from someone with a couple of million in diamonds, would you have to be found or would you be poised over the phone, waiting? Then again, there was too much hesitation before he tumbled to what was happening. If I had a plan then I would have gone straight to it. Then, he wanted her address too badly. It was all sorts of things – I don't know, it just didn't feel right.'

Pete looked across at Paddy. 'Told you, didn't I? With a brain like this on your side, you're as good as off. He'll wrap 'em in knots in court.'

'I'll kill him if he doesn't!'

Great, thought Jeremy. I knew I was in for it with this one!

'Let's just take stock of where we are. We know, or at least suspect, that Wagstaff has been removed by someone in the gang that killed Keith. We also know that the lot that are after the case knew enough of the plans to move in on Wagstaff within hours of the attack in Maidstone. What we have got, for what it is worth, is until five o'clock in the certain knowledge that these guys will expect Sandra to hand over the case quite innocently. To be honest with you, I don't know what we are going to do with the time but I have two suggestions.'

'Which are?'

'To go to the police . . .'

'I told you, old son, we don't go to any coppers.'

'Then I suggest we get this case into a safe place.'

'It's all right here, isn't it?'

'No, it's not. I was thinking that a bank vault would be a better bet, for instance.'

'I suppose there might be some sense in that,' Paddy allowed. 'If it's not here then we don't have to worry about it.'

'If that's agreed, I'll take it over to Orpington now. I need to go back to my flat for some papers, so I can deposit it on the way.'

A thought suddenly struck him.

'Oh, hell! I've just remembered. In the confusion last night I left my court case in your flat, Sandra.'

'Do you want the key to get it?'

He thought for a moment. 'I may as well. That's going to take me another hour or more. Oh, damn! It can't be helped, I suppose.'

The coffee was finished and so was the case conference. While Paddy and Pete went back to work and Sandra cleared the pots away, Jeremy put the

78

troublesome attaché case in the back of the borrowed BMW and, armed with the key to Sandra's flat, set off on his errands. Now it is one thing to decide on a course of action and another to carry it out. That case gnawed at him. Two million, was it? Gem-quality diamonds? He had never seen two million pounds' worth of diamonds and wondered what they looked like. His curiosity was winning. The bank was bypassed and he ended up back at his flat with the case on the table and an insatiable desire to look inside it.

The lock was one of those three-digit security jobs but, otherwise, there was no key. It just came down to finding the right combination. He thought for a moment. It was unlikely to be too low a number as it would be quickly found in a trial and error exercise. Start at two hundred and see what happens. For the next quarter of an hour he twiddled the cogs. At first, it was pure systematic trials but he noticed that the six seemed to click in more easily on the unit wheel than the other numbers. At two hundred and eighty-six, he abandoned the systematic approach and went up in tens, holding the units at six. At four hundred and ninety-six, the catches sprang open. He had successfully burgled his first case!

He fingered the pouch delicately before carefully opening the neck and extracting the gems. There was a sense of disappointment and anticlimax: he had expected the glitter and they were, it was true, very beautiful. However, these pieces of rock hardly seemed worth a couple of million. It struck him as a nonsense that only a quarter of the bag could have bought him a house and a car or, collectively, could ensure he never had to work again. At the same time, he could understand the criminal drive to acquire them if they had this sort of value. He turned a couple over in his hand then put them back in the bag. He smelt the perfume and

79

decided that it should, by rights, go to Sandra, so he put it on one side. Hardly bothering much, he absent-mindedly took out the wodge of documents and flicked through them.

He was about to replace everything and shut the case when something struck him with the force of a sledge-hammer. The case appeared deeper on the outside than on the inside. Why he thought it, he was not sure, but think it he did. In fact, the more he thought about it, the more it struck him that the case was abnormally heavy. He stared at it for several seconds then took out his pen and held it to one side of the case, marking the top with his finger. He transferred the pen to the inside and noted that his finger stood proud of the top by about half an inch. So it was not his imagination!

Over the next ten minutes, he could have been found running a razor-blade carefully around the seal of the lining. Then he used a kitchen knife to cut away the restraining glue. He had worked the fabric down to the base without finding anything but, as he eased away the floor, a series of translucent polythene bags were exposed to the world. With a mixture of dread and excitement, he withdrew the first bag, slit it open and prodded the white powder inside. Cautiously, he moistened his index finger and touched the surface of the powder. A few grains stayed on and he gingerly touched them with his tongue. There was a taste there all right but he realised he did not have a clue as to what he was testing for. He was assuming drugs but he had never seen any before in his life, let alone tasted them. He had a sudden fear that it only needed a few grains to send him off into a trip and he brushed the residue quickly from his hand and spat twice to clear his mouth.

This was coffee time. It was always coffee time when he had any serious thinking to do. Clearly, this called for a large pot: this was going to be at least a three-cup job. In fact, he was barely into the third cup when things started making some sense. Keith had refused to contact the police not because of any fiddle over the value of gems – for which, anyway, he could hardly be blamed – but because of the drugs. Whether it was cocaine or heroin he was not sure but he felt certain it was one of them. This was what all the fuss was about. Clever. The diamonds were an outward cover for the drug-smuggling. Who would suspect a businessman who openly went into the red gate declaring a million and a half's worth of high-quality gems? That explained why the case stank of perfume. It had not leaked: it was deliberate. It killed any smell from the drugs that might be around the case. (At least, that was his version, although he was totally wrong. Parsons had opened the bottle in the shop to smell it and the cap had not been tightened sufficiently. No subterfuge had been intended in this purchase of a simple gift for his girl-friend.)

Now the sixty-four dollar question: what to do next? Difficult. A fourth cup of coffee was called for.

The bank delayed him by only a few minutes. He exited with the secure knowledge that he was the only person, short of a court order, who could get at the diamonds. He stopped at the newsagent's and bought a *Daily Telegraph*. He had answered quite a few questions this morning, now he had another one, closer to home or, more accurately, closer to stomach: where should he eat? It was ten to twelve. Did he get it in Orpington or go to Maidstone first and then find something to eat? He decided on the latter course.

He had almost no trouble in finding Osbourne House – he had to stop and ask just the once – and parked some way from the entrance. The place was swarming with police. Two cars were parked on the double yellow lines in front of the main entrance and several officers were busy outside questioning passers-by. He decided not to risk going in for fear of being asked a series of questions he was keen not to answer. Thus, he drove back to the flat, via the Chinese take-away, and phoned Lewisham.

'Hi, that you, Pad?'

'No, it's Madonna, you prat!'

'Well, hi there, Madonna! Can I get your autograph when I come round?'

'Jackass! What do you want? I'm busy.'

'I've just been over to Sandra's place and it's crawling with cops so I didn't go in. I've decided to stay home for the rest of the day. I'm in court tomorrow with your adjournment. You might be interested to know all your papers arrived – the advanced disclosures – that's the evidence they're going to present at the trial. I'm going to spend the afternoon reading them.

'Tomorrow, on my way back to Lewisham, I'll go via Maidstone and get the case then. Do something for me, will you, Pad? Drop in the office and switch the answerphone on for me.

'Cheers, then. See you sometime after lunch. That means you'll have to get the sandwiches!'

He laughed and rang off.

The afternoon was spent in a careful study of the advanced disclosures. The defence was gradually unfolding for him and, by half past five, he had the paperwork for the day fully sorted and cleared. The evening was his own. He poured a sherry and turned the television on for the news. The first few minutes passed without any reaction: it was mostly the political nonsense of the Commons and concern for a strike that might or might not materialise. He let such matters sweep over him without arousing any emotional feelings. Then he sat up straight in the chair, his brain hurting in its efforts to soak up every word. Outside the high wrought-iron gates of a splendid house set in its own grounds, an eager young commentator was saying, 'A policeman was seriously hurt in a shoot-out this morning. Acting on an anonymous tip-off, armed officers from the Rapid Response Unit surrounded a house in Petts Wood, where they surprised four gunmen. The wounded police officer was named as Sergeant James Cordwell, from Chislehurst, in Kent. He was said to be comfortable in hospital after surgery to remove two bullets, one from his arm and a second from his shoulder. Two men were arrested late this afternoon and are being held at Paddington police station. I am told they are to appear before magistrates tomorrow on specimen charges but that more serious charges are likely to eventually be brought against the men, who police declined to name.

'A spokesman for the police revealed that a man was found bound and gagged in the boot of an abandoned car and it is understood that at least one other man was found tied up in the basement of the house. Two men escaped but, in the exchange of shots, one was believed to have been hit and seriously wounded. Hospitals in the area were alerted in case he sought treatment. Despite intensive police avtivity, the men are still at large.'

At this stage, two crude Identikit pictures were flashed on the screen and a warning given that the public should not approach them.

The commentator went on: 'It was not clear whether robbery or kidnap was the motive for the attack or whether there was something more sinister behind what was described by Detective Superintendent Colin Burnell as a most vicious and clinical operation having no concern for the lives of the police or their victims.

'Detective Superintendent Burnell went on to say that the raid was the result of information received by an anonymous caller and he appealed to him to come forward. If the person had cause to fear for his safety then he promised that any information would be treated in the strictest confidence and his identity would be completely protected. He asked that the caller should ring . . .'

Jeremy was clamouring for a pencil.

'. . . or any police station.'

Damn, he thought. Trust me to miss it!

He resolved to watch the news again at nine with the one intention of getting the number. Meanwhile, he reached for the paper and scanned the television programmes; nothing worth watching. He felt suddenly irritable. What was he to do for the evening? The news had upset him somewhat. He did not want to think about the events of the previous twenty-four hours; he wanted some pure escapism. Twenty minutes later, he could have been seen choosing a video from the local centre with the care a man might show in buying his first car. He returned with a comedy-thriller and a newspaper full of particularly greasy fish and chips.

The film lasted until twenty to nine, when he returned to scanning the paper to fill the time until the news. He had finished the sports pages (he always read a paper backwards and he often wondered what a psychologist would make of the practice – probably imply he had a mixed-up childhood) and flicked idly through towards the front. He was on that page which proliferates the gory details of the crimes of the rapists, murderers and others of no-good intent when he found a passage of particular interest. He always enjoyed this section, often musing over possible defences and usually deciding he would rather lead the prosecution. This article was about a muder in the toilets of a service station near Canterbury. A man had been knifed. He was not named and it appeared police had no leads. Immediately below, he found a passage about a second knifing.

> Police are investigating the death of a man found stabbed on the fire-escape of a block of flats in Maidstone. The body was found after an anonymous tip-off to police in the early hours of this morning. The man, named as Nicholas Carlisle, had a series of convictions for theft and one for assault with a deadly weapon. A gun was also found at the scene of the crime but fingerprint tests show that he was the only person to have fired the weapon . . . .

He read it again, up to the name. The police knew who it was. They said nothing about a Keith Parsons. They were hardly likely to have made a mistake . . . unless, of course, Parsons had used several different names. He gave the matter some thought, missed the start of the news but, luckily, the item he wanted was relegated well down the list, got the vital number and immediately switched the set off. He was straight on to a certain well-known garage in Lewisham.

Paddy answered the phone.

'Oh, it's you! I didn't think we were hearing from you until tomorrow.'

A sudden thought struck her.

'There's nothing wrong with my case, is there?'

'No, nothing. To be honest, I wanted a word with Pete and then with Sandra.'

Pete came on first. 'What is it, old son?'

'Pete. Last night. You saw the body. Could you have made a mistake? I mean, you're sure it was Keith?'

'Who else could it have been, old son?'

'Pete, did you know him?'

'Never met the guy! Why do you ask?'

'Have you read the papers today?'

'Never bother with them, son.'

'Mistake, Pete. There's this article about a guy called Nicholas Carlisle who was found stabbed on our fire-escape last night. Find out from Sandra if Keith was a cover name for this Carlisle fellow.'

There was a pause.

'Not that she knows of.'

'Can you put her on.'

'Sure.'

There was another pause before Sandra answered.

'Sandra. This is important. Did Keith ever carry a gun to your knowledge?'

'A gun? No, I'm sure he didn't. If he did, he never said anything about it to me. I think I would have seen it or felt it when we cuddled.'

'Was he wearing a leather jacket last night?'

'No, of course not. He was in his suit. Why do you ask?'

'Look, I don't want to raise your hopes but there is a strong chance that Keith isn't dead. Least, he wasn't the fellow we found on the fire-escape. If he did the killing and not the other way round then he might be hiding to avoid the police. I think this is the most likely answer. If so, he's still in a lot of trouble so don't get too excited. Can you put Pete back on?'

Once he was back on line, Jeremy asked, 'Have you seen the news tonight on the telly?'

'Naw, we've a viddy out.'

'So have I, Pete, but I also saw the news and it was most interesting.'

Jeremy then proceeded to tell Pete about the news item, though he made no mention of any intention of contacting the police.

'Try watching at ten.'

Before ringing off, he got Luigi's number then immediately called him.

'Chiaparelli's Italian Restaurant. Can I help you?'

'Luigi. It's me, Jerry. Do you remember me? Paddy's lawyer.'

'Of course Luigi remember you. I told you. Paddy's friend is Luigi's friend. What is it you want?'

'Do you have a private room I could use tomorrow night? I'll pay you, of course.'

'It depends on how many you want to eat. I can seat eight but not more.'

'I only need it for two, Luigi.'

'Then Luigi will be most excited to help.'

'That's splendid. Could you have the room ready for eight o'clock tomorrow?'

'It is done, Mr Jerry.'

The next call was made from the public box at the end of the street.

'Put me through to your top man. I'm not staying on the line long enough for you to trace me so don't hang around.'

'Who's speaking, please?'

'The Fox.'

He felt the tingle in his spine and sensed the stiffening of the man on the other end.

'One moment, please, sir. Don't ring off!'

It took less than five seconds before a distinctive voice said, 'This is Detective Superintendent Burnell. Please don't ring off, sir. I assure you, nobody is going to try to find you but we would appreciate some information.'

Jeremy cut in sharply.

'Listen, don't talk! I want a meeting – on my terms and my timing. There is an Italian restaurant in Lewisham

87

called Chiaparelli's. You or one of your men can meet me there tomorrow night at eight o'clock. Introduce yourself as the Blue Pig.'

He rang off abruptly and walked back slowly to the flat, childishly chuckling at his silly sense of humour. The Blue Pig. He liked it. He had reached the driveway just as a blue flashing light caught his eye. He ran up the steps, ducked into the cover of the porch and watched as a patrol car fled by, lamp flashing but no siren. So the honourable superintendent was not interested in tracing the call, was he? So much for trust.

6

If nothing else, Parsons was caution personified. If anyone was waiting for him to emerge from a sixth-floor room then he would check. That did not mean blundering up the stairs. No way. If he did that and there was somebody there then he would be risking his neck and effectively telling them he had come from a lower floor. In turn, that might endanger Sandra and the case. He did want to know, however. It might tell him if the chase had been abandoned or whether they were on the look-out for him still.

He stopped at the stairs and checked to make sure that Sandra really had gone inside, then went up a floor. He crossed to the fire-escape and opened the door with the minimum of noise, easing himself onto the platform. He gently pushed the doors to and turned to creep up the stairs with the intention of looking through the glass onto the sixth-floor corridor. He was destined to get no further than the first step.

'If you don't want your brains exposed to the air, you'll keep very still and not say a word.'

Parsons froze. The voice was from above him.

'Very good! You have some intelligence, at least. Now, turn round very slowly and grip the rail with both hands.'

He turned very, very slowly. He wanted thinking time.

He also needed to recover from the shock; a shock that had frozen him but now was causing his heart to pound and his hand to shake. Bluff or action? Was he known or might he yet get out of it? The bluff was useless, he decided. Even if he was believed, how could this man allow him to walk away? No, his best chance lay in not pretending to be other than he was. Indeed, he should emphasise it.

'You're a patient bastard, I'll give you that.'

'Shut up. Just move those hands round where I can see them.'

Where he could see them? In this light? No way. So long as he made no exaggerated move, he could cover any action against his body. He must appear to the gunman as little more than a dark shape moving against the background of the striations of the railings. He continued the turn, allowing his right hand to drop easily into his pocket. He brought it out, flicked the blade and let the thin stiletto slip well up his sleeve. By keeping his elbow parallel with his wrist, the weapon nestled snugly in the fold of the jacket. Both hands gripped the top rail; he looked down at the blackness of the courtyard below and waited.

He had not seen the gun but he had no reason to doubt its existence. He knew that at least one of the men in the car had a weapon but it had not been silenced. That was of little comfort. Even if someone did hear a shot, it would matter little to him if the bullet had gone through his head. On the other hand, would the man use it to fire blindly as he ran down the staircase? The stairs themselves would offer considerable protection and it was still quite dark. He liked his alternative plan better. The knife was a possible match for a gun only if he was close. The man was coming to him and that had to be good news.

He judged the steps to be almost down to his platform.

'How about a deal?'

'I told you to shut it.'

'Sure. I thought what I was carrying might interest you.'

'It doesn't. You're going to tell us all we want to know very quickly anyway.'

'Don't you get Brownie points for getting the diamonds as well as the man?'

He heard the laugh almost in his ears. It was cold and mirthless.

'Don't worry. We shan't be leaving without everything. Spread those feet!'

The last command was pure snarl. Parsons obeyed. He felt the gun hard against his ribs and his captor ran his left hand expertly down his torso and legs. Apparently satisfied, he moved to the right side. He tried to keep the gun jabbed into Parsons's midriff but it turned slightly as he leant down to check his captive's right leg. That was all Parsons wanted. He pushed himself backwards from the railings, turning sharply as he did so. He felt the searing pain as the gun went off; he had pulled away enough to sustain no more than a flesh wound, though he had no time to think about it then. His life was in the balance. As he spun round, he grabbed at the gun with his left hand and simultaneously let the knife slip through his fingers until he could feel the handle in his palm. The gun went off a second time but the bullet flew into the side of the building and ricocheted away into the night.

It was all over. The knife travelled in just below the bottom rib and sank into the flesh until his hand was pressing into the jacket. He twisted the blade viciously through as great an angle as he could manage and pulled it out. The man coughed and the gun went loose. Parsons

91

took a smart step backwards and watched as his victim let the weapon fall clanging onto the metal platform then clutched at his stomach. His right hand came away and hooked over the railing for support.

Enough was enough. He flicked the knife closed and started down the steps as fast as he could. He was past the second-floor platform when the next shot rang out. His assailant had recovered his weapon. The bullet went nowhere near him and he continued his flight. There was a fourth shot that whistled close to his ears as he sprinted the short distance across the courtyard and down into the underground car park. There he was safe. From half-way between the third and fourth floors, his assailant's spirit flagged totally with the disappearance of his quarry. The gun slipped from his fingers once more, bounced on the stairs and spun off into space. With consciousness fading fast, he partly staggered and partly fell onto the third-floor platform. He pulled himself up to the door and hammered on it. The blows quickly weakened and he slumped forward.

Parsons stopped in the shelter of the entrance and took in air. His side was giving him hell. While he had been running for his life, the pain appeared insignificant but now it was really getting to him. Gingerly, he pulled his shirt and vest away and looked at the three-inch channel the bullet had cut through his skin. The blood was coming out far too rapidly – the whole area was saturated in the sticky stuff. He took his handkerchief and folded it to form a pad, which he laid directly into the wound. Just touching it caused him to feel faint and he stopped to regain his full senses. The next bit was going to be worse, he knew. He pulled his belt from his trousers and passed it around his waist and over the handkerchief. Bracing himself, he pulled on it until it held the pad firmly in the hole. He leant back against the wall and waited for the pain to subside a little.

He was ready. He tucked his shirt partially into his trousers and steadily made his way towards the Granada. The car park was apparently deserted; he could not be sure in the semi-darkness. Only the auxiliary lights were on and they did no more than show the outlines of the cars and highlight the exits. If he was observed, there was little he could do about it: he was not in any shape to run or put up much of a fight. He reached the open door of the car unchallenged and gratefully slumped into the driver's seat. If he could now straighten the thing, he could drive through the other entrance. He was only vaguely thinking what he would do then. Certainly, treatment for the wound figured high but he was not sure where to go. A hospital seemed a last resort: they would ask questions. The matter, however, was about to take on academic interest only.

'Don't try anything clever. There's a sawn-off twelve-bore pointing at you through the seat. If I have to fire, I can't miss and there won't be a lot left of you. Got it?'

Parsons's mind was crystal clear again, the bullet wound momentarily forgotten.

'Very slowly, switch on the ignition and put the window your side half-way down.'

Slowly suited him: it gave him time to think but what was he going to do this time?

'Good. Now switch the window to fully closed and put both hands through it as it goes up.'

Damn these automatic devices. The man in the back seat could not have tried this trick with a good old-fashioned manual system. There was no choice: he had to do as he was told. The glass cut into his arms before the motor stopped. His captor leant over from the rear and switched off the ignition. He professionally ran his hands across Parsons's body; he certainly saw the padding and the blood on his shirt but he showed no reaction to it. He stopped at the pocket, fished inside and withdrew the knife. With a sharp flick of the wrist, it looped over the seat into the back. He continued the search. Finding nothing else that concerned him, he leant back to consider.

'How did you get that wound?'

'Your pal up there shot me.'

It would do no good being awkward or belligerent. He was in no position to do anything and risking a beating for nothing was not Parsons's idea of common sense.

'Where is he now?'

Now lying might be sensible. However, it was obvious that they had fought and that he had got away. It was unlikely that he could bluff this one out. Nevertheless, he might try.

'He fell down the fire-escape chasing me. I didn't look to see what had happened to him. I had enough problems without looking to him.'

'How far did he fall?'

'A hell of a long way. He's likely to be pretty badly hurt at the best.'

At least he had not admitted to knifing him and the man had been slack: he had not examined the blade. If he had, he would have seen the blood.

'Where're the diamonds?'

'Find them yourself.' He had to resist this one.

The man stuck the barrel of the shotgun hard under his chin.

'This can go off ever so easily.'

Parsons could hardly move his mouth. He waited for the gun to come away a fraction and said, 'Pull that trigger and you'll never find them.'

The gun went back into his throat. He waited for what seemed an interminable time, fully expecting to have his head blasted open. Then the gun came sharply away, leaving him gasping for breath. His captor let out an expletive and brought his hand down in a vicious chop on his unprotected neck. He could do nothing about it. The follow-up was a punch into his damaged side. He blacked out.

Parsons had no idea how long he had been out. Indeed, he came round slowly and took some time to realise what had happened and even longer to appreciate where he was. All about him was in darkness. Through the red mists, he was aware that he was moving. His mind started to clear: he was in the boot of a car travelling at a very steady speed. Motorway. That was the likely explanation. He lay still and thought. His side was giving him hell but he appeared not to be tied at all. He wriggled a bit and made himself slightly more comfortable.

The passage of time had no realistic meaning in the dark. Parsons explored the floor of the boot with his hands and managed to find a small spanner, which he pocketed. It was hardly a weapon but was better than nothing. He tried prising the rubber away from around the lock and squinting through the pin-hole of a gap in the vain hope of discovering where he was but it was useless. There was little to be done except to minimise the jolting on his wound and await developments.

The car came to a stop but it was some time before the boot opened. When it did, there were two men outside. The one who had done the driving held a sawn-off shotgun at the ready while the other fellow pulled Parsons from the boot. With the gun jammed into his back, he was hustled across the pavement and into a large warehouse. He had time for a brief glimpse of the dingy street and the row of depressing black buildings. It was a faceless world wearing an oppressive air. Despite the captivity, entering the warehouse was almost a relief. It was lit from high in the ceiling by a series of strip lights, two of which were flickering badly. Nevertheless, there was sufficient light to see clearly all that was around him.

Once inside, he was chivvied along through miniature streets amongst a city of stacked crates to the far end, where a set of rickety stairs led up to a gallery running the length of the wall. At the end and at right angles to the corridor were a series of rooms; it was into the first of these that he was led. Without any fuss, yet with a ruthless efficiency, his hands were firmly tied, he was thrown to the floor and his feet also trussed up, the rope being passed from the feet through the loop of his arms and back down to his ankles, leaving him trussed like the proverbial Christmas turkey. The men left, locking the door as they went. He just caught a fading voice saying, 'Get over and fetch Clive. Mr Smith wants him up here immediately.'

7

The following morning, having first thrown a few clothes and toilet materials into the boot of the car, Jeremy set out for the court-house. He decided that the future day or so was not predictable, so a change of clothes in the car would be no bad thing. Providentially, as it turned out.

He spent an hour hanging around in the ante-room to the court while he waited to be called but the affair inside took very little time. The case was adjourned for hearing in two weeks. He took out full witness orders on both of the Pallister brothers and accepted the statements of the police and medical staff. In his plan, he did not want any great play made about the injuries or the details of police activity – he intended to rely purely on making a mockery of the main prosecution witnesses.

Thus, at twenty past eleven, he set off again for Maidstone. This time, he found Osbourne House clear of blue uniforms and he drove into the underground car park unchallenged. He noted that Keith's white Granada was still where Pete had left it but, otherwise, paid no attention to the other half-dozen vehicles scattered about. He took the lift in cavalier fashion, walking to the door of the flat with no qualms. The key turned smoothly in the lock and he pushed the door open but one pace into the room was enough. He froze in horror at the sight. Chaos reigned everywhere: furniture scattered and overturned, fabric torn and ornaments smashed. If the place had been hit by a tornado it could not have been in a worse mess.

He lost control of his feet as an invisible energy source locked onto him and sucked him into the room. Common sense should have warned him to retreat at once but it did not. As he strove to take in the destruction and mayhem, he drifted further into the flat. The door slammed behind him and he spun round. The trap had been sprung.

'What the . . . who the hell are you?'

The man behind the door was dressed in black jeans, with a black shirt topped by a leather jacket. Even as the question was being asked, he produced an ugly-looking, thin-barrelled hand-gun and proceeded to screw on a silencer, each twist being delivered with a lazy, unhurried action.

'Exactly the question I was going to ask you.'

The voice was silky smooth, even sickly, but dipped in venom. Jeremy turned again and found a much older man neatly attired in a grey suit and sporting a relatively tasteful tie. He was emerging from the kitchen, drawing on a thin cheroot and letting the smoke puff out of his nose as though he were some mythical dragon breathing fire. Jeremy fought to control his initial fear.

Lie.

'Carrington-Fox. Jeremy Carrington-Fox. Now who the hell are you and what do you think you are doing here?'

He considered. That was a pretty good lie and the question showed great intellectual merit.

'Fox, eh? Not very cunning, stumbling in here like that.'

The man behind the door sniggered. The older man

continued.

'Now, it was you who was about to tell me what you were doing here.'

I was not! Lie this time, you idiot.

'I've come to get a case I left here the night before last.'

That was good! Quick thinking, that.

'I had my papers in it.'

'Did you really? What colour was it? Perhaps one of the boys has seen it.'

'Black.'

'Funny, that. We've been looking for a black case as well.'

I bet you have, thought Jeremy, but you haven't found it, have you?

'You're not going to let me just recover my property and go, are you?'

'Real bright, this lad, isn't he, Clive?'

'Shut it, Butch. I'll do the clever bit. Where's the case?'

'I don't know. I left it here somewhere.'

'Don't try and be funny. You heard what I told Butch. Same applies to you.'

'I don't know anything about any other case.'

While all this was going on, two other men had entered the room from the main bedroom. One was scruffy, with highly greased hair that was plastered into something of a sculpture and jeans and jacket that were ripped in several places. The other was in total contrast: he was immaculate in every detail from the short curly hair to the trim beard, the white shirt bright against his black skin, the bow-tie and pin-stripe suit. He looked directly at the man called Clive and nodded briefly. Clive moved two paces forward and, with no warning, smashed his fist into the lawyer's groin.

Jeremy bent half forward, paralysed with pain, unable even to move his hands down to protect this vulnerable area. Clive stepped smartly back and smiled wickedly.

'Does that help your memory?'

'You sodding bastard.'

The words were forced between clenched teeth. He did not normally swear; it was hardly done in the society he used to live in but things were changing.

The black fellow came round so that he was nearly square on with him.

'He is nice: I am not. Now, Mr Carrington-Fox. No! That's too much of a mouthful. Perhaps you would have no objection if I simply called you Mr Fox?'

He smiled sweetly and waited for a second or so before he went on.

'Perhaps you would like to reconsider before you suffer any further needless pain.'

'If I knew, do you think I'd tell you? I might be stupid but I like living. I doubt if I'd last ten minutes if you had what you wanted.'

'Let's start from the beginning, shall we, Mr Fox?'

'Start where the hell you like. I'm not helping you any.'

'Oh, you are, Mr Fox. I assure you, you are.'

He nodded again and Clive put the toe of his boot in just at the base of his left knee-cap. Jeremy went down, writhing in agony and clenching his numbed limb with both hands in the fruitless attempt to stop the pain. Despite his wish to do otherwise, he was sobbing. A stream of four-letter language flooded his brain but a deeper instinct for survival was fighting for supremacy. Save energy: you will need every bit before you are through, he thought. Antagonising them more might satisfy a superficial pride but he would suffer for it. Better to appear weaker than he was: better to be in one piece for as long as possible.

'Let's try again, shall we?'

The voice was velvet and barely above a gentle whisper. Jeremy gave a surly nod.

'Good. Now, why are you here?'

'I told you, I came for my case.'

He was hardly able to speak between the tears. He looked at the boot poised above him.

'It's the truth. The damn thing is here if you look!'

His voice had miraculously risen in volume and picked up in speed as he desperately strove to fend off the next blow. It did not land.

'That sounds very like the truth, Mr Fox. That's better. You seem to be learning. It's wonderful what a little bit of pain will do to bring a man to his senses. We will try another question. How is it you had a key to this flat?'

The brain was working better. The lies needed to be consistent and plausible.

'The girl who lives here, Sandra, I was seeing a lot of her. Nothing sinister in that, is there?'

'Nothing, Mr Fox. You would like us to believe that you are nothing more than a boy-friend?'

He was getting somewhere.

'Yes.'

'No, Mr Fox. You have not shown the slightest concern for your so-called girl-friend. You knew she was not here when you came in.'

'Of course. She phoned me to say she had to go up to London.'

The man placed his hands together and held them across his mouth with the fingertips touching his nose. He stared intently at the frightened man on the floor. Jeremy tried hard to look the innocent lover stumbling blindly in on a nasty robbery. Had it worked?

'Ronnie, help Mr Fox to his feet, if you please.'

The scruffy individual came forward and grabbed the unfortunate solicitor by his hair and, over the sound of the involuntary scream, hauled him to his feet.

'Butch, put that little toy of yours up against Mr Fox's ear.'

The gun barrel forced his head to jerk violently to the side, the cold metal biting into the flesh of his ear.

'Say goodbye, Mr Fox. I don't think we need you any more.'

Until the words were spoken, Jeremy's heart had been thumping wildly and the sweat forming around his neck and the palms of his hands. Now, he became illogically calm. Death has that effect: when it cannot be defeated, the terror of it fades. His brain was as clear as it had ever been and the pain left his body.

'If your smelly little thug pulls that trigger then your precious case will have gone for ever.'

'Oh, really? Then you *do* know something about it?'

'I know enough to keep my mouth shut.'

'Then let's see if we can open it, shall we? Clive, if you please.'

He stepped back, leaving the way clear for the sadistic assistant to sweep the back of his hand across Jeremy's mouth, taking care that the ring-encrusted knuckles caught the tenderest parts. He felt the blood burst from his cheek and lips but the pain was bearable. Perhaps that was the intention. He looked with something approaching anger at Clive's evil eyes as the man drew his fist back. There was a sneering smile on the sadist's face as he unleashed the next blow hard into Jeremy's unprotected stomach. The third was again up into the groin. That was enough. The swirling red mists enveloped him and he swayed semi-consciously. If he had not been supported by the hair, he would unquestionably have collapsed on the floor. He vaguely heard the voice say 'enough' before he passed out.

He only lost consciousness for a few seconds. He came round, unaware of what had happened or where he was. He was feeling the pain again. He ached in several places and wanted nothing more than to slide back into comfortable oblivion.

'The ammonia bottle, if you please, Clive.'

The pungent gas caused him to cough sharply. He inhaled again and the mists cleared. He opened his eyes and shook his head, trying to rid himself of the hammers battering in his skull.

'This violence is pointless, Mr Fox. You are certainly going to tell me what I want to know soon enough, so why don't you save yourself further discomfort?'

'Go to hell!'

His voice was distorted. The swelling of his lips stopped him speaking clearly. He watched as Clive sized up where to inflict the next round of pain.

'Go on, you miserable little worm. Enjoy yourself. Be my guest . . . .'

The last word was choked off by the winding fingers burying themselves into his ribs.

'Thank you, Clive. Mr Fox is beginning to enjoy himself too much.'

The man, Winston Smith, was right. Jeremy had reached the point where the victim is resigned to the forthcoming pain and it ceases to have the intended effect. The main weapon of the torturer is the mental element. If the subject does not fear the future then he is unlikely to succumb. Winston Smith knew this better than most men. Fear was the great ally he used to get his own way. It was the major factor in securing religious obedience from his own followers.

'Take him into the bathroom and clean him up. We'll

take him with us; it might take some time to get what we want out of him and I've no wish to be around here too long.'

The physical abuse subsided. He was pulled into the bathroom but without the vindictive bullying he had just endured. Ronnie pushed the plug into the basin and turned on the tap. Both men stood back.

'You've got a choice. Either you clean yourself up or we do it for you.'

'I can manage.'

He bent over the basin and gingerly dabbed water onto his swollen mouth. He looked with little more than academic interest at the changing colour of the water. His actions were slow and studied but they did not hurry him: he was allowed to clean his damaged face as much as he wanted and to dry it on the towel lying across the bath. He would hardly want to confess to it but he felt considerably better when he emerged into the main room. The pain in several parts of his body was still intense but he was not the cowed animal of ten minutes previously. The assault had been most professional although he did not appreciate it. Clive had produced maximum pain with minimum long-term damage. He was, after all, capable of walking relatively normally.

Winston thrust his black court case into his hands. Jeremy looked slightly quizzically at him as though surprised at the act. The unspoken question was interpreted.

'I don't want anything to be found to associate you with this place. There is no saying when our friends in blue might return.'

His voice took on a harder edge.

'Now, Mr Fox, we are all going to walk out of here as though we are all good friends. If we meet anybody in the corridors, you will say absolutely nothing or make any sign to them. Understood? If you are so stupid, we will ensure that person travels with us.'

The cold bastard. It seemed he was prepared to kidnap and probably murder any unfortunate they happened to meet if he thought they posed even the most outside of threats.

'You don't have to spell it out.'

'Excellent. Butch, the door.'

Butch edged the door open, peered out and pronounced that all was deserted. The men left quietly with Jeremy in the middle, still clutching his case, and took the lift to the basement. The corridor and car park were empty, which, given Winston Smith's attitude, was probably as well. They stopped in the middle of the central corridor while Ronnie went for the car. Smith looked at Jeremy.

'Presumably, Mr Fox, you came by car. Where is it?'

'Find it yourself.'

'Not helpful, Mr Fox. Still, there are ways. Clive get his keys.'

Before he quite knew what was happening, Clive had twisted his right arm hard up behind his back and reached into his trouser pocket. He adroitly extracted the keys, releasing the arm in the same motion.

'A Porsche.'

Winston looked pleased.

'Only one in the place, Clive. Get it, will you? We will remove the evidence of Mr Fox's little visit.'

For all the predicament, a grim amusement played on Jeremy's mind. Before he had time to weigh up the effects, Clive had inserted the key and turned it in the lock. The wailing was immediate and the note echoed around the concrete walls of the basement.

'How do you switch the thing off?'

'You can find that out, too, you clever bastard.'

'Stop it now or Butch puts that bullet straight through your brain. I do not want police down here.'

The point struck Jeremy but for a slightly different reason. He could well have more than just his own death on his hands. He strode straight across to his car, took the keys off Clive, locked the door again and reset the alarm. The noise immediately ceased.

'Now open it without that infernal racket.'

Winston was at his side. Jeremy went through the routine of turning the key to the unlock position, a half turn back towards the locked position and then, finally, unlocked the door.

'Your alarm is certainly non-standard, Mr Fox. I trust you have no more little surprises.'

'You'll have to find that out as well.'

'There's more, is there?'

'Your Clive will have, let us say, an entertaining time driving my beauty.'

'I think he may be disappointed, Mr Fox. My original intention was to stow you away in the boot but I've just decided you will now drive. Giving you something to do may prove the most practical way of containing your rebellious spirit. Butch, let Clive have your gun.'

The last statement was directed at an increased volume towards the black Mercedes that was now purring softly a few feet away. Butch, it seemed, was reluctant to part with his weapon and must have said something, as Winston scowled and walked across to the window, now half open. A few words were exchanged then Butch got out of the vehicle and walked across to the Porsche. It seemed as though he was not to have the pleasure of Clive's company in the car after all.

'Get in, Mr Fox. Butch is highly expert with his unfortunate little toy and loves to use it. He has

106

instructions to shoot you in the thigh if you put a foot wrong. You will drive at a sedate pace, obeying all traffic regulations to the letter, and will take the exact route given to you. Only thus can you hope to arrive without a nasty hole in your leg.'

Jeremy said nothing. What was there to say? This was a time for compliance. However, he was feeling marginally better. Despite the presence of the gun and its trigger-happy owner, the odds were cut. It was not just the numbers. This Butch was hardly your regular intellectual – in fact, Jeremy doubted if he had ever passed any examination in his life. If he could keep his nerve, he might escape with his neck. However, the first few miles did nothing to encourage that view. They drove steadily through the town and onto the motorway with the Mercedes a meticulous five car-lengths behind. As they picked up speed, so it dropped back slightly but never wavered from its attachment to the Porsche. Any thought of attempting something dramatic with the car's performance was discouraged by the tip of the gun barrel nestling permanently in his upper thigh.

They had merged into the London traffic and its never-ending succession of traffic lights when Jeremy's numbed brain graciously agreed to put some effort into retrieving the seemingly impossible situation. Up until then, it had been fantasizing. The ways out it had attempted ranged from ramming the brakes on hard, crashing into the Mercedes, then fighting for the gun, to hooting the first police car he saw and praying that Butch would not dare shoot. Neither had any likely chance of success.

There were two cars in front of them at the lights. As they went green, he let the clutch out too fiercely and stalled the engine.

'What the hell are you playing at, punk?'

'Sorry,' said Jeremy, desperately trying to sound scared and rattled. 'I suppose it was nerves.'

'Nerves might just make me pull this trigger.'

He started the engine again, slipped the car into third and bucked to a halt straddling the white line.

'You do that again, pal, and your leg's going to look one hell of a mess.'

'Sorry. Honestly, I didn't do it on purpose.' He tried to sound scared. It required only minimal effort.

'I'd have pulled the trigger already if I thought you had.'

The lights went amber. He started the engine first turn of the key. The light went red. He let the clutch out rapidly but smoothly this time. The tyres screamed an indignant protest and laid five hundred miles' worth of rubber on the road but the car was accelerating wildly. Jeremy ignored the hoots from the cars starting from the lights and concentrated everything on speed.

'Pull up, you stupid bastard. The others haven't followed.'

'Tough on them. Incidentally, you pull that trigger now and like as not we'll crash. Think about it, punk.'

'You think about it, punk.'

The gun had been moved very quickly and deftly to his left ear. Jeremy was gambling. The fellow would not dare shoot: a crash would be inevitable. He would at least wait until Jeremy was forced to slow in the traffic. He was up to fifty and catching the cars in front; the natural gap that develops between the changing of the lights had evaporated. In one sense, he was no longer thinking: imagination was dead. He could not see his corpse slumped across the wheel but he could see the small gap in the oncoming traffic and he could see the parked lorry on the other side of the road. The gun being raised to his head cleared the way to the gear-lever. He changed, dropped his hand naturally back and found the button to Butch's safety strap. In one motion, the wheel twisted sharply and he released the belt.

'Look out, you bloody fool! We're going to crash!'

Butch let his eyes focus on the traffic, stiffened in fear and then brought his hands up in front of him as he felt his body propelled forward. The brakes were hard on. The car coming towards them was also braking and swerving. In the half-second before impact, Jeremy heard the sound of cars behind hitting, then it was their turn. The Porsche was into the side and running straight at the front of the lorry. He braced himself and instinctively shut his eyes.

The front of the Porsche buckled under the blow. Jeremy felt the sting of the strap biting into his chest and he felt the floor moving up, pushing his feet, still on the pedals, into the underside of the dashboard. He heard the splintering of glass close to his ear and he felt the slap on his face, then all was suddenly still. In reality, it was not. The world outside continued almost unabated but Jeremy heard nothing for several seconds. He opened his eyes and saw the screams and cries from the pavement before he heard them. It was the sight of Butch, half-way out of the car via the windscreen, that galvanised his mind and body into action. He unfastened his own strap and pushed at the door. It was stuck. For a second, panic surged through his body. Somebody from outside was tugging on it as well: it came open in a sudden rush.

Jeremy prised himself out from the wreck, twisting his body to get his legs out first. In so doing, his eyes caught sight of the gun on the floor. He grabbed it, levered himself out and looked around. He was aware of the noise, of the shouting, the screaming and the roar of the traffic as a bass background to it all. He could see the still form lying across the bonnet, the head touching the radiator of the lorry. He could feel the blood trickling down his face. As yet, he did not comprehend what it was but he still felt it.

Two voices penetrated. The first asked if he was all right. The stupid man! Had he no intelligence? Of course he was not – any fool could see that! He was on his feet and able to use his limbs but that was about all. Perhaps he would have been more sympathetic if he could have seen his face and, then again, he might have felt less angry if he had not been so shaken. The second voice was not directed at him. It was shrieking to the crowd that he had a gun.

Suddenly, he was the fox, not just in name but in reality – the hunted animal, the creature of the wilds, driven by an instinct for survival that transcended everything. He fixed his eyes on the men around him, pointed the gun deliberately, watched the natural recoil and sprang for the gap. He was off down the street like a gazelle, side-stepping, dodging, leaping. Forty yards brought him to the entrance of a departmental store. He was through the door and weaving through the aisles, getting as deep inside as he could. As he entered, he had managed to slip the gun into his pocket so that, although some people were indignantly brushed aside and some looked on in outraged curiosity at his headlong flight, he drew less attention than he feared. Indeed, had it not been for his bloody face, he could have hidden in the crowd. The further he delved into the place, the more he slowed until he reached the escalator at a mere brisk walk.

The second floor offered toilets. In some relief, he went in and viewed his face in the mirror over the first wash-basin. He was cut in several places, presumably from glass fragments, but there was nothing that a good

110

wash would not greatly improve. He did what he could, surveyed the results in the mirror and decided he would pass muster. A quick comb of the hair and he ventured out once more to face the world. The question was, where to go? The fire-escape: there had to be one. That way, he could leave without having to use the front entrance.

The fire door opened onto a typical wrought-iron stairway which led into the delivery yard at the rear of the store. Fortunately, it was deserted and he was able to get down the stairs and out through the back of the yard without attracting attention. In a mixture of short trots and brisk walks, he threaded through several back streets until the road opened into a rather poorly built residential area. Scruffy children were playing on the streets and several women were chatting on the doorsteps. A mongrel with a perfectly disgusting coat and worse smell decided he was intruding and barked harshly at him but was sufficiently cowardly to refrain from approaching too closely. The sight at the end of the street, however, gladdened his heart: it was a red telephone box.

For all the graffiti and broken glass, the telephone itself was still in working order. What was more, it was answered quickly by a comforting voice.

'McBear Garages. What can I do for you?'

'Pete. Oh, thank God! Pete, it's Jerry. I'm in big trouble.'

'Steady, old son,' Pete cut in. 'Can't be anything we can't fix.'

Jerry realised he was having difficulty speaking. The traumas of the previous few hours were taking their toll. His voice was disrespectfully refusing to do as he asked of it. It shook and cracked, requiring brief pauses before agreeing to continue.

111

'I've crashed the Porsche. Deliberately. I had a gun at my head . . . .'

He stopped. This would not do. What would Frobisher, his old housemaster, say to this disgusting lack of self-control? Damn Frobisher. *He* had never had a gun pointed at his head.

'Where are you, old son?'

'I'm sorry, Pete. I'm all in.'

'Come on, Jerry. I've got to know where you are.' There was more than a hint of concern in the voice.

Jeremy looked around him. A broken street sign was a few yards away.

'Connaught Road. The phone box on the corner of Connaught Road but I've no idea where I am. No, wait a minute. The crash. I was in Deptford High Street just before I turned off. I can't be far from there. No. The car must be still there. Oh, God! The police will find it and then trace it to me. The body will still be in it.'

He was half sobbing, the tension finally breaking him.

'Listen, son. Stay where you are. Got it? Stay where you are. We're on our way. I'll get the breakdown truck and see if I can find the Porsche; Paddy'll come for you. Have you got that?'

He managed to give a stifled yes and then the phone went dead.

The next quarter of an hour was the worst Jeremy had ever spent. Even the beating in the flat was not as bad. Now, the adrenalin had soaked away and the pain from his earlier ordeal was mixing with the shock from the crash and utter dejection at all that had happened sent him into a flood of uncontrollable tears. He slumped down on the floor of the box and sobbed. A woman walked past, looked at him with disgust and continued on her way. There was no pity, no comfort to be had. The dog approached the box and sniffed at him through the shattered window. He could not even find the energy to shoo it off. He was miserable beyond description.

It was a nadir only lifted by a familiar voice saying, 'Don't think much of your pal. He smells something awful.'

8

Jeremy remembered little about the journey back to the garage. He afterwards assumed he had walked up the stairs to the flat but everything was hazy until he was in bed. Perhaps this was no bad thing. In reality, he caused more consternation than he realised. For most of the short return journey, his teeth chattered furiously with the delayed shock and the story he tried to tell barely made sense. In fact, about the only thing he managed to convey was that he had been beaten up and had deliberately crashed the Porsche. It was, at least, enough to stop Paddy's flippant quips as she grasped the seriousness of the situation. Paying attention to his story and giving some deference to his mental state, she even drove in a nearly normal manner.

He did indeed manage to walk up the stairs to the flat, where he almost bumped into Sandra. He stuttered and spluttered a partial apology then started to blubber. It was enough to set her off as well and she became almost as distressed as Jeremy until her sister snapped, 'We can do without any bloody histrionics, ta very much, sis. Make yourself useful instead of slobbering around. Doc Masters's number's in the book. Give him a ring and tell him we need him quick. Then put the kettle on.'

Paddy took Jeremy into the spare bedroom and started to undress him. As he objected, the gun tumbled out of

114

his jacket. She picked it up and weighed it expertly in her hand.

'Nice balance. Where did you get this beauty from?'

'Th-that's the thing I had stuck at my head. F-f-for God's sake, g-g-get rid of it!'

'Not likely. Never know when something like this might come in handy. I'll practise with it. Shouldn't be hard finding someone willing to sell ammo for it.'

'Y-y-you'll do yourself an injury m-mucking w-w-with th-that.'

'Rubbish! I know what I'm doing. I've been a member of the Lewisham Rifle Club for three years. I could hit a bull six out of six at fifty yards with this thing.'

With that, she departed, returning just as he shed the last garment. She laughed as he hastily covered the more vital parts of his anatomy with his shirt. Paddy tossed him a bundle of linen and laughed again as he juggled with his protective gear while at the same time trying to catch the garment. It had unfurled in the throwing and had every appearance of a thin dress.

'Put it on. It's all I can find.'

She looked at his face.

'It's a nightdress. One of mine. Oh, for God's sake put the thing on. You can't go round naked.'

She paused.

'Well, I suppose you could. Let me have it back.'

She made a grab at it but he pulled away.

'No, it's better than n-n-nothing. Just sc-scram, will you? Can't I have any privacy?'

She moved back enough to reassure him and picked up his clothes from the floor.

'Cor, your pants don't half pong! They smell like that dog went on them.'

'I'm n-n-not surprised. I w-w-wet myself w-w-when I

crashed.'

She wanted to laugh again. He was so pathetic. Suddenly, she ran up to him, gave him a monster kiss on his cheek and flounced out of the room with a parting shot.

'Better get into bed and keep warm. You've got the quack on his way.'

Indeed, the doctor was on his way and did a good job. He asked precious few questions but was painfully thorough in his examination. When he finished, he grunted in a broad Scottish accent, 'Ye'll live, I nae doot. Ye've taken a fair wee beating, laddie, but, at the worst, only a rib or two broken. Ye'll be sore a while but there's nothing a guid rest and time'll not cure. I'll give ye something tae help you sleep and I'll call the morrow to see how ye're mending.'

He left a small plastic bottle with Paddy, downed the glass of whisky she had ready for him and left just as Pete pulled into the back of the garage. He had the wrecked Porsche on the trailer.

*

Before Jeremy swallowed the pills for the night, he listened to Pete recount his version of events. He had found the scene of the crash with little trouble – the trail of flashing blue lights helped no end. He managed to persuade the officer in charge at the scene to allow him to tow the damaged car away, having honestly given Jeremy's address and sworn that he had been badly injured and, to the best of his knowledge, was under hospital treatment. It had taken a fair amount of patient chatter, coupled with sly allusions to the traffic chaos the accident was causing to get the vehicle released. The really interesting point was the lack of a body. He had overheard several witnesses giving their own accounts and there seemed to be general agreement about the fact that there had been a passenger in the car. It seemeed that a black Mercedes had pulled up a few seconds after the crash and the driver had bundled the man into the car before driving off. Unfortunately, it also seemed that too many people were also definite about Jeremy's gun. That could not be helped.

Jeremy slid gently into a drugged sleep.

*

The patient awoke well after nine the next morning and felt very stiff and sore but the shaking had disappeared. He got out of bed and dragged himself into the bathroom. He looked a mess. He could not shave – his razor was in the boot of the car – but he washed himself well then called out for the others, only to find he was alone in the flat. He crossed to the rear door that led down to the garage. Opening it, he moved to the top of the stairs and called out, 'Anyone about?'

Pete came from under a yellow Datsun and looked up.

'How you feeling, son?'

'Not so bad. A bit sore, that's all.'

Paddy appeared and giggled wickedly.

'You look a right pouff! Pink just doesn't suit you!'

'Oh, shut up. I'm not up to corny cracks.'

'Cor, touchy, aren't you? And after all I did for you last night.'

'Sorry, Pad, but I'm not that right. If you could get my clothes from the Porsche, I might be able to get dressed.'

'No way. Doc Masters is coming back this morning so you get back to bed and wait for him.'

'Isn't there any breakfast going?'

'Ask Sandra when she gets back.'

'Where is she?'

'She's gone shopping. Someone's got to get the

117

dinner.'

Damn. The thought struck him that he had missed his appointment with the Blue Pig. He returned to bed with some reluctance, spending the time until Sandra's return by thinking out a new strategy. Yes, he must talk to the police. By now, anyway, they would be wanting to talk to him about the crash. He was really eaten up by that. It needed no expert to tell him his precious Porsche was not even fit for a Demolition Derby. What was worse, it was only a quarter paid for.

He was still brooding when Sandra brought him his breakfast or, to be more exact, a mid-morning snack and a cup of tea. It was only half eaten when the honourable doctor called, declared him fit enough to get up and left him with a prescription for pain-killers.

By mid-afternoon, Jeremy was sufficiently physically recovered to borrow the BMW (Paddy had been over to Orpington to retrieve it earlier that afternoon) and to drive back to the flat but, mentally, he was far from being right. One of the effects of his accident had been to leave him flat and depressed and this manifested itself in a burning desire for solitude. The more those around him tried to cheer him up the worse it became, until escape from the garage became essential. He shaved, dressed in the spare clothes rescued from the boot of his Porsche and retrieved his black court case. Encaged once more with the veneer of middle-class respectability, he sallied forth with an unconvincing bravado.

The depression increased once he was home. The past haunted his mind and the early afternoon television programmes did nothing to dispel the fears that encroached from his subconscious to break his concentration from the screen. At last, he gave up the uneven fight and switched off the set. For the next half-hour, he sat morosely contemplating the hearthrug, his thoughts running at an uncontrolled and disturbing rate, giving him no respite or hope. At last, he managed to rouse himself and he phoned the magic number.

'This is the Fox again. I have a message for Detective Superintendent Colin Burnell. Tell him that I was detained last night and was unable to meet him. I will be at the same place tonight at eight – Chiaparelli's in Lewisham. Same code word.'

He rang off sharply. Whatever happened, he supposed he had to go through with it. Indeed, once he had got it all off his chest, he might feel better – he could hardly feel worse. Jeremy looked at his watch. It was nearly five. He must book the room with Luigi and apologise for last night's fiasco. Luigi did not seem to mind. He had found it funny. Who had thought up that stupid name, the Blue Pig! He even had large feet! The guy had not seemed very confident – could not get out of the place fast enough. He was still chuckling as he put the receiver down.

The comment had given Jeremy the information that Burnell had not gone to the meeting himself. Predictable, he thought, once you gave the matter consideration. Nevertheless he was not sorry. He had not fancied meeting such a high-ranking officer.

He made a coffee and tried to cheer up. He put on a disc, found he was not listening to it and switched it off. His ribs were hurting, his knee was so sore he could hardly walk and he generally ached all over. He put the cup down and slid back in the chair: he must prepare himself for the evening meeting.

The next thing he remembered was waking with a start. The clock showed five past seven. The initial panic that he had slept through the meeting subsided but he was still tight for time. A quick shower and a change of clothes later, he was in the car and heading once more for Lewisham. With a degree of fortune that had, for once, turned his way, he arrived at the restaurant some three minutes before eight. Luigi was clearly enjoying his private joke and ushered the solicitor into a back room. The inside was very snug and intimate: the lone table was laid for two and a soft glow filtered from an underpowered light bulb almost masked in a thick red lampshade.

Right on the dot of eight, a sandy-haired young man in jeans and an open-neck shirt entered the building. Luigi broke off from serving a young couple in the corner nearest to the door and rushed over.

'It is the Blue Pig returned, yes?'

He was chuckling with delight at the man's discomfort. An affirmative was growled.

'Is he here tonight or have I come on another bloody wild-goose chase?'

'He is here, Mr Pig. Please to come with me.'

The congenial host led the way to the back room where Jeremy had settled into one of the chairs and was sipping at the Cinzano and lemon Luigi's wife had brought in. He got up at once, slightly embarrassed and uncomfortable. The newcomer was also uneasy and this uncertainty did little for either of them but Luigi was totally relaxed.

'Do you want to eat now or talk first? You cannot do both or you will spoil the food.'

He looked from one to the other.

'Ah! I get you good bottle of wine and some capers. Then you relax, yes?'

'A good idea, Luigi. Actually, I'm starving so we might order when you come back and break the talk up.'

He held out a hand as Luigi retreated through the door.

'I'm sorry about all this clandestine activity. I feel rather embarrassed about it, to tell the truth. My name actually is Fox, Jeremy Carrington-Fox to be precise.'

His hand was shaken.

'Detective Sergeant Stanley.'

'Pleased to meet you. I trust you will just allow one further act of suspicion then I'll tell you all I can. I'd like to see your warrant card, first.'

Stanley's face flickered briefly then he produced the thin wallet from his inside pocket and passed it across. Jeremy perused it with care. Satisfied, he returned it and sat down.

'I've probably been a bit of a fool but this "Fox" nonsense started off for a very good reason. I'm a solicitor and I wanted to protect a perfectly innocent client from what might have been a traumatic experience. It was for that reason that I adopted this dumb *nom de plume.*'

Stanley nodded. He had been around a lot, despite his apparently youthful face. The crop of straggly blond hair and cherub features had a deceptively gentle air but hid a very efficient and tough policeman. For all that, he also knew when to shut up and listen and when to ask questions. Now was the time to hear what was being offered before he put in his pennyworth. Luigi returned with a bottle of red and a plate of delicious nibbles and both settled back for a long session.

By the time the soup was finished, Stanley knew about Sandra and how her boy-friend had arrived late at night with a mysterious black case apparently containing diamonds. Jeremy held nothing back and replied openly and honestly to Stanley's occasional question without compromising anyone under his nominal protection. He explained how he had found Carlisle's body and jumped to the conclusion that it was Keith's. He was into the phone calls to Wagstaff by the time the pasta course arrived.

121

'I see. So that's how you knew something was amiss. You probably saved the fellow's skin for him. When our people got there, they had already bundled him and his man into the boot of their cars and ransacked the house. They were within minutes of making a clean get-away.'

'Was Wagstaff hurt?'

'Badly shaken but I suppose he'll be OK. He came off a darn sight better than our people. Two ended up in hospital and one's pretty serious.'

'I know. I heard on the news.'

'What did you do with the case?'

'I put it in the bank vault.' He hesitated. 'That is, I put it there in the afternoon but before that I had a good look at it.'

Stanley looked quizzically at him, twirled his fork in the spaghetti and thrust it clumsily into his mouth, leaving long threads dripping disrespectfully from the corners. He sucked in the strands and waited. Jeremy gave the matter some thought.

'It seemed a bit heavy, I suppose. To be honest, I'm not quite sure what made me suspicious. No, I wasn't suspicious at all to start with, just curious. I wanted to take a look at the diamonds. I twiddled the tumblers on the lock until I opened it and then turned the diamonds over in my fingers for a bit. That's when it struck me: the case was smaller inside than it looked, if you know what I mean. I ran a knife round the edge of the lining and found some of this stuff underneath.'

He dug into his pocket and took out a small twist of paper, which he passed across the table. Stanley put down his fork and carefully unfolded the paper. He pushed the powder around the paper, wet a finger, picked up a couple of grains on the end of it and gingerly held them to his nose. One light sniff was enough.

122

'Heroin. Unless I'm mistaken, it seems very pure. How much was there?'

'A few pounds. Ten or twelve, maybe. I didn't weigh it.'

'You put it back?'

'No. It's still in the flat.'

'We'd better go and get it.'

'Yes, OK. I originally intended bringing it tonight but thought better of it. You'd better hear the rest. There's a hell of a lot more yet.'

Stanley nodded.

'I told you I put the case in the bank. Then I came home and listened to the news. That's how I knew to phone you but it wasn't that simple. I got in contact with Pete again and found he had never seen Sandra's boyfriend. It seems we had both jumped to the wrong conclusion when I found the body. I didn't want Sandra drawn into this – she knew nothing about the corpse and, for all I knew then, the whole thing might have been a ghastly coincidence so I decided to keep the *nom de plume* going a bit longer. I must say, I don't think much of your promises of preserving anonymity – I had hardly left the phone box when one of your squad cars came rushing up.'

'That wouldn't have been anything to do with us. An unlucky coincidence.'

'Like the body?'

Stanley allowed a little chuckle.

'No, not like finding your body. It's straight. We really do try to keep confidentiality – frankly, it's in our interest. If we didn't and the word got out, nobody would ever come forward. I guess you won't be convinced but it's the truth. I'll tell you something else. Nobody's coming round tomorrow to arrest you or anything like that.'

It was Jeremy's turn to chuckle gently.

'Want a bet? You haven't heard it all yet. Any rate, as I was saying, I made our little appointment then went to bed. I was in court in the early part of the morning but I'd left my court case round at Sandra's the previous night so I went to her flat to retrieve it. I opened the door and found the place in turmoil. I shouldn't have gone in, I suppose, but somehow I couldn't help myself. That was a big mistake and how! I had hardly got inside when the door was slammed on me and I found myself looking at an ugly brute screwing a silencer onto a gun.'

He paused and launched another attack on the pasta, helping it onto his fork with a chunk of bread, which he then wiped in the sauce and popped into his mouth.

'It might not have been the mistake you imagine. If you had tried to do a runner, the fellow like as not would have shot you before you were half-way down the corridor.'

'Hadn't thought of that. Anyway, it doesn't matter much now. I went in and that's that.'

'What happened?'

Doing his best not to get too involved in the details, he told how he was beaten up and then got down to the car. He described his hare-brained scheme at the lights and how he crashed the Porsche, ran off and eventually got Paddy to pick him up.

'Frankly, I still can't understand how I got out of this alive.'

'You were bloody lucky.' The voice was dead pan.

The narrowness of the escape returned to Jeremy and he sat silently, his depression building up inside him once more. Stanley drained his glass and bent across the table, refilling his host's before going on to pour himself a generous further measure. He twisted the now replenished glass between his fingers and stared into the liquid.

'You had better let us have the diamonds.'

What was the need? Suddenly, the solicitor in him returned to his morose body. Why, indeed?

'I would have thought I should return them to Wagstaff. After all, they are his property.'

'He seems to have been defrauding Customs and Excise at best. No, we should have them.'

'You have no evidence that he was. It was only Parsons telling his girl-friend – it was probably something he made up on the spur of the moment to keep her from getting suspicious about the real reason for the chase.'

Stanley shrugged.

'I'll talk it over with the chief. If he wants them, you'd better hand them over. He doesn't take kindly to obstruction of the police.'

'Well, he should have no trouble filing for a court order, then.'

The conversation was suddenly taking a more aggressive line. Both men sensed it and neither really wanted that to happen. Stanley put his glass down.

'Reckon I've already drunk too much tonight. Drink always makes me argumentative. I'm supposed to drive as well.'

Jeremy grinned slightly. 'I'm probably the same. Let's have another coffee and call it a night. I've told you just about everything I know. The ball's in your court now.'

He got up and called Luigi.

'What's likely to happen over the crash?'

'That will also depend on the chief. He can put in the right word with Traffic if he feels like it.'

'And the diamonds might help him feel like it?'

Stanley shrugged meaningfully. The coffee arrived.

'Tell him he can have the case if he likes but not the diamonds without Wagstaff's say-so.'

'You can take it we will want to talk to Sandra at some point.'

'I expected that. There's no objection so long as I am present.'

Stanley nodded as if agreeing and changed the subject. While the coffee disappeared, the two men talked about cricket and left the world of crime behind. At last, they got up, Jeremy paid the bill and the two men walked out of the restaurant together.

'Where's your car?'

'I parked round the corner.'

Stanley indicated with his hand. Jeremy moved a little to his left, half leaving yet wavering.

'I'm just up there. I'll say goodnight, then, and . . .'

He paused, hesitating as to whether there was any trust or not. He decided that there might be.

'. . . and thanks.'

'I should be thanking you. I have the information we were seeking and I've had a good meal into the bargain.'

He grinned and thrust out a hand.

'Now take care. No more heavy stuff.'

Jeremy shook his hand.

'I'll watch it. That was enough for a lifetime.'

They turned and walked in opposite directions, Jeremy towards the BMW and Stanley wending his way up the street. He was just turning the corner as Jeremy got in his car. He turned the key, started the engine first time and promptly stalled it as he let the clutch out too fiercely. He swore to himself, aware that Stanley might well have been right – he had drunk the greater part of the bottle. With deliberate care, he tried again and, this time, set off down the street without problem. He turned the same corner that Stanley had taken less than half a minute earlier and sucked in air rapidly in response to

126

the sight in front of him.

Half-way down the pavement, four men were fighting. He did not have to recognise any of them to know that the police officer was in the fray. What was more, it was rather one-sided. Even as he straightened the car, an arm flashed across the throat of one of the men and he went very still. The other two ran to him, grabbing at his pockets. In the seconds that this happened, Jeremy stuck his foot down hard in second and ran the BMW onto the pavement, accelerating rapidly towards the knot of men. The lamp-post came up out of nowhere. The car was within inches of hitting it as he swung the wheel wildly to the right, slid back onto the road and headed straight at the first of three parked cars. Another jerk on the wheel and he once more mounted the pavement, clipped the wall with the bumper and managed to almost straighten the careering vehicle as it headed directly for the youths. He put the headlamps onto full beam, hammered the horn and literally stood on the brake pedal as he realised that he was not going to stop in time.

In those few seconds, the three young thugs initially turned to look at the oncoming car. The two frisking Stanley's pockets panicked and started to run across the pavement and to weave between two of the parked cars, continuing their run down the middle of the road. The third was holding Stanley and facing the rampant BMW. Seeing it was sure to hit them, he released his hold and turned to run after his companions, leaving the policeman staring dazzled at the twin pair of lamps bearing down on him. The car was slowing but not quickly enough. Just as contact was inevitable, Stanley came to life and leapt up and forwards. The bonnet caught his legs and flung him onto the windscreen.

The car stopped. Jeremy watched aghast as the man slid silently off the bonnet and out of sight to the side of the front wheel. It had suddenly gone very quiet. Jeremy switched off the engine and scrambled out. To his immense relief, Stanley was slowly picking himself up off the ground.

'Oh, God! I'm sorry! Are you hurt?'

There was a gasp of air.

'Black and blue all over, I reckon.'

The policeman let out another sharp burst of air.

'I couldn't stop in time. I totally misjudged it. I think you were right. I have drunk too much.'

'Bloody good thing, then. If you hadn't looked like you were going to hit me, those buggers wouldn't have run off.'

Jeremy suddenly remembered them. 'What about those three?'

'Half-way to kingdom come by now. No point chasing them, even if I felt like it.' He rubbed his side.

'Gosh, I am sorry.'

'I told you, don't be. Here, I owe you one, Fox. You've only to ask.'

He stuck out a hand. Jeremy was embarrassed: he had nearly killed the chap and he was actually thanking him.

'Ah, forget it. Honestly.'

'You aren't driving back to Orpington, are you?'

'I was.'

'I shouldn't let you.'

'I'll go to the garage and get Paddy to run me back.'

'How far's that?'

'No more than a quarter of a mile. I'll manage, I promise.'

Stanley rubbed his side again. 'I'll follow you, just in case, and, for God's sake, take it carefully. I really shouldn't let you drive.'

He sounded worried but made no move to stop him. No harm was done and they reached the garage without mishap. As Jeremy pulled up on the forecourt, Stanley gave a toot on the horn and sped off, leaving Jeremy to break the news on the state of the bumper to Pete. He came down none too delighted to view it, walked round the car twice, slid onto his backside and felt underneath.

As he emerged, he said gruffly, 'Don't know why I drive in Demolition Derbys. You're much better at it than me.'

Thank God, he had been forgiven.

'I suppose you need another brandy.'

'Not this time, Pete. A coffee would be great.'

'OK, then Pad can run you back to Orpington, I suppose. I doubt if she will mind.'

9

Paddy drove him back to his flat in her customary manner, having little regard for minor details such as speed limits – she claimed the signs were only there to tell you the average age of the population in the area – and rarely leaving her right foot anywhere else than on the boards of the Cosworth. Jeremy was becoming used to this ridiculous way of traversing the countryside and had worked out a strategy for remaining sane and dry in the pants. He pulled the safety strap very tight about his middle, grasped the upper part with his left hand and hung onto the side of the seat with the other. Now, with his eyes firmly fixed on the front dashboard, he attempted to shut his ears to the heavy metal assaulting them from four speakers. The journey was mercifully short – it had to be at that speed. Paddy slowed at the edge of the town.

'Which way now?'

He had forgotten she had only been to his place once before. Great! She would have to slow down to his pace or near it. Did she hell!

'Take a right at the lights.'

The car slid gracefully through the corner at over forty in second, swept smoothly into third and accelerated past a Nissan with go-fast badges on its backside.

'Pad, slow it! My nerves won't take much more of this!

Left here! Oh, never mind. The next one will do.'

Two more turns and he pointed to the house. She had recognised it and was braking almost before he spoke. The Sierra nipped skilfully round a Granada parked close to the driveway and rolled gently to rest on the tarmac area about a yard from the steps leading up to the front entrance hall.

'Coming in for a coffee?'

'Sure.'

She bounced out of the car, flicking the door shut as she went then hung back while Jeremy went up the steps. The house was an old Victorian three-storey affair that had been recently modernised and converted into three self-contained flats. He had bought his first-floor apartment the previous September. Since then, the value of the property had fallen and his mortgage was higher than the resale price, a factor that had further worried him at the time of his redundancy.

The flats were all reached from a wide hall that opened from the double doors at the entrance, ornate glass tastelessly spoiling an otherwise attractive façade. Once inside, a wide flight of stairs swept up to the two upper front doors.

Jeremy was about to open the glass door when a voice spoke from the bottom of the steps.

'You Carrington-Fox?'

Jeremy turned at the voice and looked down at the three men arranged across the drive. They looked the sort you might want to avoid on a bright day with hundreds of people around. This was a dark night and he was alone but for Paddy.

'If I am?'

'Mr Smith sent us.'

The cold tingle ran the length of his spine: he had not needed to be told, however. There was only one person in the world who might want to send out a personal escort for him. He was thinking rapidly; he was almost inside the building and might make a run for his front door but Paddy was less than three feet from the nearest man, who clearly had a part time job doubling for the Whipsnade Zoo gorilla.

'Two ways to do it, pal, and we much prefer the hard way.'

'What about the girl?'

'Here, don't mind me!'

'Shut it, Pad.' It was more of a frightened hiss than a command.

'Mr Smith made no mention of her. Take yourself off, bitch, before you get hurt.'

Paddy had turned fully round to face the men. There was no hint of fear in her voice as she said, 'I don't take kindly to being called a bitch. You'd better apologise, punk.'

The gorilla laughed openly and genuinely but it was a harsh, unfriendly rattle.

'You'd better get your hide out of here, bitch, before I kick your arse in.'

Paddy walked very slowly down the two steps she had ascended and stopped a couple of feet from the animal. She shook her head sadly.

'My pa's always telling me my temper will get me into trouble but I'm sorry, I can't help it, I just can't help it. Being called a bitch always gets me riled up so you'd better apologise quickly, pal, and then get your ugly butt out of here before I get real mad.'

The gorilla uttered an expletive.

While this was going on, Jeremy remained more or less motionless, his hand still on the doorknob. It was difficult to say if he was more scared for himself or Paddy. He had a horrible feeling that he was spectator to an

132

impending Greek tragedy and he had no mortal way of averting it. As the next few seconds unfolded, he became aware more of the black comedy of the situation and less of the tragic element.

The gorilla certainly did not see the funny side of things. He was holding his groin and whimpering like a child. His two companions gaped in amazement, frozen by the audacity of the blow. They still watched as the young woman pirouetted neatly on the spot, coming out of the spin with an outspread left hand that caught the creature beautifully across its Adam's apple. He crumpled up, gurgling horribly. She turned to the other two.

'He really should have apologised when he had the chance. You laddies going to be sensible or do you want some of what he got?'

She was answered by a snarl from the jackal to her right and he raised his hands ready for business. It was a snarl that turned to yelps of pain as she dived forward, rolling and turning, coming up once more with both feet tucked into the man's abdomen. Her full fourteen stone went into the pile-driving kick, sending him flying backwards. One blow was enough: he cracked his head on the tarmac and lay still.

'Look out! The bastard's got a knife!'

Sure enough, the third man had stepped back, whipping a thin stiletto from his hip as he did so.

'OK, bitch. Let's see how good you are against a real man.'

He swept the blade back and forth in a series of cutting gestures. He was too far away to have any physical effect: they were done to instil confidence in himself and fear in his intended victim. It is doubtful if either objective was achieved. The Amazon below was having none of it.

'Oh, boy! This is really going to hurt you, my little

133

poofter. I'm going to carve my initials on your arse with that little penknife of yours.'

She jumped forward like a mongoose, landing squarely on both feet, her arms spread wide. The man lunged, feinted and swept the blade within inches of her throat. She sprang backwards, bounced a couple of times up into the air without yielding territory and twisted sideways as the next lunge came in. Her boot caught him on the back of his right leg, high on the thigh muscle. He caught his breath, rubbed the sore muscle, balanced himself with the knife held forward in protective vein and looked for another opening. He suddenly yelled ferociously and slashed up, across and down in one flowing movement. The mongoose jumps kept her just out of range but it was clear to Jeremy that she was deliberately letting the knife come close. At each pass, she tried to catch her assailant's arm.

The next attack was too close: she took a five-inch cut in her sleeve. That was enough. The tactics changed and she parried each new sortie with her feet. Then it came. A slight over-stretching in his eagerness to press home what he judged to be an advantage and the flaying boot flicked his ankle. Unbalanced, he pitched forward, the knife jarred from his grasp on impact with the ground. In an instant, he had recovered and made to retrieve his weapon. The sole of her boot screwed into his face and he gasped in pain. More was to come. He took the kick to the ribs all in good part but objected to her flopping on top of him with her bottom parked solidly on his mouth. He tried punching both hands into her well-padded midriff but she ignored the intrusion, bent well forward, took his ankle firmly in her hands and did a backwards somersault off him.

The scream was very effective and most genuine but Paddy appeared deaf. She let go of the leg, which stayed in the air, twitching uncontrollably, and dived for the knife.

'Now, scumbag. This is where I make my point, if you get the pun.'

She rolled him over on his side and slashed his trousers from top to half-way down the leg and peeled the material as one would deal with a banana.

'No, Pad! That's enough!'

Jeremy was down the steps and rushing up to her. He grabbed her arm and desperately tried to hold the blade away from the exposed flesh. She suddenly relaxed and let the knife fall.

'Thank God! I thought you were about to skin him alive!'

She pulled herself free and stood up. She laughed but it was not with humour, more with pent-up relief.

'I bloody well gave it to them, didn't I?'

Now she was almost crying. She grabbed him by the neck and hugged him hard.

'God, I need a brandy, Pad.'

'So do I!'

She cried properly now.

'Bloody fool I'm making of myself.'

She pulled her sleeve across her face and now, for the first time, Jeremy noticed her arm was bleeding quite badly. He glanced at the carnage before him. The three would-be assailants were still lying on the ground and it did not need a medical examination to know that she had certainly put the last creature's leg out of joint. He was writhing in agony and pleading for help. The one she had winded was choking and looking blue in the face, while the third was out cold.

'Come on, love. Up to the flat.'

She did not resist. He wound an arm round her middle and she rested her head on his shoulder and walked sedately up the stairs with him. He had to let go of her to get through the door but she instantly snuggled into his body once they were into the wide passageway. At the top of the stairs, he again let her go and fumbled for the key.

The sight inside the flat momentarily threw other matters from his mind. The place was in chaos: chairs and table overturned, drawers pulled out and their contents emptied over the floor, carpets pulled up to expose the floor-boards and even the gas fire had been pulled away from the wall. He slowly walked through to the bedroom, where the whole horrible business had been repeated. Bedding was strewn across the floor in an untidy muddle, the mattress thrown aside and, once more, the drawers emptied. The wardrobe had been left with its doors open, the contents scattered across the other side of the room. Paddy had quite naturally followed him inside and had even closed the front door but now stood dumb-struck just inside the living-room.

She came back to life.

'My God! Someone's given this place a ripe going-over. Wouldn't I like to ring the bastards' necks who done this.'

She paused.

'I guess I probably did. Wish I'd known they'd done this when we were downstairs; I'd have really worked them over.'

The mention of the men below brought Jeremy back to earth with a bang. He went back into the living-room and found the phone under a pile of table linen. It was off its hook but it had not been damaged. He pulled it clear of the mess and depressed the nine three times.

'Which service, please?'

'Police and ambulance.'

136

'Can I have your number, please, caller?'

He gave it, his voice just remaining steady.

'Police. How can I help you?'

'There's been an attempted kidnapping at 27 Armitage Road, Orpington. I'm calling from my flat – it's been ransacked. There are three men lying injured in the main drive.'

He paused to draw breath, steadied himself and went on, 'This is not a hoax. We need help and need it quickly. The injured men will also need medical attention. Can you send an ambulance as well?'

'Stay calm, sir. A car will be on its way immediately. Can I have your name, please, sir?'

'Yes, it's Carrington-Fox.'

'Right, Mr Carrington-Fox. Try not to touch anything, sir, and wait for our men to arrive. I'l have them on their way immediately.'

'Don't ring off, officer!'

'I'm not going anywhere, sir. Take your time.'

Jeremy eased a little.

'There's more! What's happened tonight needs to be communicated to Detective Superintendent Colin Burnell at police headquarters, Maidstone, or to Detective Sergeant Stanley. Get the sergeant if you can. I was with him earlier tonight. Tell him the Fox is in trouble and give him my address. I have his number somewhere . . . .'

'That's all right, sir. I'll find him easily enough.'

'You're sure?'

'Quite sure, thank you, sir.'

'OK, I'll ring off then – and thanks.'

He looked at Paddy and said grimly: 'The police are on their way. Now, let's see if the buggers left the brandy intact.'

He went to the open cabinet and found, to their

137

intense relief, that several bottles had been pulled out and three rolled partway across the floor but nothing was broken. He rescued the Napoleon, poured generous portions into two tumblers and handed one to the enigmatic young woman next to him. As he did so, he noticed the blood had run down her arm and under the sleeve onto the back of her hand.

'Let's have a look at that arm.'

She glanced down at it, gave herself two large mouthfuls of the cognac, changed hands with the glass and thrust her injured arm forward. Jeremy took a mouthful, put the glass down and rolled her sleeve back. The cut was long but not deep, running about five inches diagonally across her forearm. It was bleeding freely but was not serious. He disappeared into the kitchen, returning with a damp sponge and a tea-towel. He dabbed the residual blood away from the gash and wrapped the tea-towel as tightly around it as he could.

'It's going to need stitching. That'll only stem the bleeding until you can get to hospital.'

'Yer, I know. Oh, bugger it. I could have done without this. I'm due to fight Poison Ivy next Friday.'

He looked at her uncomprehendingly. She read the look instantly.

'Oh, Lor',' she said, 'you don't know about my little sideline, do you? I wrestle – I'm Grizelda, the Lewisham Bear! Great name, isn't it? The crowd call me "Grizzly", of course. I get fifty quid a night plus prize-money. Won three hundred the other week.' There was a ring of pride in the voice.

A curtain dropped from Jeremy's eyes: all was crystal clear. It explained how she escaped unscathed from her two would-be muggers and how she was able to despatch the trio downstairs. The Crown Prosecution Service were going to love this one! He could see it now – 'Miss

McBear . . . or should I call you Grizelda, the Lewisham Bear? I have got the name right, haven't I? Would you prefer "Grizzly"? Tell me, have you been a professional wrestler for long?' He'd give the jury at least ten minutes to return their guilty verdict. After which, she'd kill him. His lightning mind found an escape route – they might stick her in jail for a spell. That wouldn't help: Pete would kill him instead. There was no defence; he was done for.

'You look utterly gobsmacked!'

She laughed, sucked in a large mouthful of brandy, swilled it round her cheeks and swallowed it.

'God! I really needed that!'

She was clearly returning to normal. Jeremy pulled himself back to the present. The case could wait; they still had more than their fair share of trouble to be going on with. He glanced out of the window and watched without emotion as the jackal that had been kicked in the stomach tried to stand. The man nearly made it then staggered two paces forward and overbalanced. He lay still but there was no reason to think he had lost consciousness again. Indeed, he had not. Barely ten seconds later, he started to crawl towards the gatepost, where he again hauled himself to his feet. This time, he was more successful. Jeremy watched as the man moved down the street, clinging to the fencing as he went.

A sudden thought struck him – the knife.

'Pad, I've got to go down there again. Trust me. Stay here whatever happens and don't show yourself if the police arrive before I get back.'

He was out of the door and helter-skelter down the stairs. He shot out into the night then stood stock-still, scanning the ground for the missing blade. There it was, not a yard from the wretch with the damaged leg. As he moved towards it, he heard a brief wail of a police siren.

It was just two notes; presumably they needed to make the car's presence felt but were reluctant to over-use the siren this late at night. He probably only had seconds to act. He whipped out his handkerchief and wiped the handle, being careful not to touch it himself, then tossed it to the injured man on the ground. With that, he ran back to the main doors.

'Look out, Jerry!'

The call from the upper window was indeed timely. He half turned and ducked at the same time. The knife was badly aimed and flew a foot wide to bounce off the glass panel. Jeremy ignored it, continued his flight back to the flat and reached it just as the first of two police cars swung into the entrance. He watched from the window as the two officers jumped from the car and ran to the men on the ground. All the while he was talking to Paddy.

'We have only a few minutes before they are up here so listen carefully. I'm going down to meet them. Police are my territory and this is where I look after you. You leave all the talking to me until they formally want to question you. Then, you say absolutely nothing unless I'm present. Is that clear?'

She nodded.

'Right!' He reached for his brandy glass, emptied the contents into his mouth and went on, 'Don't open that door until I'm back. It's possible one of the officers might come up while I'm downstairs.'

He was away – cool, confident and in control. At least, he hoped he was in control. This was now brainwork and he had a kind of unconscious and unintended arrogance that told him he had the edge on everybody below.

He was in the act of opening the outside doors as a third policeman came up the steps.

'Good evening, officer. I am Jeremy Carrington-Fox. It was me that made the 999 call. I returned home with

140

my girl-friend, only to be accosted by three men. Fortunately for me, she is something of an expert in self-defence and stopped them kidnapping me. Two of them you will already have found injured down there and the third was knocked out in the fight but recovered while we were in the flat making the call and made off.'

'Hold it there, sir.'

He turned to the two constables on the ground.

'How are those two?'

'This one's in a bad way. He is barely breathing. Seems his throat is damaged.'

The second one looked up. 'Ambulance on its way, Sarge. This one seems to have a dislocated leg and it might be broken as well for all I know. Poor devil is in great pain, here.'

Jeremy noticed the fourth man at the radio of the second squad car. The sergeant addressed him next.

'Frank, get our vehicle clear and watch for the ambulance. It'll need to reverse right in. Let the station know what's happening and ask someone to be at the hospital for when the ambulance arrives.'

He turned back to Jeremy.

'Now, sir, do you think we could go inside and discuss this?'

'Certainly, officer. I am concerned, however, that one of the fellows is getting away. Can't you send someone to catch him?'

'I think you can leave all that to us, sir.'

'Don't patronise me, officer. I'm hardly in the mood. Has someone gone after him or not?'

The sergeant flushed marginally. His experience stopped him giving the slick rebuttal that sprang to his lips. He checked and looked into the steady eyes focused on his face.

'To tell the truth, sir, we have not seen anybody else.

There was no one in the road as we drove up.'

'Damn! Then he has got away.'

The sergeant yelled down to the men below, 'As soon as you can, one of you take a car and tour around. Apparently, one of them has got away.'

Jeremy called over the top, 'He's probably hurt and not moving fast.'

He gave his attention back to the sergeant.

'If you would like to come up to the flat, I can give you a short statement there. Do you know if a message went to county headquarters?'

'No idea about that, sir.'

The sergeant was conscious that the initiative was being wrestled from him. He was not used to this. He walked in silence up the stairs behind the solicitor, collecting his thoughts and ready to re-exert his authority. Jeremy knocked sharply on the door and Paddy opened it almost immediately. The two men entered and Jeremy closed the door as the policeman surveyed the chaos in the living-room.

'Somebody certainly gave this place a good going-over, sir.'

'The same fellows your men have got downstairs, unless I'm very much mistaken.'

'Who is the lady, sir?'

'This is Miss McBear – she's my girl-friend. We were just returning from an evening out when this happened.'

He caught the waspish smirk in Paddy's expression and shifted his position slightly so she could not catch his eye.

The ambulance arrived. Jeremy gave a cursory glance through the window and returned his attention to the business in hand.

'Do sit down.'

142

'If you don't mind, sir, I would like to put a call in to the station.'

'Certainly. Feel free to use the phone.'

'I'd prefer it in private, if you don't mind, sir.'

'We'll make a coffee.'

He ushered Paddy into the kitchen, put the kettle on and hastily checked the flour container. He was in luck: the lid was still on. The sugar was stored in a large polythene tub which had once held a litre of ice-cream. Half of it had been spilt across the shelf and this he swept carefully into his hand and shovelled back.

He gave a half-grin. 'They missed the heroin, anyway,' he whispered.

She looked puzzled.

'I didn't put the drugs into the bank: I thought I'd keep them out. Half of it's in the flour bag and most of the rest is in the sugar tub. I left about a couple of ounces in an empty pepper container.'

He put his finger to his lips.

'Shhh! That's not for our flat-footed friend next door.'

The flat-footed butt of his tongue appeared in the doorway.

'I'd like to take some statements now, if you don't mind, sir.'

'What about headquarters? Have you contacted them?'

'Appears they have reacted to the call, sir. I've instructions not to touch anything until a Sergeant Stanley arrives. I've been asked to take down some basic details before he gets here, though. Seems as though they are treating this as something special and I've had orders to find the third man at all costs. The station has another four cars on the way over.'

There was certainly a degree of respect in the voice

143

now. The kettle started to puff a little steam. Jeremy caught his eye.

'I've enough coffee but no sugar. Can I interest you in a cup?'

'That would be most kind, sir. As it happens, I use these sweetener things. Supposed to watch the weight.'

He patted a stomach that hardly boasted an inch of fat. Paddy wanted to giggle – she had a wicked thought of this pillar of the local constabulary using a spoonful from the sugar tub. The traumas of the evening were already wearing off and her irrepressible sense of fun was returning.

The next twenty minutes consisted of a clinical and staccato relation of the events of the late evening from Jeremy, followed by an exuberant and highly coloured version from Paddy. Only the occasional scowl from the solicitor spoilt her soliloquy and that was hardly effective when she got round to describing her various wrestling ploys. They had almost finished when there came a knock at the door. Jeremy opened it to find his dinner companion and two other men he had not seen before.

'Second time tonight, Mr Fox.'

''Fraid so, sergeant. I must admit, I'm not sorry to see you, though.'

Stanley looked across at the other sergeant.

'DS Stanley. I'll take over now. I don't think there's any need for you to stay.'

'I'm not sure my inspector will like that idea.'

'I'll square it with him.'

The sergeant still seemed loath to go but the choice was hardly open.

'Thank you for all you've done, sergeant. I am really grateful for the speed with which you got here.'

Jeremy felt a few flattering words could do no harm. He politely pulled the door wider – it had never been properly closed – and watched the officer to the middle of the stairs. By the time he had shut the door and turned back to Stanley, one of his two companions was already busy with a small pot of powder and a fine artist's brush.

'This is the friend of mine I told you about earlier this evening. She has had nothing to do with this affair and is only here because she ran me home.'

He allowed a wry smile.

'You will remember, it was your suggestion.'

'Paddy's the name. Jerry reckons you're all right – for a copper, that is.' She thrust her hand forward.

He smiled gently. 'So you're Paddy. From what you said, I thought Paddy was a man.'

'As you see, very definitely not. If you've no objection, I think she should get home before her father starts worrying about her. She has made her statement to the sergeant who just left.'

Stanley seemed to understand. 'There's no reason to detain you, miss.'

'That's OK. I'd like to hang around for a bit.'

'No, you wouldn't, Paddy. I'll see you tomorrow and tell you if anything exciting happens.'

'It would help, miss, if you would agree to give a set of your fingerprints. They will be destroyed when we've finished with them but we need to eliminate yours from any we might find in the flat.'

It took less than a quarter of an hour to get her away, during which time the remaining two officers had continued working as though there was nobody else around. Once they had the place to themselves, Jeremy took Stanley into the kitchen. He took down the flour container from the shelf.

'This is the stuff. What do you think?'

'It's certainly heroin and, as I told you at the restaurant, it's very pure. Even a quantity like this would fetch thousands on the streets. Is there any more of the stuff?'

Jeremy handed him the sugar packet without comment. As he did so, one of the other men entered the room.

'We're finished in here.'

Stanley nodded. 'Not much else we can do tonight.' He turned to Jeremy. 'I reckon the best thing you can do is to get a good night's sleep and clear this lot up in the morning.'

Jeremy shrugged. 'Do you know, I suddenly feel very tired.'

'We'll be off, then, and leave you to it.'

Ten minutes later, Jeremy was alone in the flat. All he wanted now was to get into bed, pull the single sheet and one blanket over him and drop off to sleep, oblivious to the cares of the world. With luck, for once he might even dream about Paddy without getting his arms crunched.

10

It was well past twelve when the anonymous Granada slid from the forecourt in Armitage Road and left Jeremy in something approaching peace. He watched from the window as the car left, then turned back to the tip that he had once looked upon as home. It gave a bitter taste to know that the flat had been systematically combed by Smith's villains. He poured another brandy, took it through to the bedroom and placed it beside the bed. He pulled the clothes over the mattress, shed his outer clothing and slumped onto the bed. He looked at the brandy, changed his mind and felt for the bottle of sleeping tablets he had bought only that afternoon. Deciding to leave the alcohol in case he woke in the night, he swallowed three tablets instead of the prescribed two, switched off the bedside lamp and prepared himself for spending the next seven or eight hours in his own fantasy world.

For all his unsettled mind, the drugs took their effect and he slept soundly, a sleep not easily broken and one in which Paddy featured pleasantly. Thus it was that the drugged slumber was invaded only slowly. At some point, he was dimly conscious of a change in the room: it was cooler and there was a slight draught. There was a hand on his shoulder. Still stupefied, he became aware of it shaking him quite violently. The moment he appeared to be waking, a second hand came across his mouth. A bright light was being shone in his eyes and it took several moments for him to realise that there were two men in the room with him.

'Get up, punk. Mr Smith ain't pleased wif you. 'Ere, come on. Wake up, can't yer?'

He was in no position to answer: the hand was still clamped across his mouth.

'Get dressed and no funny business. If we hadn't orders to deliver you in one piece, you'd 'ave been dog food by now; but don't you play on it. After what you did to Butch, neither of us 'ud be too worried at laying you one.'

The bedclothes were jerked away and allowed to fall on the floor. The hand came away from his face and he was pulled across the bed, once they were sure he was aware of what was happening. He coughed slightly and took in a large breath, swung his feet over the edge of the mattress and rubbed his face. He was well aware of the change in circumstances but sensibly used the time to give himself an opportunity to think. His limbs were heavy but his brain was beginning to function and he was almost wishing it was not. It had nothing nice to tell him.

'Come on, hurry it up.'

He was pulled to his feet.

'OK, OK. No rough stuff. I'm awake properly now.'

He held up a hand to ward off an imaginary blow. The man released him and stepped back. Somehow, he managed to pull on some clothes. Aware of the silenced weapon in the hands of his second unwanted guest, he cooperated as best he could. It was sinking in: he was being kidnapped again. However, they had orders not to damage him so long as he behaved and he had no intention of doing otherwise. He could not argue with

148

brute force but he was not quite as scared as he ought to have been and he felt a small measure of security in the thought that he had something they wanted. What was more, it was safe from their hands in the short term and they could not get it if they killed him.

It took no time at all to find his shoes. He grabbed pointlessly at his keys on the side table as he was hustled through the door and out onto the landing. The stairs came and went, then the cool of the late night air touched him. Moments later, they were at the car.

'Get the boot up!'

The second man pocketed his gun and opened the large counterbalanced tail-gate to the estate car.

'Right, you. In you go!'

Jeremy did not argue. He clambered onto the floor of the rear of the car and was helped unceremoniously to finish off the job. The door slammed down on him and he was tucked up rather uncomfortably behind the rear seat with the parcel shelf a foot or so above his head. The car started off and he had nothing else to do except worry about what was in store for him. For all his natural slant away from physical prowess, he did at least possess a good brain. Furthermore, it was a brain that was capable of working well when it was given the time. He had learned from his recent escapades that panic and the accompanying mental freezing did nothing for self-preservation.

Thus it was that he spent the thirty-minute drive to good purpose. He felt around in the boot for a possible weapon, found none and really was not too disappointed. He doubted if one would have done him any good and, in any case, he intended to try and outsmart them. By the time they pulled him out, stiff and with pins and needles in his leg, he was ready – not looking forward to the future but at least ready for it.

He briefly had time to see where he was. The road was deserted and pretty derelict; the street lamps had long ago been vandalised out of use and the immediate vicinity gave no reason for repair. As he was quickly hustled out of the boot and through the door of the warehouse, he was able just to make out the rows of high, arched windows, most with their glass missing and boarded up. The door snapped behind him and he was held for a second or so while one of the men felt for a switch. A series of fluorescent lamps flickered and the bare floor of the warehouse was flooded with light. Still keeping a firm grip on his arm, they led him across the floor to a small office shrouded in darkness.

The first man tapped firmly on the door and waited patiently. A light switch clicked on and the dirty glass in the upper partition turned yellow, the naked bulb showing clearly. It seemed to be an eternity before the door opened but the tension had magnified the time from just a few seconds. Jeremy looked squarely at the sleep-filled face of the man he knew as Clive.

'I've been waiting for this. Get him inside. Rambo, check the main door.'

He turned his back and took a couple of paces into the middle of the office, knowing without looking that he was being followed.

'Now, punk, let's get it quite clear. There's nobody around to hear your screams and I don't particularly mind how much violence I have to use to get what I want – in fact, I'd enjoy it if you do try to hold out on me.'

'You've no need to worry. I'll cooperate in any way I can.'

Clive seemed to pause for a fraction of time but his ugly composure remained intact.

'You disappoint me. Still, let's see what happens, shall we?'

'Ask your question.'

'All right. Where's the case?'

'It's quite safe.' He sniggered nervously. 'There's a bit of a pun, there. It's more than safe. It actually is in one – Orpington Branch of Barclay's Bank, to be precise. I can get it for you quite easily tomorrow morning.'

Clive considered. 'I don't believe you, punk. I think you need a little help to get you in the right mood.'

Jeremy tried to back off but found his arms pinned tightly to his side. A leering smile was about six inches from his face.

'Don't hit me!' The panic sounded in his voice: the coolness had deserted him. The fist planted itself into the hollow at the bottom of his ribs. He coughed and struggled for breath.

'Shall we try again?'

'I told you – wait!'

The fist went into his abdomen.

'There's only one way to get that case. I took out insurance against this sort of thing – I told the bank they should only hand it over to me, in person. Ask Mr Smith. He'll believe me.'

The last few words came as something between a desperate scream and a breathless gasp. Whether Clive believed him or whether the name of his boss dampened his fervour for more of his favourite sport is difficult to say but the effect was certain enough. The sadist stood back a pace and subjected his victim to a long and suspicious scrutiny.

'Get him outside.'

Jeremy was bundled through the door, which was shut firmly behind him. He heard the phone ringing and the inordinate wait before it was answered. In comparison, the conversation was short. Clive emerged with a look of considerable disappointment on his face.

151

'Take him up to the other one. See he's tied up properly but don't mark him. Mr Smith wants him completely presentable for the morning. When you've done that, you can put your heads down for a couple of hours and see I'm not disturbed.'

Clearly, Clive still had a few hours' paperwork to do.

Jeremy was led across the floor of the warehouse and through a connecting door into the next warehouse. In contrast, this one was stacked with packing-cases so that they were forced to walk down the corridors between them. He was taken up a flight of stairs, then the front man unlocked a door and pushed it half-open but instead of letting his captive enter, spun him round, grabbed his hands and expertly tied them firmly behind his back.

'Lie down!'

He bent his knees in an effort to obey but clearly did not please his captors and suffered the consequences. He did not hit the floor too hard but it was enough to make him let forth an involuntary cry followed by an expletive he had never used before. One of the men laughed but was silenced by the other.

'Just tie his feet and shut up. I could do with a few hours' shut-eye even if you couldn't.'

The rope was passed quickly round his ankles, pulled tight and knotted. The trussed-up parcel was unceremoniously rolled across the threshold of the room and then left. Jeremy heard the key turn in the lock, more with relief than regret. He was alone; alone, that is, except for the voice.

'Who are you?' The voice was thin, weak and cracked.

Jeremy was alert again, screwing his head round in a vain attempt to see some detail on the dark lump in the far corner of the room. In the total darkness, he saw nothing. He collected his breath – he had not been winded, just shaken a little by the fall.

'More to the point, who the hell are you?'

'Keith Parsons.'

'I thought you were dead.' He rolled over twice in the direction of the voice and continued, 'I'm Jeremy Carrington-Fox.'

'You seem to know me. Have we met?'

'No. I'm family solicitor to the McBears. When you failed to show up, Sandra contacted her father and I got taken along. Then I had the misfortune to find some guy stabbed on the fire-escape – at the time, I thought it was you – and, at that point, we got Sandra out of the flat and back to Lewisham. She's told me a lot about you.'

'What are you doing here?'

'Long story and I don't fancy telling it now. Briefly, I've got your case with the diamonds and our chums out there want me to give it to them.'

There was a slight pause.

'And have you?'

'Nope.'

'Are you going to?'

'They think I am. That was the only way to avoid another of their friendly little roughing-up sessions. One was enough, I can tell you.'

'Lucky you. I've had that for most of the past two days. I suppose I'm lucky even to be alive but I won't be if they get their hands on the stuff. Nor will you.'

'I had worked that out for myself, thanks.'

There was another slight pause.

'Is the stuff safe? Don't tell me where it is, just is it safe?'

'Safe as the Bank of England. Leastways, as safe as Barclay's Bank in Orpington. It can be withdrawn only with my personal signature. That's why they had to keep me in reasonable shape until they can get me to the bank in the morning.'

Jeremy sharply changed the subject.

'This isn't getting us anywhere. Can you wriggle around and get at these ropes?'

'I doubt it. I'm tied up like a sack of potatoes, I'm stiff and numb and I've a bullet-wound that's giving me hell. The bastards worked on it to try to get information out of me. I had to tell them about Sandra's flat in the end – I just couldn't take any more.' The voice faltered.

Jeremy was looking at the window. He could see that it was crudely boarded up. In the contrast of light, the night sky was relatively bright behind the cracks and he could count the slats across it. He rolled onto his back and pulled his feet up under him. Tensing his muscles, he tried to rock himself forward but only succeeded in unbalancing and rolling back onto the floor.

'Can you sit up?'

'Why?'

'Don't ask questions, can you do it?'

'Yes. What good is that going to do?'

'Listen, pal. I don't intend to lie here doing nothing. Sit up and get your back against mine.'

Parsons was hardly a willing accessory but he did as he was asked. Jeremy wriggled up against him and bunched up his knees again.

'Right. Lean forward and keep still. I'm going to try to stand up.'

He pushed with his legs and slowly clawed his way up Parsons's back. It was hard work; he could only inch his hands up Parsons's jacket. He ignored the couple of sharp pulls for air as he obviously put pressure on the wound, kept going until he was almost lying across Parsons's back, then grasped his collar.

'OK, now slowly lean back.'

Jeremy slowly came to his feet, his legs still bent under him.

'Keep still. This is where I try going completely upright.'

He took a breath, checked his balance, then pushed hard. For a few frightening seconds, he swayed precariously, then his balance returned.

'I'm up. I'm going to try reaching the window.'

'That's no use. It is directly above the river and the boards will stop you shouting, even if there was anyone to hear you.'

Jeremy ignored the pessimism. For one thing, he was too busy concentrating. He was literally inching his way across the floor by rocking from his toes to his heels. The wall touched his shoulder and he rested. The window was still a couple of feet further along the adjacent wall and the build up of lactic acid was already giving pain to his tensed muscles. It took another three painful minutes to reach the sill, where he rested. Turning his head, he could see the outline of the boards: they had been nailed across a broken pane with no great artistry but with solid enough nails. Jeremy manoeuvred himself round so that his hands could take hold of the wood. He pulled. Nothing happened. He pulled again until his hands hurt. Still the wood remained tightly fastened.

Jeremy rested until the pain left his fingers and then he took a new grip. He got some purchase with his fingers, locked them as firmly as he could manage, braced himself for the action and jerked forward. The board gave a little. He tried again. It was loose. On the third pull, it came away with sudden force and he pitched onto the floor.

He was just able to turn his face sideways and to partially get his shoulder across but none of this really

155

did much. He felt the impact on his cheek and nose. He cried out with the pain, ignored Parsons's agitated enquiry, mainly because he was too stunned to answer, and lay still. He could feel the blood running from his nose and the pain was building up. He waited for the shock to ease then spoke again to his companion.

'I think I'm OK. My nose doesn't feel too good, though.'

'I don't know what good it'll do but you got one piece off.'

'Do you think you could go through that standing-up routine again?'

He could and did. A quarter of an hour later found Jeremy back at the window. The gap where the board had been exposed a jagged triangle of glass that remained imbedded in the putty on the bottom ledge. With infinite patience, he set to work, sawing pathetically slowly up and down with his hands, keeping the bonds across the cutting edge as best he could. It took a great deal of painful work to cut the first thong but, once he had done so, the rest fell away quickly. He bent and started work on his feet, tersely giving a short commentary as he did so. He had Parsons's ropes away quickly enough but the fellow stood very shakily and seemed to have difficulty in walking. The effort was already causing him to sweat profusely.

'Legs are numb. I don't feel too good.'

He steadied himself against the wall.

'Now what?'

Jeremy thought for a moment. 'Are you up to guarding the door?'

'I can listen for somebody coming but that's about all.'

'Here, take this.'

Jeremy handed him the piece of wood from the

window. Parsons shuffled across to the door and propped himself against it, using the wood as much as a support as a weapon. Jeremy moved back to the window and pulled at the next slat up from the bottom. It held firm despite his efforts. He turned his attention to the middle of the three remaining pieces and found more success. As he struggled to prise it away, he found his mind fantasizing on the future. The first notion was to wait behind the door for the thugs to come back and attack them with the slats. That seemed hardly worthy of much thought. Then the idea struck him of somehow sticking the piece of broken glass from the window into one end of the slat. He was having more success with the wood than any plan of action. He worked it away from the nail on one side and twisted it to and fro until it finally parted company with the window.

He could see the early dawn breaking over the London skyline. Despite the restricted view, he could make out the far bank of the Thames and the row of dilapidated buildings on the waterfront. Beyond them, rows of houses and miscellaneous business premises formed a drab mosaic. He had a burning desire to stretch out a hand and pluck at it: it was freedom, safety and all the things that made life such a desirable commodity. He was frightened. It came over him in an enormous wave and he had to fight back the tremor in his hands. He could see the beating he was liable to take shortly; he could also envisage a very short life span though, for all his fears, he could not imagine how he was to be killed. Perhaps that helped. He tried to clear his brain. It was swimming with images and refused to respond. More in anger at himself, he attacked the previous piece with the slat he had freed. Jamming it against the top slat and with his arms reaching well through the window, he levered inwards.

It was while he was struggling with this next Herculean task that the wild idea of the drain-pipe overran his mind. There might just be one outside the window that he could climb down. The thought sent him into a convulsion of fear. He would prefer no pipe to actually having to make such a climb. He did not care for heights – at least, not in this sort of situation. The slat cracked in the middle. One end parted from the retaining nail and the other he could swing down against the side of the frame. He pushed his head out and saw, both to his relief and disappointment, that there was no pipe or, for that matter, any other aid to help him climb down.

'There's no one about. Were you thinking of calling for help or what?'

Parsons had moved across to join him.

The two men gazed down at the grey waters below. It was about thirty feet to the narrow tow-path and then a further six or seven feet to the Thames below that. The warehouse had been constructed almost at the edge of the river wall, so that there was no more than a couple of yards of concrete below between the base of the building and the water. The decision seemed to have been taken for him.

'I'm going to try my luck at jumping into the water.'

'Bloody stupid idea. If you are not killed on the tow-path, you'll drown in the river. Given the choice, I reckon I'd prefer to take my chances with the wood and a bit of a surprise when they come to get us. The two of us might have some luck. That way is crazy.'

Jeremy continued to stare down. 'I've never gone off anything higher than the lowest board in the pool but I got a thousand-metre badge at school. Swimming was about the one thing I was reasonable at when it came to games lessons.'

He was talking to himself as much as anything. He had untied his shoes and shed his shirt. Parsons had become a ghostly image in the room. With fastidious care, he cleaned the remaining fragments of glass from the ledge. He slowly pulled himself onto the frame, gripped the edges firmly and eased his head and shoulders through. He looked down and wished immediately that he had not. He felt himself shaking. If he stayed there for much longer he knew he would never do it. He bent his legs, closed his eyes and screwed up his nerve. His muscles were trembling with the tension. He would go on the count of five. He reached it and still his hands were gripping the side of the frame as though glued. He could not go through with it. He bit his lip. What would Paddy think? She would call him yellow. Rotten bitch! He suddenly kicked out with his legs, let go of the frame and launched himself into space.

The involuntary scream lasted the two seconds it took to travel the forty feet downwards. His feet felt as though they had hit concrete, jarring his body near senseless. Then the ice-cold water swallowed him up. He went down further than he had expected. Somehow, he had not prepared himself for this and he was ten feet under before the thought of kicking with his legs occurred to him. He came to the surface, coughing and spluttering. He looked up but the angle of the wall shielded him from the warehouse window. He felt the urge to get further away from the place and struck out into the river. After a dozen strokes, he turned onto his back and looked up. Parsons was still at the window and he waved to him. A raised hand acknowledged the action. Letting the current carry him even further from the warehouse, he struck out for the far bank with a feeling of elation. He had cheated death for a second time in two days. He would not risk the near bank in case he was discovered; he would swim the Thames!

The principle was dubious from the start but the execution of the task proved more fraught than he had imagined. In fact, in his hyped-up state, he had not anticipated anything. He was just over half-way across when the tiredness came over him suddenly and completely. His limbs became leaden and his brain numbed. He twisted onto his back, paddled gently with his feet and tried to rest. It was useless: he felt worse than ever.

Now the cold insidiously started to creep over his body. He twisted again in the water and changed to a long, slow breast-stroke. At least this made progress without sapping his remaining strength noticeably. The long minutes floated by in a dreamy unreality. Flotsam bobbed against his face and he pushed it away on the next stroke. The river wall was folded in its own darkness, the shadow melting into the river. He entered its umbra and kicked the last few feet to the rough stone.

Reaching the far bank was one thing; getting out of the water another. It was another ten minutes' drifting downstream with the tide before he reached a mooring point. He swam between a barge and the wall and got a hand onto the restraining rope. Finding a last reserve of strength, he dragged his head and upper body from the water, wound his legs around the tangled rope and pulled upwards. He managed to get one hand over the side of the wall, a leg kicked against the stone – literally found a toe-hold – and he scrambled half-way onto the tow-path. A final heave and he was fully onto dry land. For the next half-minute, he lay shivering on the cold stone.

The stubborn drive for preservation forced him to his feet and he set off along the path, found a set of steps and made his way onto the street, slapping himself about the chest with both arms as he went, in a fruitless attempt to keep warm. The pain to his sock-covered feet was ignored. As they were numb with cold, in a strange way, it was not as bad as it might have been. He cut inland at the first road junction and wandered between rows of shabby terraced houses and miserable little shops until he came across a telephone-box.

Pete was delighted at being woken at five in the morning. He told Jeremy so. When he paused for breath, the interval allowed a counter-attack.

'Listen, Pete. Just shut up and listen. There is too much to do. I've found Keith. Don't ask me how. I need a change of clothes and a lift home. Don't mess about, just get over here.'

He carefully gave his location.

'I'll ring off now. I've got to call the police.'

'Hang on, son. Isn't this something we can handle?'

'Not really, Pete. This thing has got out of hand. Keith is being held by a gang of at least four armed men in a warehouse on the other bank. This is a police job and like it.'

'OK, old son. Listen, I'll call them for you then cut over to get you. That suit you?'

Jeremy was really past caring. 'Yeh. Just so long as you make it fast.'

The line went dead and he settled down in the telephone-box to wait.

11

Jeremy was grateful for the brandy bottle, the towel and the dry clothing in that order. It took him some time to change and it hardly struck him as odd that Pete had come for him in the breakdown truck and not the usual Sierra. It almost seemed natural to be standing in the back of an open Toyota with the bottom half of his anatomy quite naked while he rubbed with considerable vigour. While this was going on, Pete was nonchalantly listening to the radio in the cab. Thus, conversation was limited. Indeed, it tended to be one-way as Pete could hear nothing through the back of the cab over the sound of the music and it remained that way until the trousers were in position and adjusted. Only then did Jeremy climb out of the back of the truck and, as he buttoned up the shirt, walked round to the front.

'Pete! For God's sake, turn that thing off! It's so anti-social!'

The music faded. It occurred to Jeremy to enquire whether the message had got through to the police.

'Not exactly, old son, but don't worry none. Reinforcements will be waiting for us by the time we get to the warehouse.'

There was something in the voice that triggered an apprehensive enquiry.

'Pete, you did call the police, didn't you?'

162

'Not exactly, old son.'

'What do you mean, "not exactly"? Either you did or you didn't.'

'Put that way, I didn't.'

'Oh, God! Couldn't you bury those hare-brained prejudices of yours for just once?'

'Don't worry. I told you, help will be there.'

Jeremy tied the laces to the shoes.

'Do that in the truck, old son. By the way, where exactly is this warehouse of yours?'

Jeremy looked up, realising that he could do no more than identify it from across the river.

'Drive to the embankment and I'll show you.'

The truck stopped at the top of the jetty from which Jeremy had climbed from the water and the pair looked across.

'That one there! See!'

He did not. However, Pete followed the instructions given to him and lined up the building. He consulted an *A to Z* and pin-pointed the road, then took a walkie-talkie set from the dashboard and pulled out the extension aerial.

'You listening in there, Paddy?'

The set crackled. 'All ready to go!'

'Meet us at the corner of Broughton Lane and Makepeace Road.'

'On our way!'

He nonchalantly tossed the set onto the shelf above the dashboard and turned the truck round. It took less than four minutes to cross the river and reach the rendezvous point yet Paddy was already there. So, it seemed, were a few friends. They alighted from the Sierra and presented themselves for introductions.

'Hi! I'm Sharon.'

'. . . better known as Hellcat Helga.'

163

The young woman weighed around fourteen stone and had arms like a man.

'Hey! He's cute, Paddy. Say, I'm Michelle.'

'. . . otherwise known as the Newham Snake Woman – she always comes into the ring with a boa wrapped around her neck.'

Paddy cut the introductions while she turned to the snake woman.

'And if you don't want me to tie a knot in your overgrown reptile, keep your mitts off my fellah.'

Next, a long black hand snaked out from a lithe, slender figure.

'Don't worry, I'll keep her off him for you, honey.'

She addressed Jeremy.

'Samantha Brown at your service. We'll really have fun!'

'You won't!'

Paddy turned to Jeremy again. 'Also known as the Black Widow, though she's never been married. This good-looking chick has a black belt as well as a black skin and is fast and lethal with it. She may look innocent but, believe me, she's far from it.'

Actually, Jeremy had already decided she was no innocent, though not in quite the way Paddy meant it.

'That's enough chatter, girls. Where's Keith?'

'He's being held in a top-floor room in that warehouse over there.' He pointed down the street. 'You can't see it from this angle.'

Pete took charge.

'Right, Jerry old son. You get into the Sierra and we'll drive slowly down, then you show us the door to the building and stay back out of the way. The girls and me'll do the rest. Right, you lovely things, into the back of the truck and keep your heads down!'

Jeremy looked at Samantha, who was doing

164

exaggerated India-rubber stretching exercises against the roof of the car, and Sharon loosening up with a series of mock kicks and chops against an invisible enemy. Beside him, Michelle was deliberately stripping off to reveal a slinky snake-motif body suit. The heads of two snakes ended in the middle of each breast and swayed in a most realistic manner as she moved. Paddy was the only one in jeans and shirt – the rest were in full fighting gear. Now, for the first time, he noticed that all the girls were in bare feet. Something approaching sympathy for the unfortunates within the warehouse welled inside – until he felt his sore groin. With luck, they would extract Keith and cause more than minimal damage to Clive and his friends. The law-abiding solicitor was being firmly suppressed by the vindictive, sadistic side of his character – a side that, until very recently, he hardly knew he possessed.

He drove the Sierra gently down the street, stopping immediately in front of the warehouse door. Pete pulled up behind him and waited in the cab as he walked round.

'They took me through this door. I'd guess the entrance to the warehouse where Keith is being held is two doors down from here.'

'OK. Now stay in the Sierra and keep out of the way. I guess we'll go in through this one. You sure the place was empty inside?'

Jeremy nodded.

Pete slipped the truck into gear and pulled over to the far side of the road. Two quick movements and the nose was lined up with the door. Jeremy understood perfectly why Pete had brought the truck.

The heavy metal grid across the bonnet opened up the door as though it were paper. The back of the vehicle sped from sight into the blackness of the warehouse and

Jeremy was left with little indication of what was occurring inside. Indeed, the initial silence was almost worrying. Then came the yells and whoops of the girls and he felt contented again.

The moment the truck had cleared a path, the four women sprang from the back and took up defensive stances. There was no need: the place appeared to be deserted. The only light in the place came from the newly constructed opening and the girls had quickly moved from its illumination. Pete switched off the engine and clambered out, a massive torque wrench swinging idly from his fingers. He strode round the side of the truck and sized up the situation.

'The bird has flown, by the look of it.'

A sharp report from behind them followed by the whine of a bullet deflecting from the side of the truck refuted the statement.

'Raise your hands, the lot of you. Otherwise the next bullet is for real.'

Rambo blinked. Where five bodies had previously been there were now none. Heads had ducked behind the side of the truck and bodies disappeared behind support pillars. Ronnie came forward and cautiously walked round the back of the truck. He stood in the halo of sunlight pouring through the hole in the warehouse door. The ghosts had vanished.

'Look under the truck!' instructed Rambo.

The hoodlum bent down warily and squinted at the bare concrete.

'Nuffink 'ere.'

'Bloody hell! They can't have disappeared into thin air!'

Rambo was right. The black octopus that uncoiled herself from the radiator bar swung out in front of Ronnie and looped across the floor in a series of handsprings, culminating in a high leap that brought her feet neatly into his face. He saw her late as she swung out of the shadow of the vehicle. It happened so quickly that he only thought to use the gun when it was too late. He fell backwards and landed heavily on his bottom. The octopus wound a tentacle about his left arm, flipped up onto her feet and twisted. He was jerked bodily upwards by the unfortunate limb, then had the pleasure of a thin foot smashing into his armpit at the instant that the hand was twisted.

The scream reached Rambo but he had no time to take any interest in what was going on behind him: he was frantically struggling with a snake-clad monster with a grip of iron that had come from the side out of the half-light. His wrist was slowly and mercilessly going backwards. The gun dropped and still the wrist folded over. Suddenly, it was released. He managed to bring the numbed hand back level with his stomach before the first of a string of forearm chops rattled into his face and body with the rapidity of a machine-gun. He grunted, doubled up and slumped in slow motion to the ground. Six inches from it, a massive boot lifted his jaw backwards and took his body back almost to an upright position. He was out cold before he started the return journey to the concrete.

Pete looked around. 'Any more about, girls?'

'Nope.'

'That's a shame. I thought we were going to have some fun. Where are the other two?'

'Gone for Keith.'

'Keep an eye on things here. I'll go and see how they're doing.'

Actually, he had no need to go anywhere for, at that moment, a pair of figures appeared at the door. Clive had one arm tightly held across Keith's throat while he forced the barrel of a short, stubby gun into his cheek with his other hand. He was half backing and half moving sideways, trying to shield his body and simultaneously watching where he was going.

'Back off or this slime gets it.'

The hiss sounded scared, for all the apparent advantage that he held. He heaved his captive slowly across the threshold and into the open space of the empty warehouse. He seemed to gain confidence as he could clearly see the opposition.

'Get away from that door!'

He changed direction and moved slowly crab-like towards the bright halo of morning light created by the truck. From the shadows of the second warehouse, Paddy slid through. She was holding the gun Jeremy had 'collected' and it was trained steadily on the retreating duo. Behind her, Sharon emerged and moved quickly a few paces to her right.

'Take it easy, girls. Don't frighten the little fellow. Give him space and don't move too quickly,' Pete advised.

'Very wise! Just listen to the man and do as he says, then no one gets hurt.'

He was near the door now. A quick sideways glance satisfied him all was safe. He gave a sudden jerk and the human shield positioned itself neatly in line with the gun. He backed three paces, stepped out onto the pavement and dragged Keith after him.

Meanwhile, Jeremy had found a spanner on the floor of the car and gained courage from its feel in his hand. He smacked it into his palm a few times then opened the door and stood by the side of the Sierra. As the interior of the warehouse quietened down, he had advanced, apparently aimlessly, towards the smashed doorway. Thus it was that he was only a dozen paces from Clive as the pair emerged from the warehouse. He had moved swiftly forward only to pull up sharply as the gun suddenly whipped round and pointed directly at his chest.

'Drop it!'

He let the spanner slip from his fingers, taking his courage with it. Clive pulled Keith backwards slowly and made the gap to the petrified statue on the pavement. Keith was unconscious; he had been slipping into this state half-way across the warehouse and now he was dead to the world. Clive realised this as the weight on his arm had increased but it had not been obvious to those inside. The time had come to change hostages. In one smooth movement, the one human shield was dropped for another. Paddy stepped across the entrance step just in time to see the gun jamming itself into Jeremy's right ear.

'It's getting better by the minute. I've got someone with enough sense to see I get out of here. Tell her, my foxy friend, tell her to put the gun down and back off.'

Jeremy found his head jerked round. He could sense the gun itching to blow his brains out and feel his heart pounding with fear. This was really it, this time. There was no way Clive would let him out of this one. He would kill him for sure, one way or another. The seconds passed in eerie silence. He was coming to terms with death and it was scaring him silly.

'Tell her!'

'All right, all right!'

Come on, brain, I need you!

'Paddy, listen carefully. I want you to promise me you will do exactly as I say.'

He waited.

'Paddy! For God's sake, promise me!'

She pouted. 'OK, then. Get on with it.'

'Listen, love. Keep that gun trained spot-on his temple. If he pulls the trigger, see he gets it straight between the eyes.'

He strove to keep his voice steady. He could only pray she was as good with the thing as she had bragged back in the flat.

'Hey!'

His head was wrenched upwards and the gun bore deeper into his skull. His whole body was almost totally shielding Clive.

'Shut your mouth, punk! Tell her to put the gun down!'

It did not seem to matter that Jeremy could not do both.

'Thinking about it, love, count to ten and if he has not put the gun down and raised his hands, drill him anyway.'

He felt the quiver from the body behind him. Clive was really scared. This was unexpected: it was illogical, at least from his point of view. Jeremy closed his eyes and waited. He did not see Pete and Sharon slide out from the building. He did not see Pete get as close as he could to his daughter while Sharon fanned slowly away from the pair, moving carefully and perfectly balanced in a wide arc into the street and round to a position almost at right angles to the scene of the stand-off.

'One.'

Jeremy heard the voice and detected the slightest of tremors in it. She was doing it, though!

'Two.'

God! He would not be able to stand the tension. He would faint before she reached five.

'Three.'

Sharon had taken two paces slowly towards the pair. Clive had seen the movement out of the corner of his eye.

'Stay exactly where you are or I blow his brains out right now!'

She stopped in mid-pace.

'Four.'

Jeremy found his eyes opening against his wishes.

'Five.'

He had made it without fainting. It was dawning on him that his brains were still intact and likely to remain so if he used them. The question eating at him was whether Paddy could use that thing on a real target as well as she could on a paper one. Indeed, was it fair to ask it of her? No choice if he was to live. What if she was hurt? He could not let the thought cross his mind.

'Six.'

'You're pointing the gun in the wrong direction, Clive. I'm not the one with a shooter trained on you; she is and she ain't going to put it down.'

'Seven.'

'Three to go then you're dead. How does it feel now?'

'Shut up! Shut up, both of you!'

'Eight.'

The gun was gone. The pressure was off his ear. As his head sprang back like a released spring, he heard the single shot and felt the weight crushing down on him. He staggered forward and collapsed under the body of his adversary. In seconds, Pete was with him, pulling the corpse from on top of him. Sharon had got the gun and Paddy was holding very tightly to Michelle. Jeremy extricated himself from under Clive's dead arm and allowed his body a few moments to recover. He was shaking violently now that the danger had passed.

'What the hell happened?'

'He tried to shoot me.'

171

Neither voice was steady but Paddy was at least accurate. Clive had made the fatal mistake of turning the gun towards her. As he did so, he released his hostage and she fired. The bullet had gone cleanly into his skull just above the right eye.

It went very quiet in Makepeace Road as the actors in the recent drama came to terms with all that had happened.

'Pete, I think we could all do with some of your brandy.'

'Reckon we should just get home, old son.'

'For Christ's sake, Pete! Just for once, don't bloody argue! Get that brandy bottle out and give everyone a short swig – purely medicinal. Just save me some, that's all. I've a telephone call to make.'

He sat in the Sierra and dialled through to Kent police headquarters. It took very little time before he was talking to the duty officer. It appeared he had heard of the Fox, at least sufficiently to take the call seriously and to alert his superiors the moment Jeremy released the line.

*

The superintendent came in person; so did his sergeant. They arrived just as the ambulance turned into the street and exchanged words with colleagues from the Met. as a man was carried out with fractures to the jaw and ribs, a dislocated right wrist and several internal injuries. Another was found with a dislocated shoulder and a ruptured spleen. Clive could not be removed until the coroner had made a preliminary inspection. It did not take him long: it hardly needed a medical opinion to diagnose the cause of death and the body temperature had hardly fallen, a quarter of an hour at most had elapsed from the time he had been shot.

Mr Smith arrived shortly before nine, took one glance

172

at the road infested with policemen and immediately ordered his chauffeur to keep going. The car was parked three streets away and the driver walked back to see what was causing all the fuss. He did not get all the details but enough to gauge the situation and report back. Mr Smith returned home in sweet humour.

12

The journey home could hardly have been called fun. Michelle sat in the back of the Sierra with Keith, who, by this time, had recovered consciousness and probably wished he had not. Paddy drove and said nothing, the full impact of the last few minutes having got to her and plugged her natural exuberance with some force. The fourth seat was occupied by a shivering, shaking Jeremy. Try as he might, he could not stop his teeth from chattering loudly and his whole frame from vibrating from top to toe. So upset were the four that Paddy even drove at a respectable pace, arriving back at the garage several minutes before the pick-up truck – Pete had detoured to drop off the other girls.

Michelle helped Keith up the stairs, was met half-way by Sandra and gave up her charge with no hesitation. She had had enough of the affair. She stopped at the bottom of the flight and watched as Paddy passed her, struggling to get Jeremy up the stairs.

'Say this for you McBears, you certainly know how to pick your menfolk!'

'At least we've got men!'

'Nearly.'

'Ah, shut it, Michelle.' Paddy paused in the middle of her struggle and looked back. 'You off?'

'You bet! I've had enough adventures for one day.'

'Then, thanks, pal.'

'Forget it, kid. Must catch up on my beauty sleep.'

'Too true!'

The last quip was barely heard. Michelle was already half-way across the workshop floor and Paddy had made it to the top of the stairs.

Dr Masters was duly summoned and he came with his usual alacrity. Keith took nearly an hour of his time. The wound was raw and seeping. At first, he wanted him to get hospital treatment but the McBear love of such places was only rivalled by their regard for the police. Instead, Masters, to his credit, made a fair job of cleaning the wound, dressing it and making his patient as comfortable as the circumstances allowed. He finished with a jab of antibiotic and a prescription for sleeping-tablets and pain-relievers.

He looked in on Jeremy, who was sitting on Sandra's bed and refusing to get into it. At least, it was assumed by all that this was the gist of the protest but the chattering teeth distorted everything he said. He tried to say something to Masters but the thermometer cut him short.

'Noo try no' tae bite the thing, laddie.'

He extracted it intact, looked at it side-on, shook it deliberately and commented: 'It's joust shook, nothing mair. Ye're tae take it easy and rest fer a few days, noo.'

He scribbled another prescription, exchanged it for the glass, downed the liquor and made his exit.

Later in the day, Keith was transferred to number sixteen, a house occupied by a middle-aged widow with two spare beds and little spare money. The tenant was welcome and, in any case, there was no room at the garage flat. A camp-bed appeared around five and this was assembled in Jeremy's office. He had eventually been persuaded to use Sandra's bed and the tablets Masters had prescribed induced a sleep that kept him under until mid-afternoon. Once they had eaten that night, Jeremy again slept. By morning, he was more or less his old self; which was as well for, with all the events of the past few days, he was within two days of Paddy's oral committal and needed to be truly sharp.

*

The great day or, perhaps more accurately, the dreaded day arrived. Keith was still convalescing but, otherwise, the full entourage turned out. Sandra at least looked very feminine, which pleased Jeremy and Pete for different reasons. While one was just basking in secret pride at his daughter, the other wanted the two girls to go into court together, making it obvious that they were sisters and so suggesting a softer attitude than Paddy might display on her own. For his part, Pete had changed into a T-shirt exhorting all who read it to protect the ozone layer, while Paddy was once more dressed in the outfit she had worn for the earlier appearance.

They were kept waiting in the smoke-filled ante-chamber for more than an hour. At least, it was initially somewhat foggy but the atmosphere cleared after a request from Pete to think of the health of the young ladies. The only objector discovered that smoking really was liable to damage his health a little quicker than he expected and he chose a cleaner way of living. Actually, he found just about the only way of living, given the circumstances.

It was a depressing place. Everyone was on edge, waiting for the metaphorical axe to fall, praying it would not and passing the interlude in inane chatter. Paddy was more depressed than many, suddenly feeling very weak and helpless. She felt even worse when, after a brief nod from the usher, Jeremy took his leave and slid quietly

176

into the court-room.

As he entered, a colleague vacated a seat in the front bench next to the prosecutor, bowed slightly to the bench and walked back to leave the court. Jeremy waited until he had reached the door, ducked his head dutifully himself and walked inconspicuously to take up the vacant seat. The prosecutor was on his feet, reading out a list of misdemeanours of a middle-aged man with long hair and a very tattered pullover. Jeremy hardly listened as he took his own pile of papers from his court case and arranged them on the ledge in front of him. The prosecutor sat down.

Almost immediately, the chairman of the bench announced, 'We shall retire.'

'Court rise.'

They bobbed up and watched the three magistrates depart into their little room.

The prosecutor smiled amiably at Jeremy. 'Probably time for their mid-morning coffee. They can't be serious about retiring for this one otherwise. Are you doing the McBear case?'

Jeremy affirmed – this was a different prosecutor from last time; he was in luck.

'Known as the Lewisham Bear, I hear?'

No, he was quite definitely not in luck.

Oh, God! he thought, how the hell did they find that out?

'I'm going to enjoy this one, perhaps not so much today, as I assume you are only going through the motion to test out the strength of our case, but it should be really fun in the Crown Court when I get her in the witness box. I'm right through on this one. Whatever made you take the case? Needed the money?'

Jeremy gulped inwardly and forced a wan smile. 'Of course. Oral committal, briefing solicitor in the Crown

Court, the appeal, should be worth enough to keep the Porsche on the road for a week or two.'

He suddenly remembered the Porsche was unlikely to go on the road again and certainly not from the fee for this one. He won it today or he was dead.

'Well, we can give the punters a good show, anyway. We've had a pretty dull day, so far. This is the best on the list.'

Jeremy grinned weakly again. 'I'd better look over the brief, then. Be ready for them when they return.'

He dropped back to reading through his papers but the words did not register and the only image he could conjure up was Paddy's when she was told she was to go for trial. He suddenly realised that he would not be dead if he lost. These people were his friends; he would simply be devastated at letting them down. They were relying on him with a naive confidence that was far from justified. He started to think of all the things he could say to reassure them. His masochistic train of thought was broken by the return of the bench.

'We are going to adjourn your case for reports.'

The clerk to the court looked at the calendar in front of him then at the chairman.

'Three weeks? That will take us up to the fifth of August.'

'The case will be adjourned until the fifth of August. Unconditional bail is continued until then. That's all, thank you.'

The scruff departed, dejected and disorientated, the usher seeing him to the door.

'Case number twenty-one. McBear.'

There was a slight hiatus at the door: Sandra had tried to come through with Paddy and had been gently guided to the public area at the back of the court-room. Paddy came forward with more than a little trepidation and stood uncertainly in the box. Jeremy caught her eye and smiled comfortingly; at least, he meant it to be comforting but she seemed even less sure of herself after it.

The formalities concluded, the prosecutor outlined the case and proceeded to call his first witness, who was duly sworn in. The prosecutor explained that the clerk would have to write everything down so he should answer slowly and watch the pen.

'You are Arthur James Pallister of 8 Polperro Crescent, Dutton Green?'

'Yeh.'

'And do you remember the events of the ninth of April?'

'Yer.'

'Specifically, do you remember walking down Hillingdon Avenue around two-forty in the afternoon?'

'Yeh.'

'In your own words, would you like to tell us what happened?'

'Yeh. I was with Terry and we were walking up towards the town when we met this scruffy female coming towards us. That's her over there' – he pointed towards the dock – 'only she didn't look like that then. She was dressed in filthy jeans and a denim jacket. We made some comments about her appearance and she let out a right load of foul language. Then Terry said as how she ought to wash her mouth out, or somethin' like that, and he got some more abuse so I put my hand up to shut her mouth for her and the next thing I know she has slung me over her shoulder and I landed on my head.'

'And what happened then?'

'She started on Terry then. Hit him in the groin and laid into him with her tool kit –'

'Let me stop you there. You said she hit him with her

tool kit. Did you see any tools?'

'No but you could hear them jangling in her bag as she swung it around. She must have hit him a couple of times and he went down. Then she grabbed his leg and did some karate trick on it. I heard the crack as it broke and poor Terry screamed and then passed out.'

'Thank you, Mr Pallister. Would you just wait there.'

Jeremy stood up slowly, scanned his papers briefly and gave the witness a considerate smile.

'Mr Pallister, would you say you were a strong fellow?'

'Not specially.'

'Come, come Mr Pallister. Let's have no false modesty. You look pretty tough to me. It must have taken some force to have up-ended you.'

'Yeh, well, she's no skinny Liz, is she?'

'Quite so but, nevertheless, Mr Pallister, are you seriously asking us to believe that you could be thrown off your feet by a mere girl?'

'Well, yeh.'

'I find that very hard to believe. I think she caught you off balance. I don't think she could have lifted you off your feet otherwise.'

Pallister shrugged. 'Perhaps I was a bit off balance. I didn't really expect her to do anything.'

'You threw a punch at her and she moved out of the way. This caught you off your guard and she used a judo throw on you. Is that what really happened?'

'I never tried to punch her.'

'But you put your hand out and pushed it towards her?'

'Yeh, sort of.'

'And she threw you?'

'Yeh.'

180

Mr Pallister was becoming slightly sullen. There was a need to cheer him up a bit.

'I understand you were quite badly hurt?'

'Yeh. She broke my skull, she did.'

'That blow must have knocked you silly. I see from the medical reports that you were also severely concussed.'

'Yeh, I was.'

'She really caused you some very nasty injuries.'

'Yeh, she did.'

Pallister had relaxed slightly.

'So injured, in fact, that you could not have been aware of what was going on around you.'

'Yeh . . . no, I knew what was happening.'

Damn, he had spotted the trap before it was fully sprung. No matter.

'Broken skull, severely concussed, probably lost consciousness, at least temporarily, and you are asking the court to believe you saw and remember in exact detail what happened to your brother?'

'Yeh. I might have been hurt but I know what I saw.'

'Tell me, Mr Pallister, did you discuss this matter with your brother?'

He shifted slightly in the witness-box. 'We didn't discuss what we were goin' to say, if that's what you mean.'

'I never said you did. I simply asked if you had ever discussed the matter.'

'Well, a bit. Of course we did. That don't mean I didn't see what happened.'

'You did discuss it, though? Just answer yes or no, please, Mr Pallister.'

There was a long pause.

'Yeh, we discussed it.'

'Thank you, Mr Pallister, that will be all.'

The prosecutor came back with a few questions, trying to redress the balance, but he knew his witness had not done too well. Not to worry, the killer punch was yet to come.

The second Mr Pallister was wheeled into court. The chair was positioned to the side of the witness-box and the prosecutor was attentive to a fault to ensure he was comfortable and able to testify without undue strain. The witness was then duly sworn in and formalities enacted. He went on to repeat the story his brother had given with little variance, clearly pleasing the prosecutor.

'Can I get this clear before my learned friend tries to suggest to you that your mind was effected by the injuries you sustained. You were kneed in the groin and then attacked with the tool-bag?'

'Yes, that's right.'

'Then when you were on the ground, she put your leg in some sort of wrestling hold?'

Pallister looked a little puzzled. Before he could answer, the prosecutor went on.

'You could not have known at the time that Miss McBear also happens to be a female wrestler, could you?'

Jeremy was on his feet in a flash.

'I object,' he shouted.

The chairman of the bench looked disapprovingly over the top of his glasses.

'Ah . . . Mr Carrington . . . ah . . . Fox, there is no need to shout.'

'I apologise, sir.'

Damn, he had goofed again. Perry Mason would have handled it better than this. His experience was showing through. Calm down if you don't want to upset them, he told himself.

'With respect to my learned colleague, I must object

182

strongly to his questioning. It is most improper and he is making a slur on Miss McBear's good name.'

'I withdraw the question.'

The swine. He's done the damage and he knows it, Jeremy thought. He might at least have left it until the Crown Court. God, where do I go from here?

'Mr Pallister, were you in any state to defend yourself when she made her attack on your leg?'

Jeremy was on his feet again but avoided the outburst of his first attempt.

'I must ask my learned colleague to rephrase the question. He is making assumptions within it that are not true.'

The prosecutor sighed and shrugged his shoulders, as much as to indicate that his patience was dwindling rapidly.

'There are no assumptions but, if it will make the defence happy, then I will rephrase it. Mr Pallister, were you in any state to defend yourself when your leg was broken?'

He looked to see if there would be further interruptions; there were not.

'No. Like I said, I was just about paralysed with the pain.'

'Thank you, Mr Pallister. Just wait there, please. I am sure my colleague will want to put some questions to you.'

Jeremy paused. A sudden smile flashed across his brain. Be nice!

'I am sorry to see you were so badly injured, Mr Pallister. Miss McBear had asked me to pass on her good wishes and her regrets at the extent of your injuries. I'll try not to burden you with a string of questions – I'm sure that just coming here today must have been an ordeal in itself. Can I just confirm two points with you? You did advance a hand towards Miss McBear after she had thrown your brother? Is that right?'

'Yes, I might have, but I didn't try to hit her or anything.'

'No, no, I'm sure you didn't. However, isn't it possible that she might have thought you were going to?'

'I suppose she might but that don't excuse her breaking my legs and all.'

'Ah, yes! Let me come to that. When your leg broke, it must have been unbelievably painful. Did you remain conscious?'

'No, I passed out.'

'Then you were not able to see what happened to Miss McBear immediately afterwards?'

He looked puzzled.

'No . . . .' He hesitated. 'No, how could I?'

'Indeed, Mr Pallister, how could you? No more questions, thank you.'

He sat down. Inwardly, he was perspiring. One more hurdle and then it would all be down to the bench.

The second Pallister was wheeled to the back of the court, then the prosecutor half rose and sat down in one smooth motion, saying as he did so, 'That is the prosecution case, sir.'

Jeremy collected his thoughts and rose in an unhurried manner.

'The defence, your worships, is in two parts and I shall deal with them separately. The initial action followed what Miss McBear construed to be an attack on her person. I ask you to imagine the effect on her of two well-built men approaching her and making abusive remarks and then one of them putting out a hand, as he put it, towards her. I suggest to you that she, and not only Miss McBear but almost any other young girl in that position, thought she was about to be hit or, at the very least, that the man was going to molest her.

'Now, the only reason, I suspect, that Miss McBear is in the dock today is that she had the good fortune to win. The defence does not deny, nor would want to, that Miss McBear was taught self-defence when she was at school. In the situation she was in, she used it and used it very effectively but, I suggest, she did no more than she was legally entitled to do. She simply slipped inside the attack and used Mr Pallister's undoubtedly large physique against him. Off balance, he went over her shoulder and landed badly. I suggest to the court that, however regrettable, he only had himself to blame for the injuries. She made no other act of aggression towards him and, I duly submit, there was no assault but only the use of the minimum force necessary to defend herself. Thus, I respectfully invite you to dismiss the charge of assault by Miss McBear against Mr Arthur Pallister.

'I now turn to the charge of causing grevious bodily harm to Mr Terry Pallister. The facts of the case have only been half recited and, indeed, the defence does not intend to offer testimony today but you have, your worships, only part of the truth. It is not denied that Miss McBear struck Mr Pallister in the groin but this is also an act, I suggest, of self-defence. By this time, the defendant was near to panic and may well have struck out with her shoulder-bag. Frankly, she is not sure of the details but I would suggest to the court that Mr Pallister was hardly likely to have sustained the fractures to his ribs from any such brush. She would have been unable, I submit, to generate any great force from a bag slung as you see it now.'

He indicated extravagantly towards the dock, where the neat lady's shoulder-bag could be seen.

'No, indeed. The truth, I suggest, is that Mr Pallister sustained the broken ribs when Miss McBear fell on him.

Again, the defence does not deny the essence of the prosecution case but does feel that the wrong interpretation has been put on the events. As Mr Pallister collapsed on the ground, Miss McBear was, herself, close to fainting from the sheer terror of the attack. She tells me that she tried to run, stumbled over Mr Pallister and fell across him. From the unfortunate position of his leg, and may I respectfully remind your worships that Mr Pallister testified himself that his legs were in the air, the mere act of falling forward was enough both to break the leg and to also cause the breaking of the ribs. I accept that Miss McBear is no light weight and the full force of her body falling across the poor, unfortunate Mr Pallister undoubtedly caused these injuries. Certainly, the prosecution has offered no substantive evidence to the contrary. The intent, however, could not have been there and, hence, in the absence of *mens rea,* there cannot, I submit, be sufficient substance to maintain any charge of causing grevious bodily harm. I invite you to find that there is no charge to answer on either count.'

He sat down. He could do no more: he could only pray that it was enough.

'We will retire.'

'Court rise.'

The three magistrates trooped solemnly out; the atmosphere eased.

'Bit over the top, I would say. I was only trying to make sure nothing went wrong. You did say you were looking for a good fee from this one.'

'Oh, definitely. I thought the shouting would upset them and do no good. Perhaps I might have played it a little more low-key.'

He bit on a finger-nail, turned away and stood up to stretch. He was sweating mildly. He dared not look round: he knew they were all looking at him. He arched his back, turned back to his seat and very deliberately poured a glass of water, sipped at it slowly and sat back staring at the ceiling. The minutes ticked by. He risked a furtive glance to his left. Paddy was mouthing something to her father at the back of the room. She had not caught his eye so Jeremy averted his glance.

A buzzer sounded at the front of the room.

'Silence. Court rise.'

The three grim-faced justices paraded to their places and sat down.

'Stand up, please, Miss McBear.'

This was it. Another few seconds and they would know the worst. The verdict came in a sharp, staccato sentence and left Jeremy stunned.

'That's all. We will have case number thirty-four on the list . . . .'

The prosecutor leant across. 'Hard luck, old man.'

Jeremy looked suitably subdued.

'Win some, lose some,' he muttered, then gathered up his papers, bowed stiffly to the bench and left court. Win some, lose some, he thought. Hell, I'll happily lose the next fifty after this. Well, the next couple, anyway.

He was through the door. It had barely swung shut behind him when a mighty paw caught him full across the back.

'You did it, old son! I knew you would. Never a doubt! That was some real slick talking in there!'

The slap across the mouth caught him completely by surprise. He had never thought of Paddy as the sort to kiss anyone. God! It was some kiss! He disentangled himself with a sheepish smile, the thought crossing his mind that failure could hardly have resulted in a lesser assault.

'It was nothing. There really was no case to answer.'

Liar. He was not quite sure whether he really had been

187

good or whether it was beginner's luck. It was probably best not to dwell on it but to enjoy the success. He had expected the first charge to be dropped but, in all honesty, he was not sure why they had found no case to answer regarding the GBH charge – he thought there was one!

'This calls for a celebration!'

'Luigi's?'

'Sure thing. Lunch first at the nearest pub, then home and change and off to Luigi's. How does that strike everyone?'

Agreement was unanimous and the pub was near. It was barely ten minutes later that Pete was sinking his third pint, Paddy was finishing her second, Jeremy was sipping a large brandy and Sandra was toying with a lemonade. To her chagrin, she had been given the short straw – she was to drive back. Food arrived in time to stop Pete finishing a fifth pint. He took it with him and sat at the table, munching happily on his jumbo sausage in a chunk of fresh French bread. Jeremy was more than content, a state not entirely derived from the alcohol but undoubtedly assisted by it. Even without the wig, Paddy was looking remarkably feminine and almost acting like it.

The pub closed at three, ejecting a happy foursome onto an unsuspecting world. With windows down and over a hundred decibels' worth of heavy metal from the radio being almost drowned by the karaoke of the far from heavenly choir, the car more than disturbed the afternoon peace of the town. No doubt much to the relief of the locals, traffic was light and did nothing to hinder their homeward progress.

The foursome became five at the garage: Keith was certainly well enough to join them at Luigi's. At six, the party bundled into the Sierra and drove the few blocks to their favourite restaurant. Luigi had been forewarned and had the bubbly stuff ready, plus half a dozen well-wishers to help them drink it. Food and drink arrived at regular intervals until around ten, when even Pete was beyond eating further. The bill was paid and the five spilled out onto the street. The cool air hit Jeremy and he swayed slightly.

'I hate to say this but I am not too steady on my feet.'

'You need a brisk walk!'

Paddy grabbed his arm and swung him around.

'You three drive back. Me and Jerry will stroll back in our own good time.'

She winked heavily at her father. In his turn, he slapped her bottom firmly and grinned widely.

'Now don't you two get up to anything, mind, and don't you keep her up late there, Jerry. Come on, you two! Into the car!'

They bundled in and the Sierra rocketed down the road with only the slightest hint of a wobble in its forward motion. For all the alcohol, Pete appeared to be sufficiently sober to get them home.

As the car turned the corner, Paddy slid her hand through Jeremy's arm and pulled him close.

'I think you're something really special, Jerry.'

He grinned inanely. 'You're OK yourself, Pad.'

They started walking. She slid her arm out of his and around his back in such a way as to leave his arm loose behind her rear. Her head lolled onto his shoulder.

'Do you fancy me?'

He started slightly. 'I told you, you're something special.'

'Special enough for you to go steady with me?'

Despite the stupefying effects of the drink, he was not beyond deftly rebuffing the advances.

189

'I hadn't really given it any thought. Honestly, Pad, I'm still a bit too shook up over all that's happened recently to think about much else.'

'You're giving me the brush-off, aren't you?'

'No, of course not, it's just, well . . .'

'You don't have to say it. I know. I'm fat and ugly and no guy in his right mind 'ud give me a second look.'

'No, it isn't that.'

'Yes it is.'

'You aren't exactly slim but you're not ugly, not when you're dressed up. Anyway, I couldn't care what you look like – I think you're a great girl – but I hadn't thought about anything else.'

'You introduced me to that copper as your girl,' she persisted.

'Sure. That was different. I wanted to stop any questioning as to why you were with me.'

'You weren't sorry I was, not when I kicked those thugs in for you.'

'No, I wasn't, but that's no foundation for a relationship. To tell the truth, I'm just about bust and I still owe a bomb on my Porsche. I can't think about going with anybody at the moment.'

She fell silent and they continued their walk. Her head had come upright and the hand was barely holding his waist. He started feeling rather caddish. Oh, damn it! He really liked the girl and he knew it. They were as different as the proverbial chalk and cheese but what the hell. He put his arm firmly around her waist, liked the feel and squeezed gently. Her hand slipped back cautiously.

'I'll wear dresses if you like.'

He pulled up abruptly and pulled her half around.

'You do that and I'll positively ditch you for good. Whatever else you do, don't change one bit.'

He could not help himself. He kissed her. The next

second, his head was jerked downwards and his lips were clamped into her mouth as she enjoyed a second evening meal. She had the good grace to release him before he passed out for want of breath, then beamed up at him.

He grinned back. 'Just let's see how we go, OK?'

She nodded.

The two walked back to the garage with a relaxed gait, saying little but just content to be close. Indeed, so relaxed were they that they failed to notice the lack of lights on at the garage. Paddy fumbled with the key, opened the front door and climbed the stairs to the flat. She put the light on and went and muttered in annoyance about the lack of thought of some folk. She called out but no answer returned. The hairs at the back of Jeremy's neck started to prick. Either he was getting paranoid or he was developing an instinct for smelling trouble. Whichever way it was, he felt decidedly uneasy.

'Pad, something's wrong! Come down!'

She stopped, realising herself that she should have had a response.

'They're not in. Where the hell can they have got to?'

'Let's check the garage and see if the car's back.'

It now crossed his mind that Pete had hardly been sober and, by rights, should not have been driving. Nevertheless, he hardly believed he could have crashed. In any case, they should have passed them if anything like that had happened. He pushed at the garage door, expecting it to yield easily but he was in for an unpleasant surprise. The door moved about a foot then hit an obstacle and sprang back in his face. He yelled and held his nose, swearing softly. Paddy joined him.

'Oh, Lor'! I see you can't be left to open a door without thumping yourself.'

She tried with no more success.

'It's jammed on the other side.'

'Oh, well deduced. How about unjamming it, then?'

She put her shoulder to the door and shoved.

'I can't,' she panted. 'There's a ton weight behind it.'

'Can't we get in through the back?'

She grunted something he failed to catch, flounced out and ran around to the back. He followed but she beat him to it by several yards. The Sierra was neatly parked a yard or so from the back entrance; the rear personnel door to the garage was wide open but the inside was in darkness.

'Hold it, Pad,' he called out. 'Don't go in!'

She stopped and he came up to her. He moved to the driver's door, opened it and switched on the headlamps. Immediately, the obstacle blocking the door was illuminated.

'Pops!'

Paddy was across the concrete floor and down by the side of her father. Jeremy joined her but not before he had quickly glanced around the garage; they seemed to be alone.

'Is he all right?'

'Course he ain't, stupid!'

'I can't see Sandra.'

Paddy froze. She slowly moved her hands away from her father's head and stood up. She looked desperately around the garage, came to the same conclusion and burst into tears. Jeremy put out a hand; it was grabbed, then Paddy launched her head at his shoulder.

'Come on, old thing. This isn't helping.'

'Oh, shut up, you stupid sod! It ain't your sister that's disappeared! They've got her, I know they have!'

Jeremy did not ask who the 'they' were; he had the same idea. He squeezed hard and let her cry. As the initial reaction receded, so he gently pulled her away.

'Come on, old thing. Let's look after your father.'

She broke clear and he moved across the garage and switched on the lights. Immediately, he froze.

'Oh, my God!'

'What is it?' she asked.

'Look at the wall.'

She turned, wiped her eyes on her sleeve and squinted. The red aerosol had been poorly sprayed but the letters were clear enough: 'CALL THE POLICE AND SHE IS DEAD'. Their worst fears seemed to have been confirmed. At that moment, the Bear groaned and moved.

'Pad, don't mess. Get upstairs and phone for Doc Masters. Hurry!'

He pushed her away and smacked her bottom to urge her on her way. As she went, he bent down beside Pete and tried to straighten him out so she could get through the door. He groaned again and moved a hand towards his head.

'Lie still. Pad's gone for Doc Masters.'

'I don't need no doctor.'

He tried to move.

'God!'

He paused and screwed up his eyes.

'What hit me?'

'We were hoping you could tell us.'

'Never saw the bastards.'

This time, he did sit up. He took Jeremy's hand and managed to get upright.

'Come on! Upstairs and onto the bed!'

Pete must have felt lousy. He did not object. Masters was over an hour coming; he had been out on call when Paddy rang. When he did arrive, Pete was already asleep,

193

fully clothed. The doctor looked over the wound and decided Pete would have nothing worse than a sore head (he tried to make a pun about the bear with the sore head but simply had a bottle of whisky, one-third full, thrust into his hand and was pushed out into the night).

While they were waiting for their esteemed medical friend, Jeremy tried to clear his head with strong black coffee. It had failed miserably. For all that the textbooks say, it is no cure for alcohol-induced fuzziness when large quantities of food have also been assaulted. He felt sick, uncomfortable, tired without being able to sleep and highly depressed. Paddy was equally morose and not encouraged by the telephone call. She answered it then passed the receiver across to Jeremy.

'It's for you.'

Even in his state of health, that had been obvious.

'Hello – Carrington-Fox.'

'Good evening, Mr Carrington-Fox. Mr Smith speaking. I believe you have had the misfortune to lose one of your friends this evening. When I heard, I felt I must ring and offer my condolences. I am only too willing to offer any help I can to see she is found safe and well. If you could manage to extract a certain black case from the bank and bring it to where I tell you tomorrow, I am sure I can see she is returned in good health. However, should the case not appear, I see no reason for putting myself to any trouble over the matter. I trust I make myself clear.'

'Perfectly.'

'Then, good night, Mr Carrington-Fox. Sleep well.'

'Wait!'

'What is it?'

'If you harm one hair on her head, you don't get the case – and I want to speak to her before I do anything to get it for you.'

'Very touching and chivalrous. All right, Mr Carrington-Fox, you shall speak to her tomorrow.'

The phone went dead.

13

The modest Orpington branch of Barclay's Bank was situated on a stretch of brightly coloured double yellow lines in the middle of the High Street. This was most convenient because it meant that other cars had left the entrance clear so Paddy had no trouble in finding a parking space. She duly stopped the BMW outside, ten minutes before the bank was due to open. There had been no danger of her being late – due, not to the speed of her driving, but to an over-anxious father who had ensured they left in plenty of time. As it happened, a useful precaution as the early morning traffic was heavy. The idle observer would not have noticed anything particularly wrong but a keen student of the habits of the McBear clan would have noted that the radio was turned off and stayed that way while Jeremy was inside the bank.

He emerged a fraction after a quarter to ten, grim-faced and clutching the notorious black attaché case. He lobbed it into the back of the BMW and locked his door just as Paddy revved out into the traffic.

'Lock your door as well, Pad. We're taking no chances with this lot.'

He was worried that Smith's men might be waiting for them but his caution was not needed. Nevertherless, she did as she was told. He almost wished she had not; her bounce had gone completely. Like her father, she had only slept fitfully and for a short period into the night when the body refused to carry on without some concession to rest. Jeremy had also been awake for much of the night but, in his case, the mental activity was disciplined and fruitful. It was not his fault that it would all be wasted, for he could not reasonably, or unreasonably, have been expected to anticipate the turn of events of the day. Indeed, he was still chewing over the various scenarios in his mind as they journeyed back to Lewisham. There had been just the briefest of stops at his own flat while he collected all the flour and sugar he could find. It was poured carefully into the base of the case. He could not put it in packets as he had found it but he spread it evenly, replaced the bottom and trusted the weight was about right.

The garage had a funereal air to it. The workshop was in silence and the shrill whistle from the kettle was the only aural clue to the presence of anyone in the flat. In fact, there were two sitting around the kitchen table: Keith had been briefed on the night's events by Pete and he had fallen into a brown study in tune with the morbid atmosphere of the place.

He looked up as the pair joined them. 'You got the case all right, then?'

What a stupid question! He can see the bloody thing, thought Jeremy. However, he contented himself with a simple 'yes'. He banged it onto the table.

'You haven't tampered with it, have you?'

'Of course not! Do you want to check it over?'

'No, no, that's all right, I trust you.'

More than I do you, thought Jeremy. The idea was in his mind that none of this would have happened if he had not been so greedy. Why couldn't he have been content to earn an honest living?

197

'I take it that we've not heard anything from Smith yet?'

It was hardly a question; he knew he would have been greeted at the door with the news had there been any.

Pete grunted. 'No such luck. Tea?'

They all nodded. It was the third brew of the morning before the phone rang. Pete answered it, frowned deeply and passed it across the table.

'It's him.'

Jeremy took the mobile receiver and walked away from the group.

'Mr Smith?'

'Good morning to you, Mr Carrington-Fox. I trust you had no problem retrieving the case this morning?'

'None.'

'Splendid! Then we can do business. The lady in question is safe and well and desiring to return home. I should like to supervise the transaction personally but I shall be a little tied up this afternoon. Would five o'clock suit you?'

'Where?'

'Ah, yes. I suggest the seclusion of one of my warehouses. I believe you have been to one of them before. That should be good enough.'

'I know the place. Now let me speak to Sandra.'

'Of course. Have you a pen?'

'Yes.'

'Then take down this number . . . .'

Jeremy repeated it slowly. 'If she is hurt then you lose the deal and I will want her clear of the building before I hand anything over.'

'Have no fear, Mr Carrington-Fox. I am a business man. My word is my bond. If I agree an exchange then I will honour it.'

He rang off.

Jeremy turned back to the others.

'The bastard intends to make us sweat. She won't be released until five.

As he talked, so he depressed the numbers on the telephone.

'Yer, who is it?' The accent was rough.

'Mr Smith gave me this number. I wish to speak to Sandra.'

'Hang on!'

There was a long pause and then a distraught voice spoke.

'Is that you, Dad?'

'No, Sandra, it's me, Jeremy. I'll put your father on now. Are you all right?'

'No, I'm frightened. Please do what they want.'

He cut in sharply. 'We are getting you out this afternoon. Nobody is going to hurt you, otherwise they don't get a penny. Keep thinking about that. You are much safer than you think. Just trust us.'

Pete took the phone. 'Hello, kitten. It's Dad . . . .'

'Tough, Daddy, that's all you're getting. Little kitten is going back to her little hidey-hole.'

The man switched off the call, leaving Pete somewhere between total rage and near despair that he had not been allowed to talk to her. He paced across the room, smashed his fist at the wall, damaging the plaster more than his flesh, and swore softly. The words did not have to percolate: there was no one in that room who did not know what he had said or did not share the sentiment. If there was, it was well-hidden.

Paddy crossed the floor and put her hand across his shoulder. 'I'll kill 'em if ever I get near 'em, Pa.'

'You won't, lass.'

A paw swung around and clamped her in a massive bear-hug.

'You ever get to them before me, I'll wallop you. These bastards are mine and mine alone.'

There was something in all this that was getting to Jeremy but not in the way it was affecting the McBears. He stood up, flexed his shoulders as if he had been stiff from sitting and said simply, 'Standing around until five is not going to help anyone. I've a pile of work in the office and keeping busy seems to make good sense. I'm going downstairs to work.'

The Bear turned round, still hugging his daughter.

'Yeh, you do that, son. Reckon I could do worse than follow suit.'

It was some ten minutes after Jeremy had entered his little office next to the main workshop that he heard the familiar clump of Pete's footsteps across the passage, followed by the sound of the hydraulic ramp operating.

Paddy and Keith were left upstairs, still talking about nothing and everything. Eventually, the conversation swung around to the idea of lunch. Even a worried bear-cub needs sustenance.

'Somebody had better get a loaf and some sandwich fillings, I suppose.'

'Do you want me to go?'

'Say, that'd be great, Keith! Sure you don't mind?'

'Of course not. Actually, something else occurred to me. Have you still got that gun?'

She nodded.

'I have a feeling we might need it yet. How much ammunition was there with it?'

'Only what was in the clip.'

'I know this fellow who doesn't ask questions. Let me have it and I'll call and see him while I'm doing the shopping.'

Paddy retrieved it from the drawer of her bedside

chest. She looked at it and hesitated. Keith had followed her into the room.

'You sure about this friend of yours?'

'Please yourself. If you don't trust me with the thing . . . .'

'No, it's not that. Oh, OK, take the blessed thing!'

She tossed it to him and, in his surprise, he nearly dropped it. He juggled it in his hands then obtained a firm grip.

She grinned wickedly at him. 'Your reactions are slowing!'

He grinned back. She started to walk past him then half saw the gun moving across towards her. She instinctively raised her hand but not in time. The barrel caught her across the side of the head. She slumped forward, his words hardly registering.

'So are yours, my lovely . . . .'

At ten past twelve, Jeremy started to feel peckish. He finished reading the brief in front of him, stood up and stretched. He glanced at his watch then sauntered out of the office. Pete was under an old Granada, the blue dazzle of the welding arc reflecting up from the pit. Jeremy felt no inclination to disturb him so wandered upstairs in search of food.

Pete heard the cry all right. It had a penetrating urgency that defied delay. He cut the oxy-acetylene flame and pulled himself out of the pit. The second shout was from the stairs and was edged with impatience that the first had not been answered.

'Hold it, old son! I'm coming! What the hell is the fuss about?'

He found out only too quickly. Paddy was awake – just! She was also trussed up like a turkey ready for the Christmas oven. By the time Pete arrived, Jeremy was pulling the gag away from her mouth. She coughed and said nothing. They tugged at the sheet round her feet and hands and helped her onto the bed, with Pete fussing in a most uncharacteristic way around his daughter. Gone was the hard-bitten approach; she might well have been Sandra for all the gentle comforting.

Paddy was doing nothing except holding her head in her hands and letting out soft moans. For the moment, Jeremy was confused.

'Where's Keith?'

'He done it,' she whimpered.

The bolt had thumped home in one killing jolt. Jeremy stood dumb-struck; Pete let out an expletive – something that Jeremy had never heard escape his lips before – then started into a tirade of what would happen to the louse once he caught him.

'Where's the case?'

The initial shock had fallen from Jeremy and he followed the natural line of reasoning.

'Under the bed.'

Paddy was recovering enough to talk, especially as she, too, was realising what might have happened. Jeremy dived onto his hands and knees and scurried as far under as he could. One glance was enough but he looked longer in the desperate hope it would suddenly become visible.

'The bastard's taken it!'

He stood up and thought.

'If you had called the police as I asked you to instead of storming the warehouse with your female version of the SAS, then the sod would be in custody right now and none of this would have happened. How are we going to trade something we haven't got for Sandra?'

It was an unfair blow, miles below the belt. There had been ample time to hand him over after the rescue, had they chosen. Even Jeremy had not felt it fair to do so.

'Gosh, old son, you're right. I ought to have listened to

you. What are we going to do now?'

Jeremy did not have a clue. He stared at Pete and shook his head. 'Wish I knew. I suppose we had better phone the police.'

''Ere, could someone get me an aspirin? My head is giving me hell!'

'Pete, you look after Paddy. It mightn't be a bad idea to let Doc Masters look at her just to make sure there's no real damage. I'll ring the detective fellow I met the other night.'

It was twenty-five minutes later that Pete ventured into the little office of the workshop. There he found the solicitor in deep thought, eyes glued to a point somewhere in the middle of his desk, his head resting on his knuckles and with the first fingers of each hand pushing the skin of his cheeks up round his eyes.

'How did it go?'

The fingers slowly came down his face and the eyes focused on the Bear.

'Paddy OK?'

'Yeh, sure. Doc reckoned she's got a mild concussion but nothing that won't right itself in a couple of days. She just needs rest. What did your cop friend say?'

'Don't know – I haven't phoned him yet.'

'Listen, old son, it was your idea to ring him, remember? Just for once, I reckon it's the only thing we can do.'

'Yeh, may come to that but I was having another thought. If we don't have the case to bargain with, we're stuck, right? So, what do we do? I say we'll just have to get one.'

Pete looked at him oddly. 'You flipped, old son?'

'Nope.'

'Where do you reckon you're getting this case of yours from?'

'Any shop that sells them. Smith hasn't seen the case, has he?'

'How are you going to pull off this con, may one ask?'

'That's the tricky bit. I haven't got there yet but it'll come. Just for once, this is something I cannot see the police handling properly but one of your unorthodox stunts with the girls might come off.'

He seemed to make the decision for he rocked sharply forward on his chair and reached for the telephone. Unfortunately, Stanley was not in his office.

'OK. Can you reach him? . . . Do something for me, then – give him a message . . . . Yes, that's right, "the Fox is in trouble – you owe me, remember?" . . . He'll understand . . . . It is urgent, every minute counts . . . . Yes, I'm sure you will. Sorry to sound so distrusting.'

The phone went dead.

Jeremy looked up at the Bear. 'I'm starved. Reckon you could rustle something up? I can't leave here in case chummy rings back.'

'What do you want? A sandwich do?'

'I could murder a Chinese take-away.'

Pete shrugged. He had no appetite and found it hard to comprehend how this slight figure seemed hungry in the middle of a crisis.

Jeremy was three-quarters of the way through sweet-and-sour chicken, prawn chop suey, beef strips with onions and double fried rice when the phone rang. Between mouthfuls, he went about gaining the information he so desperately desired.

'I've a registration number – at least, I have enough to make it worth while trying to trace it – and I need the address of the owner.'

'And you expect me to get it for you, is that it?'

'Yep. It's a black Mercedes belonging to a Winston

Smith, reg. W . . . I . . .'

'I don't need the number, I know the guy and can find his address without trouble. The real point is whether I agree to do it. Why do you want to know?'

'Remember a certain case I told you about? Well, our charmer is very eager to get his hands on it. So eager, in fact, that he has kidnapped one of the McBear girls and is threatening nasty things if we don't deliver at five this evening. There is just one snag, we don't have the case any more and I don't think he'll believe us.'

The expletive was almost whispered, then there came a long pause.

'Tell me where the drop is supposed to be made and I'll see we have enough armed officers present to get her back.'

'She would be dead before you even showed yourselves. That's a hopeless course.'

'It's the only one you've got.'

'Give me the information I need and there might be another.'

'No way. You're mad to try anything. This is a straight police matter.'

'Do you fancy heading a murder inquiry?'

'No more than you. Have you still no idea what you are into? Christ, this man is in the top three wanted men in the country.'

'Then why haven't you arrested him?'

'We have twice and each time he walked away scot-free for lack of evidence. He's known as the Black Panther – he's reckoned to be the drugs baron for half of London and is into a whole range of other nasty stuff on top.'

'Tell me what I want to know and I might just be able to give him to you. Come on, Sandy, you owe me one, remember?'

'I haven't forgotten.' The voice had become

defensive.

'One address, that's all I need. If I blow it then we do it your way. It's my neck that's going on the line, not yours.'

'I want to know exactly what you plan to do.'

'It's a deal. Now what's the address?'

'I'll have to get back to you.'

'OK – but make it quick, will you? There's something else. You know I said I didn't have the diamonds any more, well the guy who originally brought them into the country has nicked them and done a runner. Can you get him picked up? His name's Keith Parsons. If you want anything else beside the theft to hold him on then try nailing him for the murder of Nicholas Carlisle at Osbourne House, Maidstone, a week ago.'

'Can you give me a description?'

'Send someone round and I'll let you have a photograph.'

'Christ, Fox, you are a deceptive bastard. How the hell did you get into all this?'

'Don't worry about that, just get me that address.'

'Stay around! I'll think it over and get back to you.'

The phone went dead. Jeremy let the receiver slide slowly back into place and looked up at Pete.

'Do you know how to get in contact with Sharon and the rest of the girls?'

'Of course I do. What do you want them for?'

'If I read my man right, I'll have that address in half an hour. I don't want to waste time when I do. Get the girls – you had better use the upstairs phone in case Stanley tries getting back to me – then pop back in here. I'll have a shopping list for you.'

He gave a twisted smile.

'You Bears will be the death of me. A month ago, I was just any other solicitor working in a boring office but it was safe. Now I am close to breaking the law, even if I haven't done so already, and I'm putting my neck on the line. Do you know the really worrying part?'

Pete did not.

'I'm actually enjoying it in a funny way. I like the Mr Hyde side of my character. Until I got involved in all this, I never knew it even existed.'

He rocked back in the chair and laughed to himself.

'I must be stark, staring mad.'

Pete rose and lumbered across to the door. 'Yeh, I guess I know what you mean, old son. I was in the Marines when I was your age. Loved every minute of it, even when I was scared to death.'

He departed, leaving Jeremy wondering how this Bear could ever be afraid. Then he realised he was now. Really scared, not for himself but for his cub.

By the time the telephone rang again, Jeremy had just about refined his plan.

'Right, what do you intend doing if I give you this address?'

Talk to the guy. That was all. Simply talk. No, he would not be going inside unless invited and then he would feel perfectly safe. Smith was not going to do anything, knowing that he had involved the police. Jeremy was as honest as Nixon over Watergate but it got him the address.

Pete returned with the news that the girls were all on their way over. He took the shopping list and left Jeremy once more to his musings.

Sharon arrived first.

'Hey, you dishy thing! I didn't expect to find you on your own. Where's your chaperon?'

He answered and her face lost a fraction of its easygoing expression.

'Can I go up and see her?'

'Actually, I hoped you might take her home with you.'

He explained. Samantha and Michelle arrived just about together in time to see Sharon helping Paddy into a rather beaten-up Mini, which she drove away in a cloud of blue smoke.

It fascinated Jeremy the way these girls viewed the outrageous plan he put to them.

'Honey, have you got to be the greatest! I can see why Paddy goes for you and, sister, am I jealous!'

Samantha wound her long arm round his neck, pulled his head up and kissed him hard. He decided not to mention the fact to Paddy. Michelle grinned and got in on the act. He definitely was not telling Paddy but that did not stop him enjoying it. He had never been the centre of hero-worship before and, what is more, could not understand why he was.

*

It was a quarter past three when a red BMW slid past the entrance to The Wirrals. They had had great difficulty finding the place. The address consisted of a house name and the name of a village it was supposed to be in but it was actually three miles beyond the village boundary. The brakes went on and, thirty seconds later, the security camera panned across its tail as the BMW reversed onto the red brick drive and parked with its front wheels still on the road.

The house could not be seen from the road, protected as it was by a thick twelve-foot-high thorn hedge that could only be penetrated by something the size of a vole. A short wall looped just round the entrance to the drive and served little other purpose than to support the iron gates and the camera. The drive itself was lined with tall trees artistically highlighted by tasteful bushes and sweeping lawns.

Jeremy took all this in as he approached the gates. He rang the buzzer over an intercom unit and waited patiently until a low voice enquired his business.

'Mr Carrington-Fox to see Mr Smith.'

'Is he expecting you?'

'In a way, you might say he is. I was due to see him at five but the venue was proving inconvenient so I thought I'd drop round. He wants this.'

He raised his left arm to the camera to clearly show the notorious black case. It also showed the set of handcuffs attached to the handle and his wrist.

'Wait there.'

As if he was going anywhere!

Jeremy continued posing for the camera in case anyone was watching. As it happened, it was a wasted performance but it did help to sustain his confidence.

The voice returned.

'Mr Smith says he'll see you. Drive up and wait in the car for someone to come to you. There are dogs off the leash.'

He was right in a way but the word 'dog' hardly fitted the brutes. The smallest had apparently auditioned for the part of the Hound of the Baskervilles. As the baying brutes clambered round the doors, the occupants were only too pleased to sit still and wait. Three men came down the steps of the imposing country seat and whistled at the dogs. With some reluctance, they withdrew enough to allow the car to disgorge its contents. With more than a concerned backward glance, the bearer of the case and his two female companions moved swiftly up the steps and into the hall.

They had this desire to search them. Jeremy was happy enough to be frisked but he drew the line at the girls being touched. The men were prepared to accept that neither could have concealed anything. Indeed, the scant clothing did not cover much of their bodies. However, they were very insistent about the case.

'This is for Mr Smith and no one else. Check with him if you don't believe me.'

A tall, pretty, black lad came out of the lounge.

'What seems to be the trouble, David?'

'This guy won't open the case.'

'Not correct. I'll not open it for him. The contents are for Mr Smith and only when he has honoured his part of the contract.'

'It's all right, David. Leave the case alone. Just you and Peter come in to make sure this fellow behaves himself.'

The trio were ushered into a large and expensively furnished lounge. Tasteful paintings hung in profusion and the carpet soaked up all sound as they penetrated into the centre of the Smith empire.

Mr Smith was sitting in an elegant high-backed reproduction period chair (actually, Jeremy was not very good on such things. It was a genuine antique). He swivelled round and eyed his guest with a mixture of amused contempt and mild astonishment. His feelings about the girls were not likely to be complimentary, the more so as Samantha ejected a sexy 'I say, he's cute' and wiggled forward with her hand outstretched. It was ignored.

'Well, Mr Carrington-Fox, this is an unexpected meeting. I had rather thought you would have followed my instructions.'

'They would have upset my social life. Anyway, I decided to do things my way. The deal is still the same as far as I am concerned. You let me have the McBear girl and you get the case.'

'What makes you think I can't just take it?'

'You probably can. However, that is hardly necessary when a civilised exchange can be made. You don't want the girl and I'm not going anywhere for the moment. Anyway, I had another reason for calling in. I thought it was about time we understood each other and stopped this unnecessary feuding.'

Samantha tried to stroke Smith's head but her hand was flicked away as though it was an irritating fly.

'Can't you keep your bimbo under control?'

'I am so sorry. Come on, Sammy love. I pay you for keeping me happy. Work on him when you're on your own time.'

She shrugged provocatively and moved a little to one side. As she did so, the black youth became silhouetted between them. He was now immediately behind Smith's chair. In that instant, the veil fell from Jeremy's eyes. His adversary was more than a trifle bent. He inwardly smiled – had he found a weakness, an Achilles heel, perhaps?

Jeremy took a couple of paces forward. 'Give it a feel. It's the real thing.'

Smith went to touch it then brushed it aside. 'You would not have come if it wasn't.'

'How about producing the girl, then we can talk in a relaxed manner?'

Smith smiled slowly. 'Yes, indeed, Mr Carrington-Fox. Why not? Unfortunately, she is currently in central London.'

'I am sure a simple telephone call could have her on her way without difficulty.'

Smith turned in his chair.

'Adrian, be a good fellow and have Ronnie bring the girl.'

He swung back.

'Does that satisfy you?'

211

Jeremy nodded and watched as the elegant Adrian dialled on the mock 1920s phone. Once the receiver had been replaced, Jeremy showed outward signs of relaxing. He walked across to a chair similar to the one his unwilling host was occupying and indicated to it with his hand.

'May I?'

He hardly waited for the wave of agreement before dropping into it.

'As I was saying earlier, our feuding is doing nobody any good. By my count, you have lost three dead and four injured, while I have had one of my men killed and three put out of action. I am most annoyed about what you did to my courier, actually. The poor fellow is completely shattered. I daren't use him again and, until I find somebody reliable to take his place, I'm having to do the runs myself. You will appreciate, I am sure, that I do not take kindly to putting myself at such risk with the law.

'Anyway, I think the point has been made. I suggest we agree to respect each other's areas of activity and concentrate efforts on avoiding the police rather than each other. As an act of goodwill, I am happy to withdraw from the heroin side of my business. It was only a dabble, to be honest, and I do much better on the local crime. For your part, I want your agreement not to upset my diamond-running fraud and to keep out of my locality. What do you say?'

He threw his arms wide and smiled.

The Black Panther stood up and stretched. He paced towards the window and stared out for some time. Still with his back to Jeremy, he said, 'You are asking me to believe you control a major syndicate in east London. No, sorry, Mr Carrington-Fox, I don't buy it. How is it I have never heard of you before?'

'If I had my way, you wouldn't now.'

Well, that's honest if none of the rest is, thought Jeremy.

'Unfortunately, even if you had not heard of me, most police forces in the South East have. Take the Carrington part away and there you have it. I am known as "the Fox". However, unlike you, I keep a low profile – one that is in keeping with my name. I don't believe in flashy cars with personalised plates. Too much of a give-away. Play the cover for all it's worth – that's my motto. It even fooled you.'

Smith turned round, mildly curious. 'What makes you think that?'

'When you had me in the flat, you abandoned the search and took me off without leaving anyone to continue looking. Funny, really. You could have saved yourself a lot of trouble. This famous case was there. Why else do you think I had gone along? Oh, I admit I was a trifle careless as well. I never dreamt you knew where to go. You will note, though, that you have twice had me and twice I slipped through your fingers – and you lost men each time. You know, you really should take my offer seriously. Underestimating the opposition is most foolish, if not downright dangerous.

'I may not look as though I am old enough to command anything but I was lucky. My dear father worked up the patch, sent me to public school on it and then schooled me in the family business. When he met with an unfortunate accident, I inherited and I reckon I have not disgraced his memory.'

'I will tell you what I will do, Mr Carrington-Fox. I will think over what you have said and give you an answer by the time the car arrives.'

'How long do you think it will take?'

'An hour, perhaps a little more.'

'Perhaps you would allow me a room where I could be

private with my friends while we wait?'

The Black Panther made no attempt to disguise his disgust. Nevertheless, he said, 'Adrian, show our guests to one of the spare bedrooms.'

Jeremy slightly bowed his head. 'Most kind of you. Come on, girls, time for fun, fun, fun!'

Samantha was accentuating the wiggle to near-ridiculous proportions as the two women followed the men out of the room, up the wide, flowing staircase and along an impressive corridor to an oak-panelled bedroom. They entered in fine spirits, shut and locked the door and listened to the soft receding tread of footsteps on the carpet. The façade dropped. With an efficiency not easily bettered, the girls went across the room, testing furniture for weight and strength. Satisfied, they called on Jeremy's help and the trio struggled to manoeuvre a George the Third oak chest across the door.

Contented, the girls lounged on the bed and watched as the solicitor deftly opened the case and extricated a walkie-talkie set. He walked to the window, looked out suspiciously then drew back into the shadow of the frame and pulled out the aerial.

'Cuckoo to Magpie. Have you got your ears on?'

'Magpie receiving loud and clear, old son. What news?'

'Stand by. Decoy pigeon needed in about half an hour. Cuckoos safe and undetected but high in the nest and may have to fly to leave, if you get my point.'

'Can have a good guess. Anything else?'

'No. Just keep your ears on, that's all.'

He closed the aerial and put the set on the chest. Next, he opened the bottom drawer of the chest. It was empty. He pondered over it for a minute or so then removed it totally. With infinite care, he taped a small freezer bag filled with white powder to the back of it and closed it once more. It failed to shut flush by an odd fraction only. He then sloped over to a wicker chair, pulled it close to the window and dropped into it to observe the view. Indeed, the view was all he could see, which was a pity as there were interesting events taking place.

Almost thirty-five minutes later, an old Rover 3500 saloon came into the range of the security camera. It was being pushed by two rather scruffy young men who, on balance, were only slightly more respectable than their vehicle. The voluminous quantities of grey paint that had been used to cover the points on the body where rust holes had been covered by fibreglass suggested a certain disquiet with the original yellow. It took considerable effort to force the battered contraption over the slightly raised edge to the brick drive and they were blowing hard by the time the car was clear of the road. Having caught his breath, the older of the two opened the bonnet and half disappeared over the lip of the radiator.

The news was greeted by Smith with something considerably more than disquiet. Instinct suggested that the event was more than coincidence but it was a quarter of an hour before the decision was taken in the house to investigate. Adrian set off on his moped, accompanied by the baying hounds.

'Are you having trouble?'

The younger man came up to the gate. 'Yeh. I reckon she's really had it this time.'

'You can't leave it here. You're obstructing the gate.'

'There's no need to worry, pal. Bob has already rung the garage. They're sending a breakdown truck out. Should be 'ere any minute. We can push it back a bit if yer like, only we didn't want to block the lane.'

Suspicious or not, Adrian had to concede that they had

a point. The lane was so narrow that it was a very tight squeeze for two cars to pass each other. Indeed, their drive made a natural widening of the road that was regularly used for the purpose. Careful observation also showed that the entrance was not blocked – a car could go in and out through this gap without too much trouble. The elder man came round from the boot, where he had been repacking the tool kit.

'Ready for off as soon as the guy from the garage gets 'ere.'

Adrian was not totally convinced, however, but shrugged and turned back for the house, leaving the dogs to launch themselves half a dozen times at the gate before seeking fresh sport. Smith seemed less than happy at the report, though there seemed little to be done other than have the camera monitor the situation. He almost relaxed when the news came a quarter of an hour later that a breakdown truck had indeed materialised.

The mechanic spent a couple of minutes inspecting the inside of the bonnet before driving the van up the road, to return in the opposite direction and reverse up to the front bumper of the Rover.

The Granada slowed at the entrance, tooted belligerently and grudgingly waited. The truck-driver left the van and walked back for a casual conversation. It was difficult to say exactly what happened but it appeared that he had carelessly left off the handbrake, for the driver had to leap clear and was almost pinned by the truck as it slowly rolled onto the front wing of the Granada.

It must be said that the two fellows from the Rover reacted remarkably swiftly. Seeing the problem, they ran to the truck and one reversed it while the other politely enquired of the front-seat passenger to see if he was hurt. It seemed he was not because he got out of the car smartly enough and proceeded to use some quite unpleasant language on the fellow who, after all, was only trying to help.

As the young man protested his innocence and expressed his philanthropic intentions, the truck-driver picked himself up from the ground and in an unseen but rapid movement produced an eighteen-inch wrench – it had originally been intended to turn 1¼-inch-diameter nuts but now was to double as a sledge-hammer. With one clear swing, it caused rather severe damage to the rear window. There was no protest, however. The sawn-off shotgun at the head of the nearest man saw to that.

In the space of fifteen seconds, two more men appeared from behind the hedge to the rear of the Granada, opened the doors and pulled out the guard and the young woman jammed in the middle of the rear seat. She was whisked into the back of the Rover, its engine being the subject of a miraculous cure. The vehicle sped off with remarkable acceleration, leaving the two men who had got out of the Granada to enjoy an early and enforced afternoon nap.

The truck ploughed forward once more, pummelling the Granada backwards through the hedge and into the cornfield beyond. One of the rear wheels dropped into a deep rut and the whole car turned at a drunken angle, finishing up with its bonnet pointing in the general direction of the sky.

'Mission accomplished, Cuckoo. Caged bird freed! Get your butts out of there!'

The commotion at the door suggested a slight difficulty.

'Sorry, Pete. We have a problem. We are in a first-floor bedroom with gorillas prancing around outside.'

There was an uncomfortably loud report from outside

217

of the door and the wood around the lock disappeared.

'Oh, dear! The gorillas are intent on getting in. Looks like we could do with some help!'

'Hang in there, old son. Cavalry on its way. Can you get out of the window?'

'No problem.' He had not even looked.

'I'll get the truck underneath and you can drop in. Wave so I know where to come.'

There was a second report and the rest of the lock disintegrated. The girls were throwing furniture into the barricade as fast as they could, while Jeremy went to the window to signal to the relief forces. Thirty seconds later, a large breakdown truck careered up the drive, still dragging part of an iron gate that had become entangled in its front bumper. Jeremy leant out of the window and waved for all he was worth. The truck skidded to a halt and, without the wheels apparently stopping, reversed up tight to the wall.

'You first, Jerry.'

'That doesn't seem right.'

'Shut it!'

Michelle was very firm.

'Our job is to protect you, right? Then you do as we say. Onto the window-ledge, face inwards and get your legs over the side.'

He did as he was told. As he momentarily swung in space in the iron wrist-lock of the two women, he began to doubt the wisdom of the venture. There was no time for further philosophising: he was falling through space backwards. The floor of the truck was hardly receptive to the impact and he lay, jarred and winded, trying desperately to recover his senses. Before he had done so, there was a thump immediately beside him and a soft, feline body rolled across him. The second percussion was hailed by a roar of 'go, go, go' and the truck was

218

picking up speed and heading for the entrance, while a couple of hounds attempted the impossible by trying to leap into it. Jeremy had a dim sight of a red BMW following and flames leaping from the entrance hall to the house. As Pete said afterwards, it is wonderful what you can do with a jerrycan of petrol and a bit of oily rag.

14

Mr Wagstaff was not a happy man. He had no love of zoos and certainly no regard for venomous snakes but here he was, standing in front of a sluggish puff-adder in a most humid reptile house on the hottest of summer days. He really had little choice: it was that or kiss goodbye to his two million in diamonds and risk who knows what from the fraud squad. At least, that was the threat made by the mysterious man on the phone and he could hardly take the chance. He had been standing in front of the inanimate creature for nearly ten minutes and was just beginning to wonder if the whole thing might actually be a macabre joke when a young couple wandered through the steamy corridor and stopped in front of the tank.

'He's a real beauty, isn't he?'

Wagstaff conjured up a false enthusiasm. 'Really lovely creature.'

The girl seemed to prefer a thin black worm that was slithering up a piece of dead wood two tanks further down.

'I love snakes but, personally, I prefer mammals.'

'They are all fascinating.'

'Foxes. They're my real favourites.'

Wagstaff tried to look innocent but his pulse had quickened slightly. The code had been triggered. It was a stupid code and a stupid idea meeting in such bizarre surroundings. Perhaps this had added to his ill humour or perhaps any venue suggested would have annoyed him. He was a worried man but would not admit it.

'Tricky things. Never really know where you are with them. Had one in the garden the other night. Cheeky thing came right across the patio and barely trotted off when I opened the door. Personally, though, I prefer them to panthers.'

The right reply had been given.

'There's one particular one I know that is a really cheeky fellow. He's over by the wolf cage. Fancy a stroll across to see him?'

Wagstaff nodded. The contact had been made. He was to be taken to meet the Fox after all. The young man's girl-friend seemed loath to leave the African black mamba, calling out as they walked past that she would catch them up.

The two men picked their way slowly between the hordes of holiday-makers teeming through the gardens and took nearly ten minutes to reach the enclosure containing not a fox but a prowling black panther.

'A beautiful creature, don't you think? One, however, that is rightly behind bars. It's not safe to have a fellow like that roaming around.'

Wagstaff said nothing. The conversation was either inane or too obtuse for him. He wondered when the Fox would show himself.

The young man was getting into his stride. 'I know a panther on the loose at the moment. A black one in all senses of the word. Really nasty character with a façade of fine living. It was his mob that raided your house and his lot that intercepted your courier on the last diamond run.'

Suddenly, Wagstaff was interested. There was a point

to the conversation after all. The panther turned at the end of his silent walk across the front of the cage and paced back, the powerful muscles rippling with controlled rhythm.

'How do you know about such things, assuming, of course, that they are true?'

'Oh, I know.'

He smiled falsely. The face muscles held their position briefly then dropped into a sombre mode.

'I am remarkably well-informed about all that we're about to discuss –' he broke off sharply. A couple of children had taken up position next to them and were calling to their mother to join them.

Jeremy swung away from the cage and strolled idly along the walkway.

'. . . and you would do well not to underestimate me. This panther creature has already done that and he has come off worst so far. It's the way I intend to keep it. I am not going to get bogged down with detail but I know a lot more about this little affair than you do. As well as having you roughed up when your house was raided, he has also seriously inconvenienced me and my friends. I want this animal more firmly behind bars than his namesake here.

'Anyway, as I said on the phone, I am in possession of all the details about your little bit of deception to Customs and Excise and I am fully prepared to give the lot to the police if I don't have cooperation from you. If I get it, I will tell you what I know about the whereabouts of the last consignment and do what I can to recover your diamonds for you. In other words, go along with what I want and you'll benefit as well. To trap this Black Panther guy, I need another diamond run from Amsterdam.'

Wagstaff stopped walking and considered the position. 'Where is the last lot now?'

222

'Interesting question. Probably with Parsons and likely to be out of the country by now, if I guess right. In simple terms, he's nicked them.'

'Do you think you can get them back?'

'I don't know for sure. I have passed the word to a – "friend", let us say. If Parsons can be picked up, he'll do it.'

They came to a seat. Jeremy dropped lazily into it. He was about to continue the conversation when he spied Paddy ambling up with a swarthy character in tow. The awkward walk and close proximity of their bodies was enough to alert him to the situation. As they closed, he could see the pained expression on the man's face.

'Hi, Pad. What have you trawled up?'

She twisted the fingers gently and wrung a throttled cry from her companion.

'He was following you.'

'What is this? This is my bodyguard and butler, Carlos.'

Jermy looked quickly from Wagstaff to the man and then to Paddy.

'Let him go. Not much of a bodyguard, is he? Is this the chap that let the Black Panther's men raid your house?'

Paddy seemed upset that she had not caught a more worthy prize and pouted as she released her bone sandwich. Carlos massaged the damaged fingers and scowled viciously at the young woman. Wagstaff took up the gauntlet.

'He couldn't be blamed for that. What would you do if you were faced by a sawn-off shotgun when you opened the door?'

'Then it was lucky for you that I tipped off the police.'

It was a morning of surprises for the diamond dealer

but he hid them well. For all that, Jeremy noted the slight start. He smiled briefly.

'Can you two keep the rabble from getting close?'

It was not really a question. He turned back to Wagstaff and grinned boardly. For the next ten minutes he briefly outlined how he had tumbled that something had been wrong at the Wagstaff house, finishing with a side-swipe by intimating that Wagstaff owed the solicitor a favour.

'Do you trust Carlos?'

It seemed a strange question with the man in earshot but he had a purpose.

'Of course I do. He has worked for me for seven years now.'

'Good. Then I can talk freely; my proposition will be known to just the four of us. So long as that's not one too many, I am content to let him stay. I want to see the diamond runs continue. You have lost a courier; that's too bad but I'm willing to do it as an interim measure.'

He broke off sharply.

'I say, Pad, could you and Carlos get a cup of coffee for everyone? I'm absolutely parched.'

'Got some money?'

He pulled a ten-pound note from his pocket and flipped it across as though it was nothing. Ignoring his girl-friend, he continued the conversation but as soon as Carlos was out of range the tone changed. He rapidly explained what was on his mind and Wagstaff took some more surprises on board.

Jeremy watched as Wagstaff and his pseudo-bodyguard walked through the exit gate and were lost in the crowd. He and Paddy turned back and sauntered through the gardens for another half-hour, holding hands and chatting earnestly about all manner of things.

They left by another exit, strolled through the park and made their way to the underground station. In less than an hour, they were back in the large detached house in Croydon that they had rented a mere three days after their return from rescuing Sandra.

It was not just luck that had stopped them from being roasted in their beds: it was Stanley's cautious attitude. He had said little in his debriefing session with Jeremy but he had immediately put a discreet watch on the garage and its occupants. Thus, the two men who turned up a little after three a couple of nights later were not as inconspicuous as they intended. They had hardly finished pouring the petrol through the letter-box to the flat when two unmarked cars caught them in a pincer operation.

Pete was none too happy at leaving the flat but the threat from the Black Panther could not be lightly ignored and even he accepted that the girls had to be protected. It had taken less than a day for Jeremy to come up with his scheme: Smith had to be permanently. rendered harmless and in a way that destroyed his reputation as much as possible. If they did not do something, they would be looking over their shoulders and jumping at shadows as long as they lived. A single day of that was too long for the Bears so they had turned to their resourceful family lawyer, who, in turn, had needed little prompting to put his brains to work.

Now, Jeremy quickly briefed Pete on the trip to the zoo.

'The bargain has been struck. I'm going to do a run Tuesday next. Wagstaff will arrange for a bag of paste diamonds to be collected from van Hoffner's. Outwardly, everything will be the same as usual: he will make sure that Carlos knows I'm doing it and that there will be drugs in the case as well as the diamonds.'

'And you reckon you can square all this with your tame cop?'

'Yes, I think he'll play ball. He wants the Black Panther as much as we do but I'll only tell him the bit he needs to know. I'll keep quiet about the drugs until after-wards.'

He grinned boyishly. It was exciting. He was taking a risk with the drug-smuggling bit but there was little choice and, he reasoned, he was likely to get away with it even if he was caught. He only had a couple of ounces of the heroin – left in the pepper-pot – but even that was worth several thousand pounds. There would be no problem on the return trip as that was all rigged – he would be fine just so long as no over-zealous customs officer wanted to examine the case on the way out. Anyway, he hoped Stanley could be relied on to get him off as a last resort.

As far as he was concerned, the essential thing was to get a charge of possession to stick on Smith and that meant he had to have a reasonable quantity in the case. The really dangerous part was letting the Panther's lot grab the loot. As yet, he did not have this bit really worked out, though he would not admit it. There was an unjustified confidence that he would have it all sorted by the time he set off.

*

Wagstaff kept his own counsel for the most of the homeward journey and Carlos had no cause to make conversation. He was still nursing his sore fingers and inwardly fuming at being taken by a mere woman. About a mile from the house, however, the diamond merchant seemed to have relaxed somewhat, at least enough to open up.

'He's a cool bastard, that Fox. I don't like being manipulated or ordered around but I've got to admit he's clever.'

'That young kid?'

'Indeed, Carlos, "that young kid". I've no idea of the size of his operation but it is clearly substantial, yet he manages to be almost totally anonymous. For instance, had you ever heard of him before today?'

The driver thought for a moment. 'No, I can't say I have. What's he in to?'

'Most organised crime in his part of London that actually succeeds. He masterminds our little diamond business, for instance.'

'I thought that was your show.'

'That's where he is so diabolically clever. He never shows his hand. Instead, he lets others do the fronting. No, he's the real brains behind it all.'

There was a slight pause as Carlos thought matters over.

'I'd like to get that bird of his alone on a dark night.'

Wagstaff allowed a slight laugh. 'Don't feel too bad about it. Nobody would've expected a female body-guard. You see, another example of his cleverness. He's not called the Fox for nothing. Do you know, I actually pity that Black Panther character for trying to muscle in on his territory. He's liable to get his fur singed. Think about it, Carlos. By tipping off the police when we were raided, that guy probably saved your neck for you, and mine as well, for that matter.'

A taxi cut them up from the inside and Carlos muttered a gentle expletive. Wagstaff allowed the driver to settle and continued, 'No, that Panther guy had better watch it. It seems as though he has put the usual courier out of action and that's made the Fox really narked with him. It must be serious, as the Fox is doing the next run himself.'

'I thought you had decided to stop after the last lot went astray.'

'No, the Fox won't hear of it. He has it all set up for next Tuesday. He's not content with just bringing in diamonds, either. He's intent on carrying a supply of heroin as well.'

The trap had been set. Carlos knew the plan and, according to Jeremy, would pass the information on to Smith. Despite Wagstaff's protestations, there could be little doubt that Carlos was the leak in the diamond operation. The one trouble with all this was that Wagstaff really did know Carlos and his faith in Carlos's loyalty was not misplaced. Carlos had heard of the Panther for the first time that day. The arrogance of youth had tripped the intrepid solicitor once more: the carefully prepared hype was in vain yet, without Smith getting word of the run, the whole venture lost meaning.

15

Now a lot can happen in seven days and this was a week that more than proved the point. There they were, enjoying a well-earned evening meal on the Friday, when the telephone rang. It was Stanley.

'Thought you might like to know that the French police picked up your mate at Orly airport, trying to catch a flight to Buenos Aires. They're holding him while we apply for extradition. It might take some time before we see him back here, though. I'm sure he'll fight it.'

'That's great news! Thanks for ringing. By the way, are we all set for Wednesday?'

An affirmative came down the line and then the detective rang off. All set! Excellent! The die had been cast the day before at a lengthy and not always straightforward meeting between the two. Stanley might be on good terms with the solicitor but he was still a policeman and disliked intensely the game Jeremy was playing. As he knew only part of it (little bits like the pepper-pot contents were discreetly omitted), his attitude to full knowledge would have been totally predictable and equally uncooperative.

The meal continued, with considerable conversation centred around Parsons and his error in striking one of the Bear's offspring. They joked and laughed, drank a couple of litres of wine and sank back contented in the fantasies of Parsons's future discomfort.

'Pity the guy couldn't be persuaded to return voluntarily, then he would get out of jail quicker and we could get on with his corrective training.'

'No chance, Pete. Would you come back voluntarily?'

'Nope, but then I ain't easily fooled. He might be.'

'Forget it, Pops. Let him rot as long as he likes in a ruddy froggy jail. Then he gets over here and starts again. Guess he should stay inside longer that way and that's fine by me.'

'Unfortunately, that will not happen. The time he spends inside over there will be taken into account if and when he does get before an English judge.'

The conversation flagged a little. Perhaps the third litre had something to do with it. Whatever, they drifted into a lethargic nothing that was only broken when, sometime in the middle of the fourth litre, Paddy suggested a walk. Now it was not Jeremy's nature to take idle rambles about the countryside (the family walks, as a boy, after Sunday lunch had been enough to put him off the idea for life) and the notion of walking in the town was even more of an anathema. Unfortunately for him, Paddy was not in a reasonable mood. Happy both at getting her own way and from the drink, she thrust her arms around his waist as, a quarter of an hour later, they chugged out through the gate and toddled along contentedly.

It took Jeremy less than a hundred yards to realise that he was steering and partially supporting her. In about another fifty yards, he came to the conclusion that even his relatively modest half-litre plus was slightly more than was good for either his legs or his head. For all that, some guardian angel saw them safely to the town centre, where they found a convenient seat and, both relieved and delighted at the sudden discovery, flopped onto it.

230

'I still feel sorry for Wagstaff. I rather liked him. When will he get his diamonds back?'

'Oh, could be a year or more; it all depends on the extradition, I suppose. Anyway, there's no need to feel sorry for him – he's a crook.'

'So are most people I know. Perhaps they're the only really honest ones.'

'That's daft but I guess I know what you mean. Might teach him a lesson.'

'You're being mean. He is helping us land the Panther, isn't he?'

Jeremy gave the matter some thought. 'Yeh, perhaps you're right. Still, I don't see what we can do.'

'Couldn't you get your tame cop to help?'

'I do wish you'd stop calling him a tame cop. He's nothing of the sort.'

'OK then, your Blue Pig friend.' She giggled.

'He can't do anything.'

'Be nice to me. At least ring him up and see.'

'I will if you can walk home without falling over.'

'Cinch!'

He got up very carefully, managing to sustain the sixty-degree angle Paddy found herself at as she attempted to stand unaided. Despite everything, she did remain on her feet until she got home and even toddled off to bed without sister Sandra's assistance.

Jeremy turned in as well, slept soundly and woke with little memory of the previous evening. Unfortunately, Paddy displayed another feat of unbelievable fortitude in remembering every detail of the conversation. Thus, Jeremy spent another hour thinking hard in his room while she beat hell out of a chewed wing from an old Fiat in the small garage attached to the house.

Oh, God! I'd better try, he thought and picked up the telephone.

'Look, Sandy,' – the friendly touch seemed the only way in – 'I've been thinking.'

That bit was certainly true.

'This Parsons business. What's he charged with?'

'Theft of diamonds, of course. What else did you expect?'

'No mention of the heroin?'

'What's with you? How the hell could we hang the dope charge on him when there wasn't any in the case?'

'You know that, I know that, the French know that but does Parsons?'

'Where is all this going?'

'You want him back quickly, don't you?'

'Silly question.'

'I had this notion that I might persuade him to return voluntarily. After all, if he engages me as his lawyer, I am not going to disclose information about the smuggling. However, if I am not so bound, it would be my duty to tell the French police about the false bottom to the case.'

There was a slight pause.

'You're a real bastard. You certainly chose an appropriate *nom de plume.*'

'Am I on? I need the fee badly after my smash-up.'

Jeremy's voice had taken a slightly pleading tone.

'I'll talk to the Super.'

'I'm around all morning but I shall have to cross to France tomorrow if I'm to get to Amsterdam by Monday and see Parsons in the middle.'

'It might be late this afternoon but I'll do what I can. I still don't know why you have to go to Amsterdam, anyway. Simply crossing the Channel should be enough to trigger this dodgy trap of yours.'

'What if the tip-off is from the Dutch end? No, I have to go through with the whole thing.'

'Who knows the gems are paste?'

'Only Wagstaff and van Hoffner.'

'Still don't like it.'

Jeremy gave an artificial laugh. 'You just persuade the Super to let me try Parsons.'

He rang off.

*

Over the sandwiches at lunch, Paddy dropped her bombshell.

'Pops says he doesn't mind me coming with you to Holland. Isn't that great!'

Hell, no! He was not sure what to say. This difficulty, however, was resolved.

'Well, old son, seemed good sense to have someone to look after you and I couldn't object since you two are going to get hitched; though, to be honest, I wished you had asked me formally, like. Suppose that's too much to ask these days, not that I'm not delighted. She needs a steady fellow and I liked you from the day we met.'

Now he was absolutely sure what to say but, somehow, the words were stuck in his throat. He managed 'engaged?' then half choked on a piece of corned beef. By the time he had stopped, taken a long drink and recovered his breath, he was able to say, 'Well, not officially engaged . . . .'

The pain in his left shin warned of further expressions of denial. He made a mental note to have it out with Paddy as soon as the Bear had gone back to work. It was quite marvellous how this pair seemed to find beaten-up wrecks to resuscitate, even in suburban Croydon. Fortunately, she seemed in no hurry to follow her father and quite expected his tirade.

'What else could I tell him? He'd never have let me go if I hadn't let him think that we were steady.'

'But that's less than honest, Pad. I told you, we'd see

233

how it went but I'll not see Pete hurt just so you can get your own way.'

Tears suddenly welled in her eyes.

'What's wrong with a little white lie? I do want to look after you and I've never been out of the country before.'

He looked at her despairingly. If there was one thing he could not cope with, it was Paddy crying. Oh, God! He was done for! Well, he could always say they had fallen out at a later date. He was not so angry as he first thought.

'I'll go along with it just so long as you don't pull any more of your stunts.'

'I won't, I promise.'

She was far too suppliant.

'And there's another thing. I drive. I've waited too long to get a go in that Sierra and I couldn't stand several hundred miles of your high-speed work. In any case, with you driving over there, they would like as not stick us both in jail.'

She pouted heavily.

'OK, that does it. Pete's getting the truth!'

'No! You drive. I don't mind!'

Paddy disappeared for the whole afternoon. She claimed it was necessary to get her passport but her slight evasiveness suggested she had other business she was not prepared to divulge.

They left Croydon at around eight-thirty and reached the port just after ten. The hastily booked crossing was at peak time and peak prices but that was all they could get. They ate on the boat and then meandered up to Paris at a leisurely pace. Paddy was relaxed, enjoying the journey with a passion born of a previous lack of contact with anywhere south of the Channel. She had a naive charm to her at times and this was one of them. Every street sign,

234

every field, every car that passed – in fact, everything she could see – was a thrill in itself. They had to stop three times in what Jeremy thought were nothing more than very ordinary villages while she explored the shops in near-ecstasy. Beauvais was another matter. He intended to show her the sights there and was rewarded by her delight.

They reached the capital midway through the evening and had little trouble finding an hotel. The boot of the Sierra was carrying a mass of trivia that had caught Paddy's eye in the shops. Taking it all in was tiring. Thus, they were content to enjoy an evening meal and to turn in early.

The next morning, Jeremy rang the contact number he had been given by Stanley. Half an hour later, a small Citroën arrived outside the hotel and he was whisked off to the jail, leaving Paddy to kill time as best she could.

Parsons at first refused to see him but grudgingly agreed after Jeremy had a written note sent in. They met in a typical barren interview room; there is little difference between an English prison and a French one. The same depressing concrete is everywhere and the air hangs with hopelessness. Perhaps there was one small difference: the duty officer on this occasion could not understand their conversation.

'How are they treating you?'

Parsons had not lost his cool manner. He smiled coldly and rocked back in the chair.

'You haven't come to ask after my health. Let's cut the small talk, shall we? What are you after?'

'I was looking for a client.'

'They supplied me with a lawyer. Why do I need another one?'

'I see you don't trust me.'

'Why should I? I would expect you to want my guts.'

'The Bear certainly does and Paddy doesn't feel too kindly towards you. In fact, it would be better for your health if you never saw any of the family again; but me, I've no grudge. I am fairly broke and a lucrative brief is something worth chasing. Take it as truth, this is a purely business venture on my part.'

'I never believe anyone who protests so much that he isn't lying.'

'OK. The deal falls flat. You're the loser more than me.'

Jeremy got up to go.

'You're a fool, Keith. I had a slight sympathy for you and I hadn't forgotten that you helped me get out from that damned warehouse. I had already done some work in the hope you might trust me, but – he shrugged his shoulders – please yourself. You obviously like jail.' He walked across to the door.

'Wait a minute! What are you offering?'

'Do I have the work?'

'Let's hear what you have to say, first.'

Jeremy returned to his seat and opened his case. He extracted a batch of forms.

'First form. This requires your signature for the legal aid. I assume you have no money.'

He caught the look in Parsons's eye.

'Let us say that you have no money you wish an English court to know about.'

He slid the form across the table and dropped a pen on top of it. Ignoring Parsons's inaction, he went on, 'The second one retains me as your solicitor. This one is also for signing; it states that you wish to return to the jurisdiction of the English courts and waive contest against extradition.'

236

Parsons gave a sharp laugh.

'Are you mad? I'm told I have a reasonable chance of getting away with it. The papers in the case were legal and I haven't broken any French laws. Is Wagstaff going to press the matter?'

'Actually, yes. Surprisingly, he puts more stock on getting his diamonds back than anything you might say against him. Anyway, he is almost certain to get Crown immunity for testifying.'

Parsons's face hardened slightly.

'At the moment I haven't told the French authorities about the false bottom to your case . . . .'

He caught the involuntary start.

'. . . but I assure you the Kent police know all about it. However, I have their assurance that no charges will be pressed if you return voluntarily.'

Parsons's face was a picture.

'Oh, yes! I had the bottom out of your case before I took it to the bank. I know all about the heroin game.'

He continued, almost without pausing for breath.

'Choice is yours. Don't sign me up and I spill the beans to the French. They'll not want to keep you – then you get back to jolly old England facing four years on the drugs charge as an extra. Given the circumstances, the old judge will probably load another couple of years onto the theft charge as well. Come back of your own free will and you have only an attempted theft charge to answer. I'll brief a good barrister and you'll get three years, I promise. Good behaviour and you're out in one.'

'And you expect me to believe that?'

'I don't expect you to believe anything.' He pushed the forms together and started to pack them into the brief-case.

'Let me think about it.'

'Think all you like. I shall be here until about nine-thirty tomorrow morning, when I leave for Amsterdam. You might be amused to know I've taken your role as courier. It appears to pay rather well.'

Parsons stared in disbelief.

'Goodbye, old chap.'

*

The afternoon was idyllic. It may be an old cliché – that hardly destroys the truth – but there is a magic about Paris, especially when you are young and it's summer. They walked the sights until they were close to dropping, then they found a cosy café with excellent wine and very mediocre food. It was gone midnight before they tumbled out of the taxi in front of the hotel. However, the night porter was alert enough to give Jeremy the message from the Sûreté; it had come in somewhere around seven.

> *'Parsons agrees to return voluntarily to England.*
> *Phone as soon as you arrive back.'*

The close cooperation between the forces was still working well and a car arrived at seven-thirty sharp the next morning. By nine, Jeremy had cleared all the paperwork, phoned Stanley and he and Paddy were on their way. They had eaten before leaving the hotel but they hardly called that a meal. Croissants and coffee were little more than an *hors-d'oeuvre.* They managed an hour before the lure of a small village café won the day and the pair tucked into warm rolls, slices of ham and cheese and lashings of coffee. They even put in another couple of hours' drive before lunch. Somehow, the adventure had given them both an appetite.

Amsterdam was reached just before nightfall and Jeremy, for one, was not sorry to sleep. In the few minutes before his subconscious took over for the night,

238

he let the joys and excitement of the past days run through his mind. This, he decided, was better than house conveyancing. There was a slight smile on his lips as he nodded off.

16

In looks, van Hoffner could well have been a Dutch clone of Wagstaff, even down to the thin moustache. In personality, however, he was very different. He had an open, cheery disposition and rose immediately to greet his guests and to offer a coffee and schnapps. The former was accepted but a clear head was required for the drive back. He quite understood.

There seemed to be no hurry to get to business and it seemed that Hoffner was pleased to show his prowess with the English language. At length, he produced a small bag, drawn together at the neck, which he opened casually and let the glistening objects tumble out onto the velvet cloth on the desk top.

'They are beautiful, are they not?'

'Absolutely.'

'And only worth about a few hundred guilders.'

Jeremy picked up a couple and let them move in his fingers.

'You could have fooled me with this lot.'

Hoffner smiled broadly. 'That is the idea, my friend. I wish you luck with your enterprise. John and I have been doing business for eight years now and it would be a pity if we had to stop because of this Panther man.'

He opened the second drawer down in the desk and pulled out a sheaf of papers.

'These are all you need. They say you are carrying imitation diamonds to the value of six hundred and two guilders. They confirm that all duties have been paid. You are sure the customs side is set up? You will not want the Panther people to think you have imitations.'

'Buttoned tight.'

He caught the slight frown.

'Don't worry. Our police have put an undercover man on one of the booths in the red section and there will be someone to make sure we're directed to him when we land.'

Jeremy opened his black case, put the gems and the papers in with great care, locked the case and spun the combination wheels on the lock. Satisfied, he looked up at the dealer.

'I guess that's it. We'll say goodbye.'

The Dutchman's face went very serious. 'I wish you luck, my friends.'

Jeremy acknowledged the good wishes. They both shook hands with van Hoffner very formally and descended the stairs to the small reception area below.

'Oh! Bother! I've left my shoulder-bag in Hoffner's room.' Paddy looked irritated.

'I'll get it for you,' he said.

'No. I was the stupid ass that left it; I'll go. Don't go away!'

She turned and bounded up the stairs. In less than half a minute she had reappeared, swinging the bag from her shoulder.

'No harm done. Where are we going now?'

'How about an hour or so looking at the city? We've plenty of time.'

They had indeed. It was a little before eleven and the ferry was not until three the following day. The car meandered through the centre then turned towards a convenient car park. The pair walked along the banks of a bustling canal, stopped on the top of a bridge to watch the water bus slide along underneath them, then continued along a street lined with houses, each having a quaint staircase roof. They paused at an ice-cream vendor's van and purchased two enormous cornets with chocolate flakes and wafers. The cost was also enormous. Licking the sickly ooze, they leant across the protective rail over the canal and fell to idle observation of the water and its traffic.

'This is ace!'

'Enjoying yourself?'

What a silly question – of course she was! The last of the cornet was sucked in and Paddy wiped her mouth with the sleeve of her denim jacket.

'I love you, Jerry Fox!'

'Yeh, I was afraid of that!'

He flicked the end of his cornet into the water and slid an arm across her shoulder.

'There's no hurry to say anything to Pete when we get back – I mean, about us not being engaged.'

She turned her face up towards his.

'Hey! You've got lipstick on!'

'I found it lying around just before we left. It was the lot I got to go to court with.'

She blushed ever so slightly and they were suddenly both laughing.

'Can't waste it, then, can we?'

He kissed her and this time she made no attempt to cut off his oxygen supply.

They had lunch in a small restaurant which had a dozen or so tables scattered under a large canopy that enfolded over half the pavement as well as the front of the building. They sat as close to the street as they could and enjoyed the bustle of city life as they ate. In no great rush, they went back to the car and drove out of the city and in the general direction of the Belgian port of Zeebrugge. They spent the night some hundred and twenty miles out and were still on the dockside by one, despite dawdling over breakfast, the drive and the coffee-break. There was nothing to do but to sit out the boredom of the wait and to prepare for the real adventure.

The ferry duly docked at six forty-five, London time, and they took a further twenty minutes getting to the customs post. There was a reassuring uniformed police officer at the red entrance to the customs house who promptly directed them to a bay already occupied by two cars, despite there being a free unit next to it. They patiently relaxed in the seats but did not have long to wait as the officer seemed barely interested in whatever was being declared by those in front. Two shuffles of the car and they were in position. Jeremy had rehearsed the next few minutes in his mind many times on the crossing. He got out with absolute confidence, rounded the car and withdrew the black case from the boot. He handed over the papers that he had earlier transferred to the inside of the car, waited while the officer scanned them and responded nonchalantly to the request to follow him.

They went into the same interview room that Parsons had gone to only a few weeks before. Once the door was shut, the officer introduced himself.

'Detective Sergeant Spencer, Kent Constabulary. I understand I am to call you "the Fox".'

Jeremy held out a hand. 'That will do nicely.'

'The trap appears to be set. We have instructions to let the duty officer know if anyone enters the port carrying diamonds. The instruction is not to apprehend or raise suspicion but to pass on the information as soon as possible. Hang on here for a moment and I will do just as

I am told. It seems reasonable to give them as much time as possible.'

He left the room, returning less than a minute later.

'All done. I've a message for you from D.S. Stanley. He seems concerned about you and wants you to be careful – same applies to your lady-friend. You're to tell her not to break a leg!'

Jeremy allowed a mirthless smile. Stanley probably meant that a different way from his colleague's interpretation.

'No fear. We are going to behave to the letter.'

They spent an awkward ten minutes not really knowing what to say but feeling some polite conversation was needed. At last, Spencer glanced at his watch and said, 'I think that's about long enough for the paperwork to have been done. On your way and good luck!'

Jeremy walked steadily back to the car, carefully put the case on the back seat, got into the driving seat and started to do up the seat-belt.

'They've taken the bait.'

A hand stopped the metal clip making contact with its other end.

'Swap over. Let me drive.'

The voice was slightly unsteady. He looked at her concerned eyes.

'If there's trouble, you can't drive this beast half as fast as I can and you'll think better in the passenger seat!'

God, he thought, you're really concerned about me, aren't you, lass?

'OK,' he said, 'but remember to take it steady.'

They swapped over.

The Sierra purred out of the dock, turned up the Jubilee Way and climbed smoothly up the hill. Jeremy threw a worried look over his shoulder. There were several cars behind – it was impossible to say which might be the tail – and beyond that the sea sparkled in the evening sun. He turned round and settled back in the seat. Nothing could stop the adrenalin flowing. He just prayed the action would start soon; the waiting was the worst part.

Three miles from the docks, Paddy quietly said, 'Our tail is in place, a hundred yards back. Call your cop friend then get on the hand set to Pa. He'll be listening OK.'

The McBears had not really trusted the police and had settled on their own back-up.

'The Fox is running and the hounds are behind! Out!'

That done, Jeremy picked up the walkie-talkie.

'You listening, Pete?'

'Sure am, old son.'

'Paddy's driving – we have a tail in place – be ready, pal.'

A large trailer with a beaten-up American saloon on the back pulled slowly out from a lay-by a mile in front and built up speed to a steady seventy. The convoy continued in peace, eating up the miles, until they reached the motorway.

'They're closing fast!'

'OK, Paddy, speed up!'

Speeding up they were. A sudden expletive from Paddy prefaced the news that there were three cars chasing them. Why they had not noticed the other two before this they would never know. Perhaps it was psychological: they had only expected one. They had noticed them now, though. Bastards! thought Jeremy, we're easy pickings. They were now on the motorway with no hope of turning off. All they could do was to trust in the back-up.

Jeremy switched on the radio.

'Fox in trouble! Three hounds, repeat, three hounds baying at our heels.'

No time for more. He jettisoned the radio to the dashboard ledge and slewed round in the seat. He had to undo his safety strap to reach it but he managed to retrieve the case.

'How are we doing?'

'We're still in front – just! There's a Sierra, a Merc and a Jag. The Sierra must be souped, it's giving us the most trouble!'

The car swerved sharply across the two lanes, onto the hard shoulder and then back again. Paddy was just keeping the Sierra from overtaking. Now they were closing rapidly on two cars, one overtaking the other.

'Oh, hell! Hang on!'

The car veered sharply onto the hard shoulder and rounded the two on the inside to the accompaniment of a melody of horns. What these two law-abiding drivers thought as they were cut up by another three cars is left to the imagination but was undoubtedly unprintable. In front, an American car slid off the back of its trailer and accelerated hard, shedding rubber everywhere as it did so. Paddy slid through on the outside easily enough but the following Sierra had a nasty shock as the car hit it side-on, taking it into the safety barrier. As it bounced off, it found to its surprise the American was nowhere in sight. Any respite was momentary. The car reappeared behind it. The jolt shook the car out of any possible recovery and, under the impetus from the rear, it skewed across the motorway and ended its life rolling down the embankment.

Pete drew up on the edge of the drop and stuck his head and half his body out of the glassless window. He gave the wreck a brief glance, dropped back into the driver's seat and revved up the stock-car once more. As he let the clutch out, he knew the worst: the rear tyre had blown. His chase was over. Cursing under his breath, he drew a torsion wrench from the back of the car, got out and ploughed down the embankment to the remains of the Sierra. As he went, he was still making up his mind whether he was going to pull the occupants out or slug them with the wrench. He had just reached the back of the car by the time he had made his decision. He would do both.

From the pursuing cars' viewpoint, the crash left the outside lane clear and the pair sped through without more than a passing interest in the fate of the Sierra. The intermezzo had, however, been more than useful from the Fox's viewpoint. The fleeing Cosworth gained a vital hundred and fifty yards over the pursuit.

'Keep it steady, Pad!'

He wound the window down, held the case firmly with both hands and pushed the thing out into the slip-stream. The wind tore at his hands and they went blue with cold in seconds. He grimly hung on, took aim and launched the case high into the air and into the path of the Mercedes.

It braked sharply and swerved. As the Jaguar went past the case, Jeremy could see the Mercedes reversing back down the road. A man jumped out, grabbed the case, scrambled back inside and the car sped off once more but this was no longer in Jeremy's field of vision.

He flicked the button to the window control and watched with some relief as it wound up. He took up the radio again and called up.

'Fox to Blue Pig. Come in if you can hear me!'

'I hear you well enough, Fox, but I wish you would drop this "Blue Pig" nonsense. What do you have?'

'Sorry. They've taken the bait OK. Unfortunately, still one hound in pursuit. Can you do anything?'

'Do my best, my foxy friend. Look after yourself!
Out!'

'Don't worry, Jerry, I'll lose him!'

Jeremy never heard the helicopter that came over the
motorway and hovered above the Mercedes. He was
grimly fastening his seat-belt as the Sierra's speedometer
climbed even higher. He had it on at a hundred and
thirty but somehow it hardly seemed to matter. A sudden
trust had replaced his fear of her driving. The other cars
on the road hardly caused any concern, they were so
quickly in front of them, as often as not passing them on
the hard shoulder. Still the speedometer climbed. He
gave up looking at it or the road or anything in
particular.

Somewhere in the distance, a blue lamp flashed, then
it was behind them.

'Pad! For God's sake, slow down! You'll kill us
both.'

She was not listening. Her every ounce of concentration was on the road in front. Now she could see the two
cars abreast, the blue lamps flashing. Hell! There were
three! She had no choice. The brakes went on and the
whole car rocked forward but the speedometer refused
to alter. Slowly, oh so slowly, the needle crept away from
the far end of the dial. They were closing too quickly on
the cars in front. A crash was inevitable.

At the last moment, the police cars moved apart enough
to allow the Sierra through and then closed again.

'Pad! Stop, for Christ's sake! They're protecting our
butts! We're safe!'

She reacted. The car was no longer being braked but
was slowing naturally. She let it glide onto the hard
shoulder, switched off the engine and let out a long, loud
breath of air. Behind them, the three police cars had
sealed the motorway. Nothing could get at them now.

Jeremy slid the strap off and got out of the car. He needed air. Vomit was in his mouth. He swallowed hard, walked a few paces back and viewed the road-block.

Even as he did so, the end police car shuddered, moved a little forwards and sideways and the Jaguar forced its way through on the inside. The massive car was accelerating hard up the road towards him, with one of the police cars in pursuit. Jeremy instinctively drew back towards the Sierra but not quickly enough. Too late, he saw the gun protruding through the passenger window. He half ducked and launched himself at the Ford. He heard the crack and almost simultaneously the pain hit his arm. The force of the blow helped him to the ground, where he lay stunned and shocked as a second bullet hit the tarmac inches from his head and whined away. Then the assailants had gone, followed by two wailing Carltons, their blue lights flashing.

The third car limped across the gap, its rear wing badly bent and the lamps across the whole of the back smashed. It pulled up on the hard shoulder and a constable ran across. Jeremy was lying in Paddy's arms and whimpering with the pain.

'Don't you go dying on me, Jerry Fox. I won't find another fellow half as good.'

The constable bent down.

'Is he badly hit?'

He did not wait for an answer but turned his head and shouted, 'Hey! Mike! Get an ambulance. This chap's been shot!'

'My arm! The bugger got me in the arm!'

He looked up at Paddy.

'No, I'm not going to die on you. If you think I'm going to miss the celebration dinner at Luigi's, you're sadly mistaken!'

He winced with the pain again, then lay back and tried

to relax. It was over now, once and for all.

*

The party was delayed for a week while Jeremy recovered from the wound. Initially, he was kept in hospital overnight before being released into Paddy's charge. It was her insistence that kept him convalescing for the week, nursing what the duty doctor in casualty had referred to as little more than a simple flesh wound. It is true, however, that he rather hastily revised his diagnosis when Paddy pointed out the seriousness of it. Even Stanley fussed a bit in his own way and posted an armed officer in the corridor outside Jeremy's room. He was withdrawn only when word came through that the last of the gang had been detained. Jeremy found the pampering was all right for the first twenty-four hours but became too much of a good thing as time wore on. Mostly, the arm was just stiff and pretty sore.

Stanley dropped in a couple of times to see him. The chopper had seen to it that the occupants of the Mercedes had all been arrested, including Smith, who had made the crucial mistke of going along to view the kill. Adrian had been the real prize: the thought of prison had sent him into a fit of depression. It seems that a small quantity of heroin had been found behind a drawer in his bedroom. Although he swore blind that it had not been his room and, anyway, he knew nothing about the stuff, he was not stupid. He also understood exactly what they meant about a pretty boy not enjoying life inside and, when he was given a promise of immunity as a Crown witness in return for full cooperation, sang like a nightingale, sweet and clear, fingering Smith for everything he could. Stanley gave Jeremy all the details.

'We also have Wagstaff's housekeeper under lock and key. Seems she spilt the beans to Smith about what was

250

happening. God! You are a lucky bastard, Fox! She only found out about your run forty-eight hours before the off, as a result of a chance remark by Carlos. Your suspicions about him were totally wrong.'

Jeremy decided to say nothing. Can't win them all, he thought. Well, all's well that ends well.

The convalescent period gave Jeremy more time than he wanted to go over the affair. He knew he had been lucky but now it really came home to him. He had escaped death on at least four occasions and mostly by good fortune. He had miscalculated more times than he cared to remember and even his attempts to stitch up Smith by loading drugs into the case were a waste of time and silly. The police neither wanted the plant nor would use it. He was left to ponder whether or not he was even a good lawyer. He was not even sure if he wanted the relationship with Paddy to get too close; they were so different – would it ever work? By and large, he decided, the whole Panther affair had done little for his ego. Then again, he found he had got a kick out of it. He started to think about all the very real people he had met. He had made more true friends in a month than he had done all his previous life. What was more, they liked him for what he was, warts and all. Not, that is, that Paddy or any of her wrestling friends thought he had any. He grinned inwardly and decided life was what it was. There was nothing to be gained by too much dwelling on the past and the future appeared to offer some exciting times. By and large, private practice in Lewisham was tolerably agreeable.

It also seemed that Parsons was to be handed over in a couple of days. This was the excuse Jeremy needed to leave the sick bed, take a trip across the Woolwich ferry and travel up to the London City Airport to meet the plane. He still was not allowed to drive and Paddy took it

251

incredibly steadily in case his arm was jolted. Neverthe-less, things were panning out beautifully. Stanley even told him a charming tale of how a mobile police patrol on the M2 had clocked a white car at one hundred and fifty-three on the Vascarmeter only to find, when they returned to the station, that the registration number matched a sixteen-year-old Morris Minor. The superin-tendent was very reasonable about it and suggested they would never be believed in court so they dropped the matter. Paddy had always wondered what the Sierra would really do.

*

When it eventually arrived, some eight days after the shooting, the party at Luigi's was really something. To start with, the meal lasted from shortly after seven until nearly three in the morning and there is no telling how much longer it might have gone on if it had not been broken up in rather an interesting manner – but more of that later.

It was around ten-thirty when Paddy produced a packet from her trousers and offered it to Jeremy.

'What's this?'

'Yours! I made a deal with Wagstaff.'

Jeremy was puzzled. 'What deal?'

'Well, I thought it daft to carry just fake diamonds so he arranged for van Hoffner to have a second bag ready. He slipped those into my bag after we left the room. Remember, I had to go back for it?'

'Oh, my God! Do you mean we were really carrying a couple of million in diamonds?'

'No, I was.'

She grinned wickedly.

'Go on, open the envelope before I sober up and change my mind.'

Inside was a bundle of fifty-pound notes.

252

'Fifteen grand. Enough to buy a new car. Old Wagstaff reckoned it was worth more than the usual run as he avoided all duties, not just the bit on the undeclared part. There's another ten coming once the police return the diamonds Keith had when he skipped. There, Jerry Fox, you'll have to marry me now!'

He looked from one laughing face to another.

'Here, Luigi, got any champange?'

'I was saving it for later.'

'Later has come!'

The cork popped and the glasses were filled. More food arrived and the glasses were emptied and filled several times over. It was nearly three when Luigi's wife, Rosa, came in holding the portable phone.

'There's a man asking for you, Pete.'

Pete took the phone and huddled into a corner, trying desperately to listen to the voice on the other end over the raucous chatter of the party. He put his hand over the receiver and boomed, 'Jerry, old son, can you come over here a minute?'

The solicitor fumbled his way across the room.

'What is it?'

'Guess we are going to have to break up the party. Mike's in trouble. Guess he's going to need your wizardry with the courts.'

'Who the hell is Mike?'

'Mike? He's my eldest boy. Runs a scrap-yard in Dagenham. Get all my best bits from him. He's a good lad, really – chip off the old block. Normally, he keeps his nose clean but he's run into a spot of bother. Seems like he's been wrongfully arrested. Anyhow, he's at East Ham police station. Appears this car he was driving had a body in the boot when he was stopped but he swears he knew nothing about it. Anyway, he says he only rammed the cop car because his brakes failed and . . . .'

253